Girls Only!

VOLUME ONE

Books by Beverly Lewis

GIRLS ONLY (GO!)
Youth Fiction

Girls Only! Volume One
Girls Only! Volume Two

SUMMERHILL SECRETS
Youth Fiction

SummerHill Secrets Volume One
SummerHill Secrets Volume Two

HOLLY'S HEART
Youth Fiction

Best Friend, Worst Enemy • *Straight-A Teacher*
Secret Summer Dreams • *No Guys Pact*
Sealed With a Kiss • *Little White Lies*
The Trouble With Weddings • *Freshman Frenzy*
California Crazy • *Mystery Letters*
Second-Best Friend • *Eight Is Enough*
Good-Bye, Dressel Hills • *It's a Girl Thing*

www.BeverlyLewis.com

BEVERLY LEWIS

Girls Only!

VOLUME ONE

BETHANYHOUSE

Minneapolis, Minnesota

Girls Only! Volume One
Copyright © 1998, 1999
Beverly Lewis

Previously published in four separate volumes:
  Dreams on Ice Copyright © 1998
  Only the Best Copyright © 1998
  A Perfect Match Copyright © 1999
  Reach for the Stars Copyright © 1999

Cover design by Eric Walljasper

Published by Bethany House Publishers
11400 Hampshire Avenue South
Bloomington, Minnesota 55438

Bethany House Publishers is a division of
Baker Publishing Group, Grand Rapids, Michigan.

Printed in the United States of America

Library of Congress Cataloging-in-Publication Data is available for this title.

ISBN 978-0-7642-0461-6

BEVERLY LEWIS is the bestselling author of more than eighty books for adults and children, including the popular CUL-DE-SAC KIDS and SUMMERHILL SECRETS series, several picture books, and numerous adult fiction series. Five of her blockbuster novels have received the Gold Book Award for sales over 500,000 copies, and *The Brethren* won a 2007 Christy Award. Beverly and her husband make their home in Colorado, within miles of the Olympic Training Center, headquarters for the U.S. Olympic Committee.

Dreams on Ice

AUTHOR'S NOTE

Special thanks to the U.S. Figure Skating Association and the U.S. Olympic Committee for research assistance. Also, hugs to Heidi Van Wieren, who answered all my questions about skating competitions, programs, judging, and jumps. And to each of my readers who asked me to please write another series—*for girls only*—thanks for your encouragment and wonderful letters!

For
Heidi Van Wieren,
devoted to her own ice
dreams.

Dreams on Ice
Chapter One

Olivia Hudson pushed off toward center ice. Gaining speed, she skated a smooth, backward glide across the practice rink—the setup for her next move. She dug her toe pick hard into the slick surface.

Whoosh!

She leaped high into the air, tightening her arms against her body as she whirled around. A single skate met the ice on the back outside edge—the perfect landing for a super double flip.

"Excellent, Livvy!" Coach Elena Dimitri called from the sidelines.

Livvy clenched her hands in triumph, circling the arena. "I did it!" she shouted. Then, extending her left leg, she moved to a graceful spiral glide.

After a short cooling-down period, Livvy took her ten-minute break. "My timing's still off," she moaned.

Elena touched Livvy's shoulder. "Don't be too hard on yourself. We'll get your sparkle back . . . *and* your confidence. You'll see."

I hope she's right, Livvy thought, hurrying off to get a drink.

Two heartbreaking months had passed since the coolest mom in history had lost her battle with leukemia. Livvy would never forget that June night, standing next to the hospital bed and holding the soft, dear hand. Never, ever would she accept the unbearable moment when she said her tearful farewell.

Yet here she was, anticipating her regular forty-minute skating session, trying her best to go on with life.

When she returned to the rink, she inhaled deeply, ready to go to work on her technique. "I need more practice on my flips," Livvy said.

"Triples this time," Elena insisted.

Livvy paused a moment on the mat-lined walkway. "C'mon, now . . . *focus!*" she told herself, stepping onto the ice.

She skated backward for the setup. But she entered the jump too slowly and tilted off balance, losing her footing on the landing.

"Rats!" she muttered and got up to try again.

She waited a bit longer into the glide before attempting the jump. But her concentration was off, and she fell to the ice.

I've landed this a thousand times, she told herself. *I can do this!*

Promptly, she got up and brushed the frost off her leg.

At eleven, going on twelve, Livvy knew enough not to be discouraged over one bad skating session. Often, she'd had to force her brain to focus on winning thoughts, even at her advanced novice stage. Only one step away from juniors!

"I believe in you," her mom had always said. The encouraging words echoed in her memory. Loud and clear.

Since her preschool days, Livvy had been attending group skating classes near Riverdale, the close-knit Chicago suburb she called home. And Mom never missed a practice. *"Keep smiling!"* she would call from the stands.

Skating was the best part of the day. Any day. Livvy would rather skate than sleep, even on a summer Saturday. She'd hopped out of bed at the first musical strains of the clock radio. Even though it might've seemed like the middle of the night to the rest of the neighborhood, she hurried to the kitchen for her usual cereal, fruit, and juice. Cold (and lonely) breakfasts were common these days.

Gone were the amazing breakfast specialties Mom often prepared: whole-grain waffles or homemade cereals.

Sighing, she skimmed the rink. "Oh, Mom, I wish you were still alive. I *need* you." She glanced at the bleachers—Mom's old spot—and thought about this one-sided dialogue. *Dad would probably be upset if he knew,* she thought.

Her father was a freelance artist—and totally occupied with deadlines. Definitely, he'd frown on her endless murmurings to her dead mother. She was absolutely sure he would, because after the funeral he'd stopped talking about Livvy's mom. He didn't even mention her name anymore.

Elena had said not to worry. "Your father is facing grief his own way. He's a sensitive man. He'll learn to cope . . . eventually."

It seemed like a reasonable explanation at the time. But now—two months later—her dad was still silent. A dismal kind of silence that frightened her. Worse than that, she felt terribly alone in the world. Alone and wondering how she could possibly reach her skating goals without the support of a parent who understood her Olympic dreams.

On top of everything else, money was tight. Especially after her mom's health declined so quickly and the hospital bills started pouring in. She honestly wondered if they could even afford a new outfit for the Summer Ice Revue—in just ten days!

Livvy wished with all her heart she could talk certain things over with her dad. She'd outgrown her old costumes, for one thing. And she wished he'd show even the slightest interest in her skating. Or maybe just take her to practice sessions once in a while. Things like that.

But she knew his broken heart was stuck in the past, in those wonderful Mom-filled days before everything changed . . . for the worse.

"Try again, Livvy!" Elena's voice always gave her the strength to start over.

Livvy bit her lip. *I won't give up . . . ever!*

Everything she had went into the next setup—her speed and every ounce of strength. She dug the toe pick hard and lifted her body up, up, high off the surface of the rink.

For three rapid rotations, she was flying. But the landing was off.

And Livvy fell again.

Dreams on Ice
Chapter Two

Livvy dropped her skate bag on the living room floor. "Dad, I'm home!" she called, wandering through the house. She found him in the family room, reading the evening paper.

He looked up only briefly. "Hi, Liv. Good day?"

"Horrible." She dropped into the chair that had been her mother's favorite—a cozy, old wingback—and stared at her tall, slender dad. He seemed to be growing thinner by the day. "I'm really worried," she said softly.

His eyebrows arched as he peered over the paper. "Are you all right?"

"I'm worried about *you*," she answered.

"Olivia, let's not—"

"We *need* to talk."

He sighed and folded the newspaper. Leaning back

against the sofa, his green eyes were serious, his lanky arms folded tightly against his chest.

"You aren't yourself." Livvy felt her heart pounding like a snare drum. "You're tired all the time, Daddy. And you don't eat enough."

Without speaking, he ran his fingers slowly through his thick, dark hair. The silence unnerved her.

"I think I know what's wrong." Her throat felt tight. Achy. "I think I understand . . . because I miss Mom, too. I miss her more than ever."

He blinked repeatedly, his gaze clearly fixed on her. It would do no good to continue. The conversation was going nowhere. Same as all the other times.

Frustrated, she stood up to leave, but his startling words stopped her. "I'm thinking of moving." He paused for a moment. "There's a mountain town in Colorado . . . not too far from Colorado Springs. I'd like to move us there before school starts."

Move?

Livvy froze. This was her home—Dad's too. And Mom's! What was he thinking?

"We can't . . . move, Daddy." She stopped short of crying. There were hundreds of reasons for them to stay. Sensible reasons—more than she could count. But one of the best reasons on earth was her skating coach. How could she possibly leave the woman who'd brought her through all the early competitions of her life? Elena, who had instructed her and cheered her on all the way to novice level—incredible for Livvy's age.

She shook her head, hair swirling against her face. Standing, she faced her father. "How can you even think of doing this to me? You're going to ruin my life!"

He frowned, then a helpless look clouded his face. "Perhaps we should consider having you stay here in Riverdale. Grandma Hudson has an extra bedroom."

She could hardly believe her ears. Her father was going to abandon her? Move halfway across the United States? Hand her off to Grandma?

Livvy fought back tears and the throbbing lump in her throat. She wanted him to say he could never leave without her, that he didn't want to move anywhere without his baby girl. Or . . . no, she wanted him to say he wasn't really going to move. Let her grow up in Riverdale, let her finish middle school and later high school. All because of her skating goals. *That's* what she wanted him to say.

"We belong here," she managed to squeak out. "You know it, and so do I."

He stared at the ceiling, his feet restless on the floor. "A change would do us both good" came the hollow-sounding reply.

"A change? Isn't losing Mom enough of a change for one summer?" Livvy was immediately filled with regret. Her dad was obviously hurting, and she knew it by the dismal look on his ashen face. "I shouldn't have said that. I'm sorry, Daddy."

"No . . . no. Maybe you're right." He was studying her now. "It's just that, well, this house . . . this . . ." He was faltering, reaching for the paper again.

"I know, Dad. I know." She looked around the room at her mother's porcelain angel collection with Bible verses inscribed on each one. At the accent candles in different shapes and sizes: hearts, stars, cubes, and tapers. Everything reminded her of what they'd lost. Everything, right down to the way the drapes were pulled over with a fashionable gold clip.

———

Later, in her room, Livvy stood with her face next to her cockatiel's cage. Coco blinked his tiny eyes. "Hi, cutie-bird," she whispered, staring at his adorable white body and bright yellow head.

"Coco . . . cutie-bird" came the low-pitched voice.

"You're one crazy parrot." She puckered her lips to send kisses.

Coco didn't send any back. Not this time. He was playing hard to get.

"Okay, have it your way." She turned her back on purpose.

"Way . . . way crazy!" Coco repeated the words ten or more times without stopping.

Finally Livvy faced him again and shushed him. "Better be quiet now. Dad's in a lousy mood." She waved her pointer finger close to the cage. "And so am I."

"Ha . . . ha . . . ha . . . quiet!" was the annoying reply.

"Okay for you. If you won't behave, I'll just have to ignore you. Or cover up your cage for the rest of the day." It was a threat, nothing more. But she turned and shuffled across the room.

Gazing out the window, her thoughts flew to her dad. "He's not thinking clearly," she murmured, watching a flock of birds wing their way from tree to tree. "He's lost without Mom. . . ."

Nearly a year ago, right after she and her mother had become Christians, Livvy began to worry about her dad's disinterest in God and church. He seemed so puzzled about everything. Like he was searching his heart for answers to what had happened to his cozy, unbelieving family.

She understood his present sadness and loss, but this unexpected talk of moving to Colorado . . . What was *that* about?

When Coco didn't chatter back one of his favorite words, Livvy was surprised. Thankful, though. She needed some space, some time to think. Should she go with her dad? Or stay and seriously pursue her skating goals?

Livvy sighed and sat at her desk, leaning on her elbows. A small picture of her mother smiled back at her. "What should I do, Mom?" she asked the photo.

Asking the Lord would've made more sense, she knew. But these days it was too painful to pray. Why *had* God taken her mother at such a young age?

Pulling open the narrow drawer in the center of her desk, she found her stationery. Her Colorado pen pal—Jenna Song—was always a super sounding board. And Jenna was an avid letter writer. Same as Livvy. The girls might've been email addicts, but neither of them had access to a computer. Livvy's dad's state-of-the-art computer and printer were always in use.

Twirling a ballpoint pen between her fingers, Livvy eyed the bulletin board above her desk. There, centered among pictures of Tara Lipinski and Michelle Kwan, skating souvenirs, and ticket stubs, was Jenna. Beautifully Korean, with flawless olive skin, deep brown eyes, and dark hair down to her waist. Jenna prided herself in being "absolutely American." That's how she'd introduced herself in the first letter three months ago.

Jenna was also a minister's daughter, but she didn't flaunt it like some kids might. She *did* talk about God in her letters sometimes. Once, when Livvy had confided in her about her mother's cancer, Jenna had written back, promising to pray.

Remembering this, Livvy decided to go ahead and

share her gloomy news. Coco twittered in the cage behind her, and Livvy took a deep breath and began to write.

August 12

Dear Jenna,

Hi again! Did you place at your gymnastics meet last weekend in Denver? I hope you were psyched for it and did super great.

Well, I hate to write this, but I have some upsetting news. My dad has this horrible idea. He wants to move. Can you believe it? We've lived here my WHOLE life. And there's the big problem of leaving my skating friends— AND my skating coach. I simply couldn't exist without Elena, you know.

I overheard Daddy telling Grandma Hudson that he plans to move to Alpine Lake, somewhere in Colorado. Sounds like Podunk, USA, to me. Any idea where it is? I wonder if it's close to your town. I'll have to check the map.

If I stayed here I could live with Grandma and keep training with Elena. Then I'd end up missing BOTH my parents. So if I move with Dad, I might as well kiss my skating goals good-bye. No matter what I choose, I lose!

I wish Dad would stay put for another couple of years, then maybe I'd have a chance at junior-level competition. I can tell you all this, Jen, because we're a lot alike.

Sorry about not sending you a picture of me yet. Maybe we'll meet each other face-to-face sometime soon.

(That's IF I decide to move with Dad.) Getting to meet you in person would be the only good thing about leaving Riverdale.

Write soon!

Love ya,

Livvy

She folded her letter, then undressed for bed. After draping Coco's cage for the night, Livvy set her clock radio for 5:00 A.M.

She slipped into bed and reached to turn out the light on the lamp table. "Night-night, Coco," she whispered.

The parrot replied, "Night-night."

Livvy was thrilled to own a peculiar pet like Coco. Crazy and talkative as he was, she adored him. It had been her mother's idea to buy the exotic pet in the first place. Now Coco was one more link to her perfect past.

The room was too hot for bedcovers, so Livvy lay there in her shortie pajamas, enjoying the breeze from the window. Part of the moon shone through the curtains, casting a white light on the ice skater figurine on her bookcase. The statuette was last year's birthday gift. By far the best present ever. Livvy was sure she knew which of her parents had purchased it.

"How can I skate . . . or live . . . without you, Mom?" she whispered into the stillness. "I miss you something awful."

Dreams on Ice
Chapter Three

The flap of a screen door startled her awake. Livvy sat up in bed and squinted at the clock.

4:32 A.M.

She crawled out of bed and stumbled to the window. Below her, on the back porch step, sat her father.

What's he doing up? she wondered.

This was so unlike him. Especially because he often stayed up past midnight working on new illustrations and trying out new color combinations. The creative side of his brain switched on at night like a light bulb.

On several occasions Livvy had wandered into his studio late, only to find him boring a hole in a canvas with his eyes, a brush poised in midair . . . usually talking to himself or to the painted subject.

She stared at him through the window, her thoughts

soaring. Slowly, she began to get her hopes up. Way up. Maybe, just maybe, Dad was planning to surprise her— take her to skating for once!

Too excited to sleep again, she took a shower and dressed for practice. *Wait'll I write Jenna about this,* she thought, wishing she hadn't already sealed the envelope.

Finding it, she toyed with the notion of including a big, fat P.S. on the back. But no, she wouldn't want anyone to read her comment. Least of all Dad.

She would wait and send another note. After practice would be a good time. She'd tell Jenna all about her dad's first visit to the rink, watching her practice her jumps and spins. He would observe her stamina training . . . her technique study. Everything! This was too good to be true!

Livvy brushed her auburn hair back into a quick ponytail. She studied her full bangs in the mirror, wondering if she should let them grow out so she could wear her hair pulled back, like Michelle Kwan. Or trim them and make them fluffier, like Tara Lipinski.

She set her hairbrush back on the dresser, unable to decide about a new look. Standing in front of the mirror, her eyes fell on another framed picture of her mother. Her all-time favorite.

Holding the familiar image up to her face, she compared the picture to herself. "Mom and I actually looked like sisters . . . almost." Having made this discovery, her tears threatened to spill over.

Quickly, she placed the picture back on the dresser. Her stomach rumbled loudly, and she hurried downstairs to the kitchen. Too much thinking made her super hungry, but before she opened the cereal box, she peered out the back door.

Dad was nowhere to be seen.

Her heart sank as she poured milk over the cereal. Livvy knew as sure as she was Olivia Kay Hudson that her dad had probably gone back to bed. He wouldn't be available to take her to the rink. Not today.

Probably not ever.

She would have to catch a ride with a skating friend. Once again, she was on her own.

———

After lunch, Livvy dashed to her bedroom and tore open her letter to Jenna. She sat at her desk and wrote the longest P.S. ever.

She began by explaining how miserable she felt. How totally disappointed . . .

P.S. My dad's in the blackest cloud ever! He hardly even paid attention when I pleaded with him today. About NOT moving, that is. He's determined to start a new life somewhere else. Somewhere far away from all our happy memories.

Doesn't he know that a part of Mom will always go with him no matter where he ends up?

Oh, Jenna, you should've seen my coach's face when I told her Dad wants to move. She looked absolutely ill. And I felt as sick as she looked. I haven't told Dad yet, but I'm honestly thinking of staying here with my grandma. I can't throw away everything I've ever worked for. Can I?

Livvy found another envelope in her skinny desk drawer and rewrote the address. Without mangling the self-adhesive stamp, she removed it from the old envelope. She secured it to the new envelope with a thump of her fist.

Before mailing her letter, she took time to clean the bottom of Coco's cage. She also gave her parrot some fresh water and more food. "Say 'thank you, Livvy,' " she prompted him.

"Coco, cutie-bird." He turned his neck to preen his feathers.

"No, say 'thank you,' " she repeated.

"Cutie Livvy" came the unexpected reply.

She couldn't help but smile. "You're just too much, you know?"

"Too much . . . too much."

"I'm leaving now. Bye!" She closed her bedroom door, but Coco kept chitter-chattering.

Letter in hand, Livvy hurried down the hall to her

dad's studio. She stopped to peek inside, expecting to see him consumed in the latest art project.

Instead, she found him draped over the sketching table, snoozing. Soft music, featuring flowing water and chirping birds mingled with guitar melodies, played in the background. The music and the wilderness sounds were relaxing. No wonder he was sound asleep in the middle of the afternoon.

Tiptoeing inside, Livvy went to stand near his chair. She looked down on her grieving father and noticed dark circles under his eyes. And his face seemed horribly pale.

Oh, Daddy, I love you, she thought *and felt her heart breaking all over again. Whatever happens to my skating dreams, even if I have to give it all up, I can't let you go to Colorado. Not without me!*

Dreams on Ice
Chapter Four

It was a cloudy Saturday. Just two more days before doors opened at Alpine Lake Middle School. The *only* middle school in town.

Big whoop.

Ordinarily, Livvy would be practicing her routines on a day like this. Back in first-class Chicago! But she busied herself with cleaning and organizing her new room, trying to shove away thoughts of future competitions. Of skating buddies and the best coach in the world.

Her dreams had been put on hold. She'd even missed out on the Summer Ice Revue—something she'd worked for all year. But worst of all, she'd had to leave Elena behind. No coach . . . no skating career. Yet she couldn't blame anyone but herself for landing here in Podunk. A place precisely in the middle of nowhere!

The realtor had shown them only three houses. All of them run-down Victorians. One far worse than the others.

Amazingly, her dad had purchased the most hopeless of the bunch. He said he was going to "remodel the seventies away" and recapture the heart of the house.

Whatever that means, Livvy had thought at the time.

So here she was rattling around in an old fixer-upper, awaking each morning to pounding and sawing. "Dad's taking his misery out on this poor old house," Livvy informed her parrot.

"Poor house" came the answer.

"Right, the *poorhouse* is exactly where we're gonna end up."

"End up . . . end up."

Livvy laughed and blew kisses to Coco. "Try to behave yourself today. Is that possible? Because I'm going school shopping."

"Missing Liv . . . missing Liv . . ."

She shook her head, wondering how Coco had gotten so smart. She'd worked with him repeatedly their first years together. As a result, he could carry on like a chicken, sneeze like a human, and repeat most any phrase she'd ever taught him. But sometimes he actually seemed to think for himself. Uncanny. Never a dull moment with Coco.

At least she had *one* friend in town!

———

The shops on the edge of Alpine Lake were the poorest excuse for a mall Livvy had ever seen. She found herself buying school supplies at a drugstore, of all places!

When she'd checked off her list and paid for her supplies, she wandered over to another shop—the Cloth Mill. There she searched through bolts of bright-colored fabric and packages of sparkly sequins.

"May I help you?" a cheerful clerk asked.

"Just looking, thanks."

The woman chuckled a bit, her turquoise bracelet jangling. "Please, feel free to look around. And take all the time you need. We have plenty of markdowns this weekend."

"Okay, I'll look."

Pausing, the clerk asked, "Are you from the Midwest somewhere?"

"Chicago," she said proudly.

The woman clicked her fingers. "I thought so!"

"Really?" Livvy was surprised. "Do I have an accent?"

"I never would've guessed, except that I have some cousins who live back there. You sound just like them."

Livvy felt completely comfortable telling the clerk that she and her father had just moved to Alpine Lake. "It's a first for me . . . moving someplace new."

"Well, let me be the first to welcome you to the prettiest place on earth."

Easy for her to say. Livvy forced a smile.

"Why so glum? Our town's full of wonderful folks, you'll see."

"I'm sure it is." Quickly, she filled the clerk in on her biggest worry. "It's just that I'm an ice skater . . . without a coach."

"Oh, that *is* a problem." The woman's eyes were kind and sincere. "You'll just have to practice on the mall skating rink, I guess."

"There's a rink *here*?"

The woman nodded emphatically. "Go see for yourself." She gave easy directions. "You can't miss it."

Normally, Livvy never would have confided in a stranger like this, but the clerk had such an honest face. Like her own mother's. And there was something endearing about the way the woman's eyes focused right on her, tears glistening in the corners when Livvy told of her mother's recent death.

"Oh, I'm terribly sorry."

The more they talked, the more Livvy liked the

well-dressed clerk. She soon discovered that the sunny Mrs. Newton was a regular volunteer at the middle school.

"Then I'll be seeing you again," Livvy said before leaving.

"Oh, you'll see me, all right!"

Livvy couldn't help but feel encouraged. Grandma Hudson had told her that "small-town folks are some of the friendliest around."

She hoped Grandma was right about *all* the people here as she headed off to check out the skating rink. Along the way, she noticed several other girls shopping with their moms.

Sighing, she hated the thought of trying to survive middle school and beyond without Mom. She tried not to gawk but felt super envious and sad. Very sad.

Livvy scurried off, leaving the girls and their mothers behind. She located the mall rink quickly. It was situated in the middle of the small emporium. Tall trees with twinkling white lights dotted the area around the rink.

"Super stuff," she said to herself.

Walking all the way around, she remembered every ice skating event she and her mom had attended. Always together. With everything in her, she hoped someday she could get back on track with skating. She'd have to go through the hassle of finding a new coach to regain what she'd already lost. By not training every single day, she could lose some of the long-practiced, perfected spirals, spins, and jumps.

Every day!

It would take forever to get back her agility and strength. In more ways than one, Livvy's dreams were on ice. . . .

Dreams on Ice
Chapter Five

"But, Dad, you *promised*!"

Her father looked up from a pile of lumber and sanding tools in what had been their living room. He surveyed the mess. "Sorry, Liv. I didn't realize this project would take so long. Can we surprise your pen pal another weekend?"

"Like when? *Next* Sunday?"

"That's a good possibility."

His answer was too uncertain. Here they were, only one hour's drive away from her pen pal! They'd checked out the distance on the map. And now her dad was changing his mind and calling off the trip.

She slumped onto the bottom step, its wood stripped bare of stain. "I was living for today . . . to finally meet

Jenna," she said softly. "I don't know anyone around here."

"You know *me*." Her father's face was caked with sawdust, almost comically so.

But she refused to laugh. He'd let her down, and she felt like pouting or worse. "This town is so boring."

"Well, if you want something exciting to do, *here*." He held out the sander. "I could use a little help."

He had a point. So she spent her entire afternoon helping with her dad's latest art project—remodeling their horrid house! Livvy sanded woodwork—baseboards and trim around doorways—till she thought her arm would keep vibrating by itself. Even after the sander was turned off!

When it was time for supper, she talked her dad into driving them to the mall for burgers. "There's a skating rink in the middle of the shops," she said. It was the first she'd breathed a word of her discovery.

"There's a skating rink in a boring town like this?" he teased.

Livvy wished he would show some real excitement. For a change. "There are skaters everywhere in this world," she insisted. "*Everywhere*. You can't get away from rinks and skaters . . . no matter where we live."

He shrugged. Clearly, he wasn't interested.

But Livvy had an idea. She would take her skates

along and try out the ice, and her dad would watch. He'd have to!

She wouldn't say a thing about her plan. Not one word.

While her dad shaved and showered, she hid her skate bag in the backseat of the car. Super cool! This was the moment she'd been waiting for.

An hour later, Livvy and her dad were waiting in line at the only fast-food place in town. "What're you gonna order?" she asked, hoping that his appetite might be returning to normal.

"Probably a milk shake."

"Daddy! You've been working hard all day. You need something *real* to eat."

He chortled. "Real, eh?"

"You know what I mean. I don't want you to fade away to nothing. Please, won't you eat a sandwich?"

His cheeks flinched, and for the first time in weeks he put his arm around her. "I'll think about it, kiddo."

When they got up to the window, she was pleased to hear her dad order a cheeseburger and fries. Her hopes were high for a similar response to her personal skating revue. If she could just divert his attention long enough to retrieve her skates from the car, lace up, and claim center ice.

That's when she thought of talkative Mrs. Newton at

the fabric shop. "Can we window shop a little?" she asked as they located a table for two.

Her father groaned at the request. "You know how shopping affects me." He began to massage his temples. "I feel a migraine coming on."

"We'll just look, I promise."

He shook his head as if to say, "This is hopeless."

"Honest, Dad. I won't buy a thing!"

She waited, but he said no more. Encouraged, she assumed that his silence was a yes. She could hardly wait. "The Cloth Mill's nearby. It's a fabric shop."

"Fabric?"

"You know, to make outfits."

He frowned. "What outfits?"

"New school clothes, for one." She didn't dare mention skating costumes. Not yet.

Nodding, he continued to nibble on his cheeseburger.

Livvy didn't want to distract him from his food. But she *did* want to get him thinking about the Cloth Mill. She could only hope that Mrs. Newton was working tonight.

"I could use some new tops for school," she said. "I made a couple last fall. Mom and I—"

"We can *afford* to buy ready-made clothing," he interrupted.

"But, Dad, I—"

"There's no need for you to sew." His voice cracked, and when he reached to crumple their trash, Livvy saw that his hand was shaking.

So her plan was shot.

She didn't say a word about the fabric store again. And she didn't bother to show him the skating rink, either.

Pointless!

Dreams on Ice
Chapter Six

Br-r-ring!

The clock alarm jangled her awake. Livvy slammed her hand down on the turn-off button.

Ah . . . peace. She was tempted to lie back and snooze. Instead, she sat up and stretched.

Five o'clock seemed horribly early in Colorado. She had been getting up before dawn ever since grade-school days. Why was it so hard today?

Leaning back on her pillows, she stared past the tall windows at the opposite end of her spacious room. Sheer yellow curtains allowed her to see out into the blackness, thanks to the faint porch light below.

She craned her neck forward, looking and wondering. *Why is it so dark here?*

Getting up, she tiptoed to the stairs, heading to the

third floor. Soon it would be the studio loft. Once her dad finished the main part of the house, he planned to do some major work on his artist's getaway. Private and quaint, it was the ideal spot for his creativity.

She noticed his wall clock, the shape of an easel. Listening, she could hear its gentle clicking.

5:07 A.M. Same time as her clock.

Hurrying back to her room, she stood at the window. A dense cloud cover was the reason for the darkness. It was impossible for the sun to shine through. The weather matched her mood. This was to be her first skating day in Podunk town. A skating session on her own. Could she pull it off?

———

The mini mall was nearly deserted, except for a few early-morning walkers. Mostly older people, she guessed.

While doing her stretching exercises, she caught sight of two women. They looked closer to her mother's age than the others and chattered almost as fast as her cockatiel. But they didn't notice Livvy near the rink. They never paused to say "Good morning."

"Hello," she called just to see if they'd wave or greet her. They turned only briefly and smiled but kept going, their arms moving almost as fast as their trim legs.

"Looks like Mrs. Newton was only half right about

the people here," she mumbled as she stepped onto the ice.

Slowly, Livvy's legs began to warm up. She focused on the perimeters of the rink, eyeing it for size. Then around and around she skated. The delicate smoothness under her blades made her homesick for Elena . . . for her skating pals in Chicago. But she had to get the feel of this rink. Not Olympic size, but better than nothing.

The festive white lights in the trees surrounding the rink blurred as she sped up. Before ever attempting a jump, she practiced a long spiral, followed by a couple of sit spins.

I still have it, she thought. *I know I do!*

She remembered the thrill of competing at regionals as a novice last November. Her mother had made the trip to Michigan even though the chemo treatments had left her terribly weak. They'd hugged hard after Livvy's free-skate program. And Elena was there, all smiles, waiting for the judges' scoring.

The announcer's words rang in her ears. "Second place goes to Olivia Hudson from Illinois."

Super cool! She was on her way.

"This one's for you," she'd told her mom.

"No . . . no. You *deserve every bit of it, kiddo."* Tears of joy streamed down her mother's cheeks.

"Mom, please don't cry." Livvy had to fight back her own tears.

Please don't cry. . . .

The gentle swoosh of her skates brought her back to the present. She would allow herself only a twenty-minute workout today. Wisely, she knew she'd have to take things slowly. Steady too.

But Elena would be proud. Livvy was actually pacing herself . . . and without a coach!

In no time, though, her legs began to feel like rubber. Time to quit. No sense pushing herself too hard, especially on the first day of the school year. Besides, she had three long blocks to walk home.

Tired and a bit winded from the high altitude, Livvy hurried down the sidewalk toward the gray-and-white Victorian. The sun was making its first appearance as she walked the final block. Long pink wisps brushed the sky, as if an artist had splashed them up there.

"I believe in you, Livvy. . . ."

The memory of her mother's words encouraged her. And she slipped into the house unnoticed.

Quietly, she showered, put on fresh clothes, and headed for the kitchen. There she found a pitcher of orange juice already mixed and ready to drink. "Dad's up?" she said, smiling. "No way."

A bit hungry from her early morning skate, she plopped two pieces of wheat bread into the toaster. Then she packed her lunch for school. She still hadn't gotten over the shock at seeing the teensy-weensy middle school.

Even Dad had agreed it was peewee size when they'd gone to enroll her.

The building was as small as Livvy's grade school back home. In fact, Principal Seeley's office couldn't have been larger than a shoe box—at least her mom would've described it that way.

She forced a laugh, mostly to squash her fears. And she wondered about her locker partner, hoping whoever it was might be as friendly as Mrs. Newton at the Cloth Mill.

More worries filled her head. *Will the kids accept me?* she wondered. *Can a wanna-be Olympic skater fit in here?*

"Ready or not, here I come!" she announced to the bread as it flew up out of the toaster.

She heard footsteps. "Morning, Livvy."

"You're up early."

Sleepily, he opened the refrigerator. "Another long day ahead," he said, pulling out a quart of milk.

"More sanding and stuff?"

His eyes lit up. "Little by little, I'll make this house livable."

She couldn't help but grin. "We're *living* in it, aren't we?" Wiggling her fingers at him, she said, "Gotta run. The bus'll be here soon."

"Uh . . . wait a minute, kiddo."

She paused. "What is it?"

His eyes seemed to look right through her. "Must you get up so early?"

She sighed. "I *have* to skate. Every day!"

"But without a coach?" He placed his spoon in the cereal bowl, staring down at it.

"I'm doing my best on my own. A town this size . . ." She paused. Did she dare say it? Should she tell her dad what she really thought of his idea to come here?

His eyes met hers. "Are you trying to tell me there aren't any coaches in Alpine Lake?"

"Not for advanced skaters like me."

"I'm sorry, Livvy. I know it's *your* thing."

Quickly, she went to him. "You don't have to be sorry. Just please share my skating dreams with me. At least pretend you care about them." She touched his shoulder lightly. "I hated leaving Elena and all my friends. I despised it with all my heart. But I honestly think I can keep up without them . . . if I have *you*!"

Her father fidgeted and glanced at the wall clock nervously.

No comment. Her dad couldn't come up with one positive thing to say! Livvy wanted to shake him, to make him understand. Instead, she turned to go.

Her heart sank. She'd tried and failed to persuade him.

Bolting into the dining room, she passed the scraps of wood shavings and cans of stain.

Upstairs, she gathered up her three-ring binder and other school supplies, shoving them into her book bag. Before heading out the front door, she called to him. "I'm leaving now." She fought back tears. No sense letting herself cry. Not now.

"Come home right after school," he said from the kitchen.

"Can't I go to the rink for a while?"

"Be home by five o'clock. No later."

She snatched up her skate bag. Then, slinging her book bag over her shoulder, she left the house. She would never tell him that he sounded exactly like Mom just then. She would never dream of saying one word.

Dreams on Ice
Chapter Seven

Green and yellow gum wrappers were stuck all over the inside locker door next to Livvy's. Two girls in matching blue T-shirts shared the locker. One of them kept snapping her bubble gum.

"Hi," Livvy said, attempting a smile.

"Hey, you must be the new girl," said the gum chewer with enormous blue eyes.

"Unfortunately."

The girls turned away, whispering and giggling.

But she wouldn't let their cattiness discourage her. "I'm Olivia Hudson," she spoke up. "Most everyone calls me Livvy, so you can, too." She slammed her locker door a bit too hard.

The girls spun around. "Whoa, the skater's got a temper," declared the blond-haired gum chewer.

Livvy bit her tongue. "I'm not mad . . . not really."

"Could've fooled me," sassed the blonde.

"Wait a minute. How'd you know I was a skater?" Livvy asked.

The girl rolled her eyes and tilted her head coyly. "I just do."

Ignoring the comment, Livvy asked, "So . . . what's *your* name?"

"Diane Larson. Captain of the cheerleading squad."

Diane's short, plump friend set the record straight. "You were captain *last* year. And don't forget it." The petite girl smiled at Livvy. "Hi, I'm Suzy Buchanan."

"Nice to meet you," Livvy said, observing both of them. Diane was tall and wiry, with chin-length blond hair. Suzy was perky and cute, with big brown eyes and a sweet smile, her brunette hair pulled back in a ponytail.

"By the way, have either of you seen my locker partner?" she asked.

Diane and Suzy displayed total shock. "You're kidding! You don't know who you're sharing your locker with?" Diane gasped.

"All your stuff's in there, right?" Suzy asked.

Livvy felt nervous. "On second thought, maybe I'll just lug everything around with me. Till I meet her."

Promptly, she worked her combination lock again and yanked open the locker. Once again, Livvy noticed the upper shelf—lined with hot-pink carpet—as she checked out the place. An oval mirror with bright pink rickrack glued to its frame was tilted on its side. The mirror was attached to the inside of the door. "Whoever it is, she likes pink. Likes to primp, too."

"Don't we all," catty Diane remarked, popping her gum.

Suzy poked her. "Be nice, okay?"

"Whatever." And with that, Diane turned and dashed away.

"Wow, your locker's all jazzed up. That oughta tell you something," Suzy offered.

The brown-eyed girl was actually trying to help. "Hey, super," Livvy said, laughing. "She's probably a wanna-be teen model or something." She stared at the gum wrappers on Suzy's locker door. "And you must be into bubble gum. Do you sell it or just chew it?"

"Both," Suzy said, swinging her ponytail. She shoved her hand into her jeans pocket. "How many packs do you want?"

"Later, maybe."

"So who'd you get for homeroom?"

Livvy dug through her book bag and found her schedule.

"Smith . . . *Mrs.* Smith."

Suzy clutched her throat and made a gagging sound.

"What's wrong?"

Suzy shifted her books. "You'll find out soon enough. Diane and I had her last year."

"So you're seventh graders?" Livvy asked.

"And proud of it."

The first bell interrupted them.

"Well, is there something I should know about Mrs. Smith before I head for homeroom?" Livvy asked.

"Just don't ever let her catch you reading or writing while she's talking. It's her pet peeve. And I'm not kidding!"

"Thanks for the hint." Livvy was glad that Suzy was so friendly. Things had started out pretty iffy.

"Hope you meet your locker pal soon," Suzy called over her shoulder.

"Thanks. Me too." Livvy pushed her skate bag in the far corner of the locker and headed for Room 123—Mrs. Smith's homeroom. She reminded herself to give her undivided attention when the teacher was talking.

No problem . . . easy as a single toe loop!

———

Mrs. Smith got things started by greeting students. "It's good to see so many scrubbed faces . . . and smiling ones, too!"

A nervous ripple spread through the classroom. Nobody was smiling, at least not that Livvy could see.

"Now, let's get down to important business." She gave instructions for expected behavior, including the rule about paying attention at all times. "I assign 500-word essays for students who think I'm kidding."

The teacher wrote her name on the board. "This is just in case some of you forget."

Several kids snickered, but Livvy looked straight ahead.

Attendance was taken, and a few papers were handed out. "Please take these home and have a parent sign them. Return them by Wednesday . . . two days from now."

Mrs. Smith made an announcement about cheerleading tryouts. The girls sprang to life. "Sixth-grade girls will meet in the gymnasium at seven o'clock on Friday morning, September eleventh," said the teacher. "Seventh-grade girls, immediately after school on the same day. That's nearly two weeks to get in shape."

Livvy groaned inside. Why did sixth-grade tryouts have to be so early? Too close to early-morning skate time.

She waited until the teacher finished her announcements before jotting down a note about cheerleading. She didn't want to start the year out on the wrong foot. Especially in a new school.

She observed Mrs. Smith while waiting for the first-period bell. The teacher couldn't have been a day over twenty-five and was well dressed. She could've passed for a department-store clerk. Or . . . a judge at an important skating event.

Livvy shrugged the last thought away. No matter where she was, no matter what she was doing, her mind kept creeping back to skating.

———

During lunch period, Livvy ended up sitting alone. She was glad she'd packed her own sandwich. The meatloaf from the cafeteria looked absolutely mushy. Super ick!

Her friends back home would be choking if they could see the week's hot lunch menu. Livvy had stuffed it into her book bag—with the rest of her first-day papers.

Feeling like a stranger in alien territory, she started working on her homework. Math had always been one of her favorite subjects, so she began with the first page of problems.

Suddenly, she heard a familiar voice. "Well, hello there, Livvy."

She looked up to see Mrs. Newton. "How are you?"

"Now that you're smiling, I'm doing just fine." The woman sat across from her, fingering her charm bracelet. "How's your first day so far?"

"Oh, you know . . . being the new girl is a pain." She

hated to admit that she disliked the school and the town, too. "It takes time to fit in, I guess."

"Not if you're personal friends with the cheerleading coach." Mrs. Newton was beaming, pointing to herself.

"Really? You're in charge of tryouts?"

Mrs. Newton was nodding emphatically. "I guarantee you'll be as popular as punch if you hang out with me."

Livvy closed her homework. "You said you were a school volunteer when we met at the mall. I had no idea you were the cheerleading coach."

"Stick with me, Livvy. I'll make sure you get acquainted around here. And fast."

"Hey, thanks. Such a deal."

Grinning, Mrs. Newton excused herself. "I best be heading back to the library. I'm also the librarian's assistant."

Livvy couldn't believe her ears. "You're everywhere, Mrs. Newton!"

"No place I'd rather be." She waved, her bracelet jangling. "Come see me at the mall when you practice again."

Before Livvy could stop her, Mrs. Newton was swallowed up by the cafeteria crowd. Mostly by girls vying for her attention.

So . . . Mrs. Newton had seen her skating at the mall

rink. That meant she must work at the Cloth Mill *after* school hours. Livvy made a mental note to stop in and see the friendly woman there.

"Hey," Suzy Buchanan said, sliding in next to Livvy. "Are you saving a seat for me?" She blinked her eyes fast.

"Maybe."

They laughed together, which dismissed the tension a bit.

"I see you met our stunning Mrs. Newton," Suzy said.

"Yeah, she's super cool."

"You can say that again." Suzy opened her brown bag lunch and pulled out a napkin. "Have you met 'Hot Pink' yet?"

"Who?"

"Your locker partner."

"Oh, *her.* I've been back to my locker after every class but haven't seen anyone. Maybe she's absent today."

Suzy shook her head. "Whoever heard of missing school on the first day?" Neatly, she spread out her sandwich, some mini-pretzels, sliced apples, and chocolate-chip cookies. "Why don't you just hang out at your locker after school? That way you won't miss her."

"Super idea." Livvy watched her new friend first eat her sandwich, then her pretzels. The cookies came next, followed by three fat apple slices. "Any special reason why you save the apples for last?" she asked.

Suzy nodded, waiting to answer till she was finished chewing. "Apples clean your teeth. Did you know that?"

Livvy thought about it. "Why don't you just bring your toothbrush along and brush your teeth?"

Suzy reached into her book bag and pulled out a small zipper case. "Ta-dah!"

"You've gotta be kidding." Livvy spied a toothbrush, dental floss, and a teeny tube of toothpaste. "Looks like you're prepared for anything."

"Always!" Suzy grinned.

"So why bother eating your lunch in *any* order?" Livvy asked, noticing the remaining apple slice.

Eyebrows high, Suzy zipped the little bag shut. "Guess it's just a habit. I sorta drive people crazy that way."

"Like who?" Livvy was pretty sure she already knew.

"Diane, for one. But it's easy to annoy her, if you know what I mean."

Livvy wondered about that but played it safe and didn't ask. She thought it would be nice to talk to Suzy—friend to friend. Maybe even mention her skating goals and ask Suzy about her hobbies. Stuff like that.

She was that close to sticking her neck out and getting better acquainted when Diane Larson showed up.

"Are you trying out for cheerleader this year?" Diane asked, looking only at Suzy.

"Maybe I will, maybe I won't," Suzy sassed with a grin.

"Aw, c'mon," the taller girl said, sitting down across from them. "You have to at least try out. *Everyone* will be."

Livvy's ears perked up. "*All* the girls?"

"Well, you know." Diane seemed too eager for Suzy's reaction to make eye contact with Livvy. "So . . . *are* you?"

Suzy muttered into her brown bag, then stashed her trash inside. Turning, she looked at Livvy. "You'll come and try out, won'tcha?"

Livvy crumpled up her napkin and the sandwich bag. "Me? I doubt it."

"Why not?" Suzy persisted. "You ought to. You're tall . . . and pretty. And it looks like you're in tight with Mrs. Newton, too."

"Leave Livvy out of this," Diane blurted, her eyes flashing.

"Don't be rude," Suzy shot back.

"Don't be stupid!" Diane flounced off.

Suzy stood up, eyes pleading. "Honestly, she's totally insecure."

Livvy chuckled. "I never would've guessed."

Suzy laughed, too, and tossed her trash into the receptacle. "Hey, you're cool, Liv. See you at your locker."

Livvy felt as warm as cocoa on a winter day. Now . . . if she could just meet "Hot Pink," her mystery locker mate!

Dreams on Ice
Chapter Eight

So far, things had gone semi-okay for the first day of school. There was only one thing left to do. And Livvy was determined to do it. Even if she had to stand in front of her locker and miss the school bus, she was going to meet her locker partner!

"Any luck?" Suzy asked, gathering her books after school.

Livvy shrugged. "Beats me who she is." She surveyed the interior of her locker for the tenth time.

"Hey, wait a minute," Suzy said. "Maybe the pink carpet was glued in from last year."

Livvy didn't think so. "Except what about this snazzy mirror?" She traced the pink frame with her pointer finger. "Nobody would leave *this* behind."

"Seems like 'Hot Pink' would've stashed her books in

here by now," Suzy said, peering into the locker. "Real weird, isn't it?"

"Sure is."

Just then a girl with short, dark hair came bouncing down the hallway. "Ex-*cuse* me," she called to Livvy and Suzy. "Is that *my* locker?"

Suzy's eyebrows shot up. Playfully, she jabbed Livvy. "Could this be Hot Pink?" she whispered.

Livvy groaned. "Oh great."

Suzy spun away to her own locker just as the girl came rushing up.

But Livvy stood her ground. "I'm assigned to this locker, too. We're locker partners for the year."

The girl stepped back, eyeing the upper shelf. "Looks like you've made yourself right at home."

"It was hard *not* to. I mean, I've never seen a carpeted locker before. You did a super job of decorating."

Hot Pink frowned, staring at the top section. "I was planning to use the upper shelf, but if you really want it . . ."

Livvy wasn't going to quarrel. New or not, she didn't need a hassle. "No, this is fine." She reached up and removed her books from the carpeted shelf. Squatting on the floor, she arranged them in her book bag.

Meanwhile, Hot Pink began to organize the bright shelf with her books. "It'll be tight quarters—with all my books and yours—but let's try to keep everything separate."

"Super."

Hot Pink whirled around. "What did you say?"

Livvy stood up. "I said, 'super.' "

And for the first time since Hot Pink had arrived, the two girls looked into each other's faces.

Unbelievable, thought Livvy. Her locker partner could've passed for her pen pal's older sister. She recalled Jenna's school picture—the waist-length hair and the big smile.

Livvy continued to gawk. "Are you . . . could you be related to someone named Jenna Song? She lives near here."

Hot Pink burst out laughing. "Related?"

"It's just that you look so much like her." Livvy smiled, jostling her book bag. "Do you happen to know Jenna? Because she's my pen pal."

Hot Pink's eyes popped wide open. "You're . . . you've gotta be kidding."

"No, I've been writing to Jenna for several months now," Livvy said, wondering why the girl seemed so surprised.

"Are you an ice skater?" asked Hot Pink.

Livvy gulped. "How did you know?"

The girl gasped and covered her mouth. "Livvy? Olivia Hudson? What are *you* doing here?"

"I . . . I just moved here." She stared at her locker partner. "How do you know my name?"

"Because *I'm* your pen pal. I'm Jenna Song!"

Livvy was speechless. "You're Jenna? But your picture, your long hair—"

"The picture I sent you was last year's school picture. Besides, I had my hair cut short for school. It was a pain always putting my hair up for gymnastics and ballet."

All of a sudden they were hugging and giggling. "I wrote you a letter about moving," Livvy tried to explain. "Did you get it?"

"No, but that's because *we* were moving at the same time."

Livvy was going to burst. "I can't believe this! Why'd you move *here*?"

"Because my dad is the new pastor at the Korean church."

She grabbed her skate bag and closed the locker. "So that's why we're going to the same school!"

Jenna was still laughing as the two of them headed for the bus stop. "This is just too cool."

"I wonder how long it would've taken for us to actually meet."

Jenna smoothed her hair. "You mean if we hadn't been assigned the same locker?"

"It's super, isn't it?" Livvy meant it with all of her heart.

The girls waited for the bus together, still chattering about their first day of school.

"Where do you live?" asked Jenna.

"Main Street . . . in the tallest Victorian on the block." She didn't say the ugliest.

"My house is a couple of streets south of there. You'll have to visit sometime."

"Maybe we can have a sleepover."

Jenna's grin reached from ear to ear. "Are you trying out for cheerleading?"

"Probably not."

"How come?"

She told Jenna about her plan to keep skating without a coach. "It'll be tough, but I'm not quitting."

"I don't blame you. You were right on track for the Olympics."

"Well, not quite *that* close."

Jenna turned to face her. "You're really good for your age. C'mon, Livvy, I don't know of many sixth-grade girls who reach novice level."

She couldn't deny it. But at the same time, she didn't want to think about what she'd given up back home.

"Why'd you and your dad move to Colorado any-how?"

"Dad thought we needed a change of scenery," Livvy said. That was all she wanted to say. At least for now.

The bus pulled up to the curb just then. They waited for a group of kids to get on, then hurried up the steps and back as far as they could sit.

"So did you move because of your mom?" asked Jenna, her eyes full of concern.

Livvy felt horribly uncomfortable. She couldn't allow herself to talk about personal things. Not with Diane Larson sitting across the aisle, giving her the eyeball every other second. "Maybe we can talk later . . . in private. Okay?"

Jenna seemed to understand. "I'll call you tonight."

They exchanged phone numbers, and when the bus stopped in front of the little mall, Livvy slid out of the seat.

"Hey, where're you going?" Jenna called to her.

"To the ice rink." She couldn't help but notice Diane's hard frown. No way was *she* going to interfere with Livvy's skating plans.

Jenna leaped out of her seat. "Wait up, Livvy!"

Thrilled beyond belief, she waited for her hot-pink friend to catch up.

"You're just like me," Jenna declared as they walked toward the mall entrance. "Completely obsessed."

"That's a good thing, I hope."

"Super good," Jenna added.

And they laughed at Jenna's use of Livvy's favorite word.

Dreams on Ice
Chapter Nine

August 31

Dear Grandma,

Today was the first day of school, and you'll never guess what happened. I met Jenna Song. She's my locker partner!

I thought moving to this town was going to be the worst thing that ever happened to me. And here I have a built-in best friend! She's in training . . . just like me. Only Jenna's a gymnast.

With Jenna to hang out with, I won't be constantly thinking about missing skating competitions. It's bad enough losing my coach, but now I have someone to talk to who understands my passion. And someone I'm hoping to attend ballet classes with!

Today after school she watched me skate at the mall

rink. If I can talk Dad into it, Jen and I will be in the same ballet class.

Dad's working too hard, as always. This time it's the house. The place is going to be super nice when he's finished.

Write soon, okay?

Love,
Livvy

She folded the letter and slid it into the middle drawer of her desk. Just in case she thought of something else to write. Like a P.S. or something.

———

After supper, the phone rang.

"I'll get it," Livvy called over the noise of the sander. She picked up the portable phone in the kitchen. "Hudson residence, Olivia speaking."

"Listen, and listen good," said a muffled voice. "Go back to where you came from."

"Excuse me?"

"I'm not saying this twice—you're not welcome here!"

Livvy didn't bother to wait for more. She felt weak in the legs and hung up.

"Who was on the line?" her dad called from the dining room. He'd stopped sanding partway through the phone call.

"Wrong number, I guess."

He went right back to making more racket. Livvy was relieved. She didn't want to tell him that someone at school was trying to frighten her. Probably Diane Larson. She was almost positive that's who had called, disguising her pitiful little voice.

The phone rang again.

Livvy's heart thumped. What should she say if it was the same person? She didn't want to lose her cool. The girl had no right to terrorize her!

Cautiously, she picked up the phone. "Hello?"

"Hi, it's Jenna."

Livvy was so relieved, she started laughing.

"What's so funny?"

Livvy explained. "I just got this bizarre call. It was so mysterious and . . . garbled, kinda. Like maybe the person didn't want me to know who was calling."

"Who do you think it was?" Jenna asked.

Livvy breathed deeply. "Might've been Diane Larson. She hates me, and I don't know why."

"Who's this girl, anyway?" asked Jenna.

"She shares the locker next to us . . . with Suzy Buchanan. The locker with all the gum wrappers."

"Oh yeah, I remember. Introduce me tomorrow, okay?" Jenna said.

"I'll give it a shot, but if Diane really wants me outta

here, she won't stand still long enough to meet my best friend. Not if I'm the one doing the introductions."

"Are you sure Diane feels that way?"

"Positive."

"I wonder why."

"That's what I'm gonna find out," said Livvy.

They went on to talk about school and all their different subjects. Homeroom too.

"Middle school's so much better than grade school," Jenna said. "The biggest hassle is keeping all my teachers straight."

"I know what you mean. But maybe by the end of the week we'll know who's who." She hoped to steer their conversation away from personal things. "Isn't it cool, both of us being the new girls together?"

"Wouldn't have it any other way." Then Jenna excused herself. It sounded like she'd clamped her hand over the receiver.

Livvy could hear another voice in the background. She waited, wondering what was happening on the other end at the Song residence.

"Okay, I'm back," said Jenna. "My mom wants to know if you and your dad would like to come for supper this Saturday."

Livvy was speechless. She'd love to meet Jenna's parents, but she wasn't so sure if her dad would. He was mostly distant since Mom died. Especially around strangers.

"Tell your mom thanks, but I'll have to check with Dad. He's remodeling our house right now . . . the place is kind of trashed. Maybe when it's finished."

"Are you saying you might not come?"

She didn't want to offend her friend. Not for anything. "I'll have to ask."

"Okay. Just let me know."

Livvy felt suddenly anxious to get off the phone. "Sorry things are so messed up right now, Jen. I'll see you tomorrow."

"Everything okay?"

"Well, not exactly. But we'll talk later."

"Wait, Livvy . . ."

"I've got so much homework. Talk to you tomorrow. Bye." She hung up, feeling lousy. She'd shut out her dearest and best friend.

What *was* she thinking?

Dreams on Ice
Chapter Ten

Livvy awoke long before the clock radio sounded. She hadn't slept well. Her dreams had been disturbing.

The morning turned out lousy, too, including the discovery of curdled milk. She skipped eating cereal and had two pieces of toast and jelly and some applesauce instead.

At the rink, she missed nearly every jump. And when she tried her best camel spin, she toppled. Getting up, she worried that someone might've seen her pathetic performance. But when she glanced around, Livvy saw only an elderly man sitting on a bench near the rink. Tall and dressed for church or somewhere else special, the man looked like anyone's grandfather. No need to worry, she decided.

At about 6:45 a group of younger skaters showed up.

Three girls and two boys. Livvy wondered where their instructor might be, but no adult arrived.

She pushed herself for an additional ten minutes, inching up her total skate time to a full half hour. Back home, there had been many days of two forty-minute sessions before school. Here in Podunk, she seemed to lose her focus after only one session.

Getting up the nerve, she skated over to one of the girls. "Where's your instructor?"

"She'll be here any minute now," said the girl. "Our coach likes us to warm up on our own sometimes."

Livvy hadn't seen this group of skaters before. "Do you skate here often?" she asked.

"Three times a week. On Saturdays we drive to Colorado Springs to the World Arena. It's fabulous."

"How far away?"

"Less than an hour."

"Thanks," Livvy said, feeling all jittery. If Colorado Springs was so close, maybe she could find herself a coach there. She'd have to get her dad to agree. *That* would be the biggest hurdle!

On the walk home, she thought of all the things she wanted to talk over with Dad. Ballet lessons, the Saturday night dinner invitation, and the possibility of having a new coach. And there was the problem of the spoiled milk, too.

Should she mention everything at once? Making sure

the milk was fresh should be high on the list. Unless, of course, they could afford to have milk delivered to the house.

Livvy watched as the quaint little milk truck made its way down the street, stopping at one house, then the next.

"Things are falling apart here, Mom," she said into the air as she hurried home. "Sometimes I wonder if you can see how mixed up our lives are."

Then, just in case her mom *could* hear her complaining, she quickly added, "Please, Mom, don't worry . . . we'll make it somehow. I know we will."

For another whole block, she forced herself to walk quietly, without mumbling to her mother. It was hard, but she made it.

When the gray-and-white Victorian came into view, she quickened her pace. The skate bag bounced as she ran up the front steps and into the house. "Daddy, can we talk?" she called to him. Not waiting for an answer, she hurried into the kitchen. To the fridge.

There, on the top shelf, stood an unopened half gallon of fresh milk.

She heard footsteps and spun around. "Oh, Daddy, thanks for getting some more milk!" She ran to him, wrapping her arms around him.

"It's just milk, kiddo. No big deal."

But it *was* a big deal. One less thing on her mental

list of concerns. She couldn't remember feeling so relieved.

They sat down together and poured cold milk over
their frosted cereal. Livvy chattered all the while about
school and meeting Jenna Song . . . and skating. "It's
amazing what I found out today."

"What's that, honey?" Her dad was giving her his
undivided attention for a change.

"Colorado Springs is only a short distance from here,"
she explained. "Maybe I could find a new skating coach
there."

His face wrinkled into a frown. "What about trans-
portation?"

"Maybe I could catch a ride with other skaters, or . . ."
She wanted to say that maybe *he* could take her sometimes.

"Well, right now we don't have the money for
a skating coach," he said. "Not here or in Colorado
Springs."

"But . . . we had enough money before Mom died.
Didn't we?"

Suddenly, he fell silent, and his eyes no longer made
contact with hers.

She could've kicked herself. Right in the middle of a
great conversation, she'd made a dumb mistake!

"I'm sorry, Dad. I didn't mean to say anything about
Mom. I didn't—"

"Skating lessons are out of the question." His words were ice, and she dreaded the sound of them.

Now was not the time to bring up Jenna's supper invitation. Not ballet lessons, either. Livvy excused herself from the table and raced upstairs to shower and dress for school. She felt worse than ever. Actually, almost sick.

Her cockatiel tried to cheer her up, though. "Happy, happy Livvy," Coco chanted.

"Hush, bird." She slipped into her bathrobe.

His little white head cocked over to one side, his beady eyes blinking innocently. "Happy Livvy. Ha . . . ha . . . ha."

She couldn't stop the burst of air. It flew right past her lips. "I'm *not* even close to feeling happy, and you're one nosy parrot. That's no lie!"

"No lie . . . no lie."

Glancing at the clock, Livvy knew she'd have to rush to get ready. "I'll talk to *you* later."

"Livvy later . . . *caw!*"

In the shower, she scrubbed her body and shampooed her hair. All the while, she fretted over her slip-up at breakfast. *How long before I can talk about Mom in front of Dad?* she fumed.

She dressed faster than ever because she didn't want to be late for school. Not on the second day! Not on any day, come to think of it. Mrs. Smith had warned her homeroom about tardiness. Talk about strict.

Livvy did not want to write a 500-word essay! No matter what.

———

Jenna was waiting for her at their locker. "Well, can you come for dinner Saturday night?"

"I didn't ask my dad yet," Livvy confessed. "He was in a horrible mood this morning."

"Does he have to be in a good mood to decide about eating?"

She stared at Jenna, feeling uneasy. "Well, uh . . . it's kinda complicated." Livvy glanced around. "Can we talk at lunch?"

"Okay with me." Jenna turned to go. "See ya later."

Livvy pushed her skate bag back into the corner of the open locker. Then, standing up, she gazed down the crowded hallway. She felt terribly embarrassed and searched for Jenna, but her friend was nowhere in sight.

She stacked up her books in the lower section of the locker. And kept her math book and notebook out for first hour. "Thank goodness for homeroom," she mumbled to herself. At least she'd have time to calm down before her first class.

"Talking to yourself?"

Livvy turned to see Suzy lugging several books and her three-ring binder. She looked almost too small to be a seventh grader. "Oh, hi again."

Suzy squinted down the hall. "Hot Pink's kinda upset, looks like."

"How do you know?"

"I think she was praying . . . outside."

Livvy wasn't sure she'd heard right. "You sure?"

"Well, I saw her lips moving, and her eyes were definitely closed." Suzy twirled her combination lock, then pushed down on it.

Livvy leaned against her locker. "What's wrong with praying? It's a free country, isn't it?"

Suzy shrugged. "Just better watch out. She might try to get you on God's side, too."

Livvy wondered why Suzy was saying this. Jenna was one of the coolest girls around. And one of the best gymnasts on her team. Not to mention a really good friend.

"Lots of people pray," Livvy defended her friend. "Including me." She didn't feel like saying more. The truth was, it had been a very long time since she'd felt like praying.

Suzy taped another gum wrapper to the inside of her locker door. "Just don't expect Diane to go for any of that church stuff. From what Diane says, Jenna's dad is a pastor here in town somewhere."

"That's true, but how does Diane know so much about Jenna?"

A sly smile crossed Suzy's lips. "That girl knows everything about everyone. And don't say I didn't warn you." With that, the bell rang. Suzy darted into the stream of students.

Livvy remembered the weird phone call. "Wait!" she called after Suzy. But it was too late. Suzy had been gulped up by the homeroom rush.

Livvy dragged her feet to Room 123. She wished she'd stayed home in Chicago . . . with Grandma!

Dreams on Ice
Chapter Eleven

Lunch hour turned out far different than Livvy expected. No time to talk personally with Jenna. Not even five minutes' worth.

First off, Mrs. Newton came over and hung out at Livvy's table. Suzy showed up quickly. So did Jenna, wearing an enormous grin. Especially after Livvy informed her friend that Mrs. Newton was head of cheerleading.

Diane Larson didn't waste any time coming over, either. She squeezed in next to Suzy, her clear blue eyes merry with anticipation. "Who's gonna judge cheerleading tryouts?" she asked.

Mrs. Newton grinned. "You're lookin' at her."

Diane nodded. "Okay with me." She tapped her perfectly manicured fingernails on the table top.

"How many spots are open for just the seventh grade?" Suzy asked, glancing at Diane.

"Counting pompon girls, six." Mrs. Newton seemed excited. "We're getting new outfits this year for *all* the grades. The Cloth Mill is giving the school a discount on some expensive fabric."

Diane spoke up. "What're the patterns like?"

Suzy laughed. "Don't worry, the skirts are probably plenty cute, if that's what you're asking."

Mrs. Newton was nodding her head. "Pleated skirts, as always. But the tops are totally different this year."

Diane's face gleamed. "Like how?"

Moving her fingers, Mrs. Newton pretended to zip her lips. "My secret is sealed."

"Aw, please?" Diane begged.

Playfully, Jenna jabbed Livvy as they looked on.

"What're the school colors?" Livvy asked.

"Same as the Denver Broncos. Orange and navy blue." Mrs. Newton was obviously proud about that. "I'm a big fan of Alpine Lake Middle School," she informed Livvy and Jenna. "Betcha can't tell."

Livvy laughed. "Oh, we can tell, all right."

Mrs. Newton gave high fives to each girl before excusing herself.

"Isn't she something?" Livvy said when the woman had gone.

Jenna agreed. "Sure makes being the two new kids on the block a whole lot easier."

Diane's cheerful face turned to a scowl. "Don't go getting your hopes up about cheerleading."

Livvy shot back. "You haven't seen Jenna perform, have you? She'd make a fabulous cheerleader. She's one of the *best* gymnasts ever."

"I've heard," Diane replied, her eyes flashing with disdain. "Just don't hold your breath. Either of you!"

Livvy nudged Jenna's sleeve, trying to get her to leave the table.

"Don't bother to leave," Diane sneered. "We're outta here."

But Suzy wasn't going anywhere. "Speak for yourself, Larson," she hissed back. "I'm hanging with the new kids."

Definitely flustered, Diane batted her eyes. She shook her head and left in a huff.

———

Livvy and Jenna sat in the very back of the bus after school. In order to claim the coveted seats, they'd dashed out to the bus stop before any upperclassmen ever arrived.

"This is so cool," Jenna said, folding her arms and leaning back.

"We should do this more often," Livvy agreed as the bus pulled away from the curb. She looked ahead to Diane and several other girls in less-desirable seats halfway up, closer to the front.

She whispered to her friend about a couple of cute boys. "It's super being able to talk without Diane nosing around."

"Maybe, but I think she's having a rough time," Jenna said softly.

"Huh?"

"Diane needs us more than you think." Jenna's eyes were shining.

Livvy had no idea what she meant. "Are you for real?"

"Just watch her. She's wobbly."

Livvy observed Diane sitting with Suzy Buchanan. "Like unsure of herself?"

Jenna whispered, "No, just plain wobbly."

Livvy sighed. "You say the weirdest things."

"I do?" Jenna was laughing now. "Well, maybe there's a good reason."

"Like what?" Livvy was eager to know. Any info about Diane Larson would be helpful.

But Jenna only grinned.

"I'm waiting," said Livvy. And for the first time since she'd met Jenna face-to-face, her former pen pal seemed very mysterious.

"Waiting for what?"

"For you to tell me why you think Diane is more needy than nasty?"

"Sure, I'll tell you . . . *sometime*" came the secretive reply.

"Like when?"

"When you tell me why you moved out here."

So they both had a secret. Except Livvy was still trying to answer the "moving" question herself.

———

Grandma Hudson called right after supper and kept Dad on the phone for the longest time.

"Something wrong?" she asked as he hung up.

He was staring at her. "I guess it's time to call a family meeting."

"What's up with Grandma?"

He motioned her into the living room. "You may not be too thrilled about this." He sat at the end of the sofa. "I don't know how I feel about it, either."

Dad stopped talking for a moment.

"Is Grandma sick?" Livvy was still standing in the middle of the room.

"Better sit down, kiddo." He plumped the pillow next to him. "Your grandmother's worried about us."

"Well, somebody oughta be," Livvy mumbled.

Her father turned and looked at her, frowning. "Where on earth did *that* come from?"

She forced a puff of air past her lips. Now she'd have to explain herself for sure.

"I think it's time we level with each other." He began rolling his shirt sleeves up to the elbows. Like he was getting ready to tackle a major repair job.

She crossed her arms. "Are you actually going to hear me out?"

"Livvy . . . honey."

Her words sounded disrespectful, and she felt ashamed. "Can we *really* talk to each other, Daddy?" Her words came more softly.

Dad nodded, offering a winning smile. "Why don't you go first?"

So she did. She leaped right at the question and asked him why they'd come here. "I need to know," she said, her heart in her throat. "It was such a hard thing for me— leaving our real home behind."

His eyes shone suddenly with more than expectation. When she saw the tears, Livvy wished she'd never brought up the question.

"Back home, it seemed that your mother was everywhere I looked," he began. "I couldn't think, sketch, or create without seeing her face."

A familiar ache stabbed her throat. She thought she might cry right there in front of him.

"You and I both needed a new place in the world, away from all the memories. We had to start over, Livvy."

"Maybe you needed to, but I needed to stay. I *wanted* to stay. Mom's buried back home. I can't ever go and sit beside her grave and talk . . . not in this town."

"But you do talk to her. . . ."

His words were unexpected. "How . . . how did you know?"

He put his arm around her and drew her close. "I've overheard some of your conversations, kiddo. Mostly in the early morning, when you think I'm out cold and don't hear you getting ready to head for the rink."

Sighing, she snuggled against her father. "I can't seem to let her go. I just can't. . . ."

"I'm not asking you to."

She could hear his heart beating against her ear.

"It's going to take a long time to get used to things the way they are," he said.

She wanted to say something about that but didn't think now was a good time to talk about skating. Or ballet.

They were silent long enough for Livvy to remember the reason why they were having this talk in the first place. "What about Grandma Hudson?" she asked, sitting up. "Let's talk about her."

He leaned his elbows on his knees. "She wants to come for a visit."

"That's okay with me."

"Grandma wants to come here and try Alpine Lake on for size . . . maybe move in with us."

Livvy cringed. "You're kidding. Why?"

Dad turned and looked at her, his eyes searching hers. "She thinks you need a mother replacement."

Leaning back, Livvy covered her face with her hands. "She's my *grandmother*! No one can ever take Mom's place. She oughta know that!"

"Your grandmother means well."

"It'll never work, you'll see," she complained.

"I think we should give it a chance."

Livvy did *not* agree. But she wasn't going to let anything come between her and Dad. Not now, after their first heart-to-heart talk ever!

Dreams on Ice
Chapter Twelve

After skating the next morning, Livvy came home to find her Dad up and dressed. "We've been invited for supper," she said as casually as possible. Hoping . . . hoping.

"Where to?" He was stirring up some eggs and milk at the counter. Making a mess.

"Jenna Song's mom invited us to their house Saturday night. Wanna go?"

He shrugged a little. "If you'd like to . . . sure."

"You mean it?" She hugged him, then cleaned up the spills around the mixing bowl. "This is incredible!"

"Having dinner with your friends might help us fit in better around here."

She felt light enough to float. "I'll tell Jenna first thing." Scurrying off to clean up and put on fresh clothes,

Livvy could hardly wait to see her friend's expression. "This is so-o super!" she squealed to herself, taking the steps two at a time.

Upstairs, Coco got all excited, too. He started squawking back at her.

"Calm down, fella," she cooed, tapping his cage gently. "Nothing for *you* to get wound up about."

As she spun around the room, her feet could hardly keep from dancing. Maybe her dad was coming out of his hermit's shell. Maybe things were going to change.

Flying around the spacious room, she felt dizzy and stopped in front of her calendar. The featured world-champion ice skaters seemed to be spinning, too. Both guys and girls.

She reached up and flipped the pages back past August and July, to June tenth. The saddest day of her life, forever marked with a sad face.

Life as she'd known it had stopped on that date. For Dad, too. She knew that no matter how many Saturday suppers they attended, the pain of losing Mom was never going to disappear.

———

Jenna was sporting an orange T-shirt and navy blue pants when she boarded the bus that morning. Some of the boys cheered, and Livvy giggled about it.

"Back here!" she waved, calling to her friend.

"Why'd the boys carry on like that?" Jenna whispered to her as she settled into the seat.

"Because you're cute, silly."

Jenna laughed and fluffed her short hair. "It's probably the orange and blue colors. I heard it was school spirit day."

"No one said anything in homeroom yesterday." She looked down at her own faded blue jeans and white T-shirt. "Are you sure?"

"Well, Diane Larson called me last night. That's how I heard."

"Sounds like a trick to me."

"Well, if it is, I fell for it." Jenna straightened her iridescent orange shirt. "But, oh well . . ."

"How can you just do that?" Livvy stared at her.

"Do what?"

"You know, pretend like it's nothing."

Jenna piled her book bag on her lap. "It's not easy getting along with someone like Diane. But I have this feeling about her. Like I told you, I think she needs a true friend."

It was the way Jenna said *true* that made her wonder. Something about it reminded her of Grandma Hudson's approach to things. Her dad's mother had always been one to forgive and forget quickly.

"Hey, I have some good news," Livvy said. "We're

coming to your house on Saturday. If we're still invited."

"You sure are!" Jenna squeezed her hand. "This is so cool!"

"I didn't know what Dad would decide. He's been hiding away from the world—like a hermit—since Mom died."

Jenna nodded. "I don't blame him. Do you?"

The comment took her breath away. Her friend had a way of firing off unexpected questions. "Well, I think I understand why he'd wanna stay away from people. It's been just a little over two months since we lost Mom."

"Maybe that's why your dad picked Alpine Lake. It's far away from the past, isn't it?"

Livvy felt like she was being quizzed. "Dad and I had a long talk last night. Bottom line: He says we needed to get away from our old house back in Illinois."

"Because it reminded him of your mother?"

Livvy nodded thoughtfully.

The bus made another stop. Suzy and Diane came on board, laughing and talking to each other. Livvy was thankful that they found seats close to the front.

They waited for the traffic light to turn, then the bus jerked forward. All the while, Livvy stared at the back of Diane's head. *Is she the mystery caller?*

Livvy turned and looked out the window, watching the

old clapboard houses and the cars whiz by. She longed for the old days as tears blurred her vision.

"I've been praying for you, Livvy," her friend said.

Livvy fought the lump in her throat, still gazing out the window. "Thanks," she managed to say.

"Ever since you wrote me about your mom's illness," Jenna added.

Jenna's remark touched her heart. And Livvy was ashamed for not praying much herself.

They rode along in silence. Halfway to school, Jenna pulled something out of her pants pocket. "Before I forget . . . your letter finally came."

Livvy studied the double postmark. "Looks like it got forwarded to your new address."

"You called this town Podunk, USA, in your letter, remember?" Jenna was grinning about it. "But you know what? I think I like that name almost better than Alpine Lake."

Now *both* of them were gawking out the bus window. Livvy noticed there were fewer trees here than back home. Mostly tall Ponderosa pines. Rugged and irregular, they were different from the trees in Chicago. Everything was different here.

"Podunk's pretty tiny, isn't it?" Jenna said, snickering again. "But you should've seen the place where we used to live. My dad called it a 'one-horse town.' And I'm not kidding."

"One horse or one mall?" asked Livvy.

"Oh, we had a little mall, all right," said Jenna. "But nothing to brag about."

"Like Podunk?" Livvy said.

"Yep," answered Jenna, laughing.

Livvy couldn't help but laugh, too.

Dreams on Ice
Chapter Thirteen

Livvy stopped in to see Mrs. Newton at the Cloth Mill after school.

The woman seemed pleased to see her. "How would you like a sneak preview of the new cheerleader outfits?" she asked.

"I thought they were top secret."

"Well, I can trust *you,* can't I?" The woman's bangles and bracelets jingle-jangled as she motioned Livvy over to a wall cupboard. She reached up to turn the knob but paused in midair. "Here we are." Out came yards and yards of soft navy blue fabric and the top-secret pattern.

Livvy was still surprised that Mrs. Newton was showing her the pattern. "Who will sew the outfits?" she asked.

"Oh, you'd be surprised at the moms who'll volunteer."

Livvy nodded slowly, thinking of the many sewing projects she and her mom had shared together over the years.

"Oh, my dear, have I got no heart?" Mrs. Newton was saying. "I've gone and lost my head, it seems." And she asked Livvy to please forgive her. "Such an unthinking person I must be."

"No, not at all," Livvy insisted. Here was the perfect time to tell the woman how very kind she had been. Right from the start. "It's super nice to have someone like you as a friend."

"Why, thank you, Livvy. I'm proud to call you my friend, too." There was a glint in her expressive eyes. "I've been watching you skate," she said, her voice growing even more sweet. "During my break, I've seen you working out all by yourself."

"You have?"

"Oh yes, and you're very good." Mrs. Newton told her how she liked to stop off and have a cup of coffee at the Oo-La-La Café. "Right across from the rink, that's where I sip and watch," the woman said, looking mighty pleased with herself.

Livvy grinned, delighted with the compliment. "Well, thank you. I'm not used to people watching me practice anymore." She hesitated at first, then found herself pouring out her grief. She talked mostly of her father's lack of interest. "I don't think Daddy understands how badly I want to go to the Olympics someday."

Mrs. Newton patted her hand. "Stick to your dreams, Livvy. You must never give up on yourself." She chuckled a little. "My goodness, not as talented as you are."

She was almost afraid the woman would ask if she was going to try out for cheerleading. But they talked about everything *but* that. And Livvy was relieved.

She hated to say good-bye. But it was time to hit the ice. Today her goal was to push for a forty-minute session. Do or die!

Mrs. Newton's words of encouragement echoed in her brain, and she grinned to herself. Near the rink, she found a half-occupied bench and began to remove her tennis shoes.

The same grandfatherly man sat at the opposite end, a rolled-up newspaper in his hand. Instead of reading, he was watching several skaters as they practiced their technique.

"Excuse me, do you happen to have the time?" she asked, leaning over.

He glanced at his watch, then grinned at her. "Skate time or otherwise?"

"Otherwise, please." She didn't give his clever comment a second thought.

Promptly, he added, "It's nearly three-thirty."

"Thank you."

"You're very welcome, young lady." He unfolded his paper and shook it out. "Please, don't mind me. You go on and have fun skating."

She pulled on her white skates and laced up. Livvy could hardly wait to warm up. Skating was like flying—or better. The slick surface beneath her blades made her feel absolutely free. Like escaping from every imaginable problem and pain of her life.

Today she pretended to skate for a packed crowd, filled with hundreds of cheering fans. Soaring across the rink, she practiced some of her best fancy footwork.

Then, when she was ready, she posed at center ice. Waiting as if for the musical cue, she began her short program—the one from her last regional event. She could still hear the music in her head, the dazzling score from *Anastasia*.

She didn't have to hum the phrases to remember where her jumps and spins fit in. The thrilling strains filled her, and the performance was smooth and elegant. One of the best practices she'd had since coming to Podunk town.

"I skated my best, Mom," she whispered as she began cooling down. "I did it."

In her imagination, the fans were standing, throwing teddy bears onto the ice. Thunderous applause! She could almost see the young skaters darting here and there as they picked up bouquets of flowers. *Her* flowers! Just the way she hoped it would be someday at the Olympics.

Someday, if she ever found another coach. If she ever got back every ounce of her confidence. . . .

Dreams on Ice
Chapter Fourteen

After supper, Livvy sprawled on the couch. The living room windows yawned wide and still the house was warm. Much too hot to do homework or anything else.

Livvy decided to relax in front of the TV for a while. After a few boring scenes, she gave in to the scratchy feeling beneath her eyelids. She closed her eyes—just to rest a bit—and she was in dreamland. Lake Placid, New York, where some of the best skaters in the world train. . . .

In her dream, she heard the musical introduction for her free-skate program. The soul-stirring strains from the overture-fantasy *Romeo and Juliet* by Tchaikovsky started her four-minute routine. Her flowing green costume made her feel like an ice princess with its Austrian crystals sewn on the bodice, sleeves, and hem. They sparkled like diamonds under the arena lights, and she skated her heart out for the enthusiastic crowd.

Just as she was awaiting the judges' marks, the phone rang and woke her. The exciting dream was shattered.

She figured her dad had picked up the phone because she heard his voice in the kitchen. *Probably Grandma again,* she thought. Nestling back into the sofa pillows, she hoped she might recapture the glorious images.

"Livvy, are you awake? Someone wants to talk to you."

Groaning, she pulled herself up off the couch. "I'm coming."

Still tired from skating, she staggered through the dining room and into the kitchen. She sat down and picked up the phone. "Hello?"

"Why are you still here in Alpine Lake?" came the haunting, muddled voice.

Not frightened, Livvy confronted the caller. "Who *are* you?"

"I'm telling you, for your own good—go back home. You don't belong here!"

She wished her dad had hung around so she wasn't alone with this phone weirdo. Instead of freaking out, though, she decided to stand her ground. "*This* town is my home now."

"Not for long, Miss Livvy."

Something about the way the voice was starting to lose its raspy sound made her think of Diane Larson. Again!

"Who's *Miss* Livvy? I don't know anyone by that name." She baited the caller, hoping to trick the person into speaking more clearly.

"I know your name! It's Livvy, the loser."

With each word, the voice sounded more like Diane. So Livvy decided to keep her talking for as long as possible.

"You've gotta be mistaken, whoever you are. Because I'm a winner. I *know* I am . . . and I'm going to stay right here in Alpine Lake. You can forget about calling me anymore." She was surprised at how confident she sounded. Even to herself!

"Listen, girl, I'm not kidding. Leave town or . . . or . . ."

There was sudden silence.

"Or what? You just might get beat out at cheerleading tryouts? Is that what you're afraid of, Diane?"

A little gasp came through the phone. Then *click*— the caller hung up.

Livvy immediately dialed her friend. She had to tell Jenna the news.

Jenna answered on the first ring. "Hello?"

"Hi, it's Livvy, and guess what? I'm pretty sure Diane's the one who called me the other night, trying to scare me out of town."

"Are you sure?"

Livvy revealed every detail of tonight's phone call. Even the awkward silence. "It was like she wanted to threaten me, but she couldn't do it."

"Wow . . . I was right" came the mysterious reply.

"About what?"

"About Diane. She's not a bad kid, she's just dying for attention."

"Well, that's a bizarre way of getting it!"

"I feel sorry for Diane," Jenna said softly.

This was the last thing Livvy wanted to hear. "The girl's a troublemaker," she said. "You know it, and so do I."

"I know you probably won't understand this, but I think we oughta invite Diane to do something with us . . . soon. The *three* of us."

"You wouldn't say that if you'd heard Diane's hateful voice tonight on the phone," Livvy retorted. "So count me out!"

"Well, if you're sure," Jenna replied. "But I'd like to hang out with her a little. Maybe eat lunch with her tomorrow. Okay with you?"

Livvy despised the idea. She couldn't imagine sharing Jenna with anyone, let alone a hateful girl like Diane Larson!

Chapter Fifteen

The group of five skaters was working on circular skating steps when Livvy arrived the next morning. Their coach was a petite young woman with blond hair pulled back in a sleek French braid.

On the sidelines, the smartly dressed gentleman sat on the same bench as yesterday. She guessed he was a drifter, though she wondered about his nice clothes. Maybe he was just someone who needed a place to sit and rest. Or maybe he was a lonely old man who enjoyed watching the skaters.

The mall was the ideal shelter from the wind and rain outside. Free from the early fall drizzle that Livvy had slopped through to get here.

Stealing another glance at the man, she tightened her

skates. He seemed more interested in his surroundings than his newspaper at the moment.

Mall walkers were out in full force. Probably because of the weather. She wished that someday she could get her dad to come here and exercise with the rest of the town. And while her dad walked, she could skate. A super setup. If she could just coax him to get up early . . . and *other* important things. Like agreeing to pay for skating and ballet lessons.

She stood up and did a few back-stretching exercises. When she caught the man looking her way, she waved. "Hello again. How are you today?"

"Just dandy," he answered with a wrinkled smile. A pad of paper lay on the bench beside him. Probably checking the newspaper ads for odd jobs.

She stretched some more and did twenty-five jumping jacks, swinging her arms back and forth, before ever taking to the ice. When she'd run through her warm-ups, Livvy did several easy jumps—two double flips and three double toe loops—one after the other as she worked her way across the rink.

Sharing the ice with the other less-experienced skaters and their young coach, Livvy was careful to keep a safe distance. She practiced a combination spin, changing her feet and her position while keeping her speed. She practiced it again and again, at least fifteen times. Next, she circled the ice, shaking the kinks out of her legs.

But as hard as she tried to focus, Livvy's thoughts kept drifting back to last night's phone conversation. The oddest thing was that Jenna insisted on being kind to Diane. Her plan was absurd. It bugged Livvy. Her best friend wanted to hang out with the meanest girl in town!

Why?

The idea of having to overlook Diane's horrible, near-threatening remarks—the way Jenna had—frustrated Livvy. Made her *furious!*

Jenna should be taking Livvy's side against Diane. Wasn't that how best friends were supposed to treat each other?

She dreaded going to school. Even thought of skipping today, just this once. She could stay here at the rink and practice off and on all day long.

It was a super idea while it lasted. But she knew her father would be horrified. And knowing her homeroom teacher, Mrs. Smith would probably slap an enormous essay on top of all of Livvy's other homework!

No, it wouldn't be worth it. She'd have to face Jenna and deal with things as they were. As for Diane Larson, well . . . she couldn't even begin to think about *her!*

Gritting her teeth, Livvy was determined to turn her angry energy into something positive. She took a deep breath and, without music, skated through her entire short program.

She was careful to make every jump, including the

triple toe loop. Then came the double Salchow. There were several preparations for the jump, and up until two days ago, Livvy worried that she wasn't ready. But she did her clockwise back crossovers and moved onto her takeoff leg.

Into the air she flew, landing gracefully on the back outside edge of her skate blade—only a quarter-inch wide.

"Yes!" she shouted, arms high overhead. Her constant, everyday practice—on her own—had paid off.

The other skaters were clapping. So was their coach.

Livvy happened to look above the rink, to the bench beneath the tree. There was the old man, standing and clapping, too.

Bowing, she imagined that he was a well-known European judge at an international competition. She thought he wore a smile just for her, so she offered a second bow. Just for him.

"Hey, you're *good!*" one of the girls said.

"Thanks," Livvy said, catching her breath.

Soon, she was surrounded by all five of the skaters. Their coach, too. "Do you train around here?" the coach asked, her blue eyes dancing.

Livvy explained that she'd come from Illinois. "My name is Olivia Hudson. But everyone calls me Livvy."

"Nice to meet you, Livvy. I'm Natalie Johnston. Have you found a new coach yet?"

"Not yet." She felt uncomfortable explaining why.

"Well, if I were qualified to teach advanced skaters, I'd certainly love to work with you."

"Thanks," Livvy replied.

They talked awhile longer, and Livvy was surprised to learn that Natalie was also a ballet instructor. "I have a large practice studio in my house," Natalie explained. "On Main Street."

"That's my street, too," Livvy said. "320 Main."

Natalie raised her eyebrows. "So you must be the folks who bought the gray Victorian." She could easily have said, "The run-down piece of junk in the middle of the block," but Natalie was kind.

"It was my dad's idea to fix up the house. He's an artist."

Natalie grinned. "So . . . you're my neighbor. Just two houses down."

Livvy was delighted. She couldn't wait to tell her dad the news. She could attend ballet classes on weekends and never have to ask for a ride.

Suddenly, she was thirsty and had forgotten to bring her sports bottle along. Slipping the rubber protectors over her blades, she headed for the water fountain near the rest rooms.

Coming back, she stopped near the wooden bench to talk to the old man. Before she could speak, he stood up to greet her.

"My compliments to you, missy. You're in excellent form today."

"Thank you, uh, Mr. . . . sir." She noticed the twinkle in his gray-blue eyes, wondering if it was polite to ask his name.

"Please, excuse my bad manners," he said, extending his hand. "Allow me to introduce myself. My name is Odell Sterling. Most folks call me Sterling. It's shorter, you see. People are in a hurry these days."

She shook his hand politely. "I'll call you *Mister* Sterling, then, if that's all right."

He nodded. "And I suppose your name is Her Grace, for you are certainly light-footed and graceful on the ice."

"Thank you." She laughed a little. "That's one compliment I've never received." She went on to tell him her name but didn't bother with her *real* nickname. Because she secretly liked Her Grace better.

He picked up his pen and note pad. For a moment, he studied something on the paper. "I watched your setup for each of your jumps, Olivia," he said at last.

"You did?" She felt self-conscious.

"Perhaps you might achieve more control by gaining increased speed . . . before you go into your backward jumps."

Elena had drummed the same thing into her, over and over. And she told him so. "My coach back home was always reminding me of that."

She observed the man, this Mr. Sterling. He had to be way past fifty years old, maybe closer to sixty. She couldn't tell for sure. His hair was mostly brown, very little gray. But it was the ruddy face, populated by wrinkles, that made her guess he was older than even Grandma Hudson.

"How do you know so much about skating?" she asked, sitting on the edge of the bench.

He waved his hand as if batting a fly. "Oh, I suppose I've watched my share of skating events, like most anybody," he replied. "A person can pick up an awful lot from those slick-talking announcers, you know."

She told him she'd enjoyed watching televised sports events, too, as a young girl. "So it sounds like we have something in common," she said, getting up.

"You're the girl with talent," he agreed. "And I just appreciate what I see."

"Do you live in Podunk . . . er, Alpine Lake?" she asked.

He'd caught what she'd said. Chortling, he repeated it. "Podunk's quieter than most places I've lived. But I like it here . . . in Podunk." There was a mischievous look in his eyes.

"I guess I oughta say Alpine Lake."

"Aw, go on and call it whatever you like," he said, leaning back against the bench. "A place is only as good as its nickname."

"Where else have you lived?"

"New York . . . that's my home state."

"Ever go to Lake Placid?" she asked.

"All the time." A fleeting look of joy glimmered in his eyes. "The best years of my life."

She was more curious than ever. "Did you get to meet any of the world's best skaters?"

"Oh, a few." But he stood up with a grunt, as if he was ready to leave.

"Well, I guess we could talk all day. Sorry to keep you, Mr. Sterling."

He motioned toward the rink. "You have some more skating to do before school, Her Grace."

"I sure do!" She beamed back at him, wondering if he'd be here waiting after school.

He called his "good-byes," and she did the same.

Then she bent down to tighten the laces on her right skate. That's when she noticed the note pad. He must've dropped it. Reaching under the bench, she retrieved it. She saw his name written on the outside but didn't allow herself to peek inside.

When she looked up, she saw the man walking toward the food court. She would've run after him but couldn't risk ruining her best skates.

So she slipped the note pad into her bag and decided to return it the next time she saw him. Probably this afternoon.

Preparing to leave the rink and head for home, she thought about the old man's nickname for her. "Her Grace," she said aloud.

She twirled around, her skate bag flying as she made her way to the mall entrance. All the way home she thought about Odell Sterling, wondering why his name sounded so familiar.

Dreams on Ice
Chapter Sixteen

Livvy managed to avoid seeing Jenna before school. She even waited till her locker partner was finished getting her books and things out before heading down the hall.

When both Jenna and Diane were safely heading off to homeroom, Livvy dashed out from behind one of the classroom doors.

Just then the first bell rang.

She had to hurry—Mrs. Smith would be waiting. In more ways than one!

Her fingers fumbled the combination lock, but she managed to open the locker and stash away her skate bag. She grabbed up her math and English books and slammed the door shut.

"Whoa, are you in a rush or what?" Suzy asked, running toward her.

"Run for your life."

"What's the hurry? We're having an assembly first thing."

"I still can't be late for homeroom . . . bye!" Livvy ran to Room 123.

The tardy bell rang. Louder than usual.

She zipped past the doorway. And Mrs. Smith glanced up from her desk just as Livvy slid into her seat. She felt like a baseball player stealing home.

"Miss Hudson" came the disappointing words.

She knew to slump in her seat would be a big mistake. So she sat as straight and tall as possible. "Yes, Mrs. Smith."

"You're tardy."

"I'm sorry, it won't happen again."

Livvy felt her muscles tense up. Not a good thing for a skater on her way to fame and glory. A terrible thing, actually.

Here it comes. She braced herself for the worst possible writing assignment in all of Podunk.

"Miss Hudson, you will write . . ." The teacher paused.

Livvy realized she was holding her breath. When she inhaled, she began to blink her eyes. Fast.

"Are you all right?" Mrs. Smith asked.

"I . . . I think so."

"Very well. I'll expect to see your written assignment

on my desk first thing—well before the last bell—tomorrow. Write a 300-word letter, Olivia. Write it to a student here at Alpine Lake Middle School."

A letter?

She was super at letters. She'd write one to her old pen pal. This was too good to be true!

She pulled out some paper to take notes.

"In the letter, I want you to describe the meaning of tardy. Why it's important to be on time for school . . . and for life."

Livvy began to take notes. While Mrs. Smith was still talking, Livvy jotted down the guidelines for the assignment.

"Excuse me, Olivia."

She looked up. "Yes?"

"Please, you must *never* write when I'm talking."

Livvy gasped.

The pet peeve!

How could she have forgotten?

Instantly, she put her pen down. But she knew by the teacher's stern face she'd committed an unforgivable flub.

"Make that two letters, to two different students. One, explaining the importance of being prompt. The second, describing the significance of following rules in general."

Mrs. Smith was ticked off. No question.

Livvy didn't know whether to apologize or to keep

her mouth shut. In the end, she wished she'd stayed at the rink. But who knows what sort of letter *that* misdeed would have required.

She was in hot water, and she knew it. Now . . . how to keep from drowning! With the homework assignments of the day yet to be given, and the after-school practice session at the rink, Livvy wondered how she would pull off two acceptable letters. And to students!

Mrs. Smith continued. "I expect to receive these written assignments directly. In other words, bring your letters to me."

———

If she hadn't been so angry at Jenna, Livvy might've weathered the blow. But lunch period turned out to be another disaster. "One after another," she said to herself, gazing across the cafeteria.

She could see Jenna and Diane sitting together, laughing and talking. And she could hardly stand to watch. Too many glances toward her best friend and her worst enemy wouldn't do. So she made herself look only at her brown lunch bag.

"What're you doing way over here?" Suzy asked, sneaking up.

"None of your business," she snapped. "Go sit with your locker partner."

"If you say so." Suzy must've spotted where Diane was sitting. "Okay, I see her. Bye!"

Once again, Livvy was alone.

She dug around in her book bag and found the small note pad belonging to Odell Sterling. Fighting nosiness, she tried to imagine what might be written inside. She had no right to read someone's private writings. So she placed it on the table, while she had several more bites of her chicken and tomato sandwich.

Several times throughout her lunch, she caught herself staring at Mr. Sterling's note pad. *What was he writing while I skated?* she wondered. *Why was an old man taking notes at the rink?*

At last, her curiosity got the best of her. She opened the flap and saw line after line of scribble. Scanning the first page, she tried to read the words.

When she'd finished, she flipped to the next page. Soon she'd read every word.

"He knows skating," she whispered. "Who *is* Odell Sterling?"

Wanting to take good care of the old man's tiny notebook, she slipped it back into her book bag for safekeeping.

Then, to save time, she began working on her assigned letters for Mrs. Smith. While she nibbled on pretzel sticks, she started writing the one on the tardy theme.

Dear Jenna,

This is a required letter. It's to you from me, and I hope you'll understand what the word "tardy" means by the end of it.

I was a few seconds behind the bell for homeroom this morning. It's not the first time I've ever been late, though. Once, when I was in fourth grade, I forgot to set my alarm and missed my skating session. It messed things up big time for me.

You know why? Because I didn't get to skate in the local competition. I should have learned my lesson back then.

She stopped writing. Someone was staring at her. Livvy was sure of it.

Slowly, she looked up. There stood Diane.

The spiteful girl glanced at the chair across from her. "Mind if I sit down?"

Livvy tried to cover the letter, but she folded it instead and pushed it down into her sock.

"Look, I've been a jerk," Diane said, her clear eyes holding their gaze.

Livvy nearly choked. "Excuse me?"

"Your best friend just filled me in and—"

"*Jenna* talked to you about me?"

Diane nodded her head up and down. "I decided the day you enrolled for school that I didn't like you. I heard you were a star skater or something."

"A novice."

"Well, that's supposed to be really good . . . for a sixth grader, anyway."

Livvy didn't know whether to say "thanks" or "get lost."

But Diane wasn't finished. "I didn't want to get squeezed out of my chance at cheerleading. Or anything else around here. It's a small school and . . . and I was jealous of you."

"What did Jenna say about me?" Livvy asked.

"Just that you're the coolest friend ever. And that your mother died last summer." Diane's eyes blinked awkwardly. "I can't imagine not having my mom around . . . and I can't think of going off somewhere new to live, where kids like me act like morons." She stopped to find a tissue in her pocket. "What I'm trying to say is, I'm sorry, Livvy. I never should've called you on the phone like that. It was a cruel thing to do."

Livvy shook her head. "You didn't scare me—not really. I was mostly just mad."

"So . . . can we be friends?" Diane's eyes were pleading.

Out of the corner of her eye, Livvy spotted Jenna. She was smiling that winning smile of hers. "Friends? Sure."

After Diane left, Jenna wandered over. "You shouldn't be eating alone over here. You know better than that, girl."

"Yeah, so?"

"I see Diane talked to you." Jenna pulled her hair back, then let it float free.

"Very funny . . . you set it all up." She gathered up her trash. "You're a real peacemaker, aren't you?"

"That's what friends are for."

Livvy took a long drink of her pop while Jenna picked at her pretzel sticks. She told her about being tardy for homeroom. "Now I have to write a long letter to someone as an assignment. I picked you, but you'll never read it."

"That's what *you* think!"

Livvy took another sip of soda and felt something tickling her leg. "Why you!"

Jenna had reached down and pulled the letter out of Livvy's sock.

"Give that back!"

"No way." Jenna pretended to scan the letter, holding it high, out of Livvy's reach.

Mrs. Smith strolled by just then.

Livvy didn't want to chance another humiliating scene with her homeroom teacher. "Oh, so what. Go ahead and read it," she said, giving up.

Surprisingly, Jenna returned the letter, eyes smiling. "I know what tardy means, silly. I wasn't *too late* with Diane, was I?"

"Somehow, you knew it was time."

Jenna glanced up. "It helps to talk things over with Someone who knows all things."

"I figured you'd say that."

"He's never too late, Livvy."

"I know."

Dreams on Ice
Chapter Seventeen

The table at Jenna's house was lit with several tall candles in a floral centerpiece. Jenna's mother insisted on serving each person. And Livvy was amazed at the way the Saturday night supper was presented. The dishes were ornate with Oriental themes and swirling, colorful designs.

"It's wonderful to finally meet our Jenna's pen pal"— Reverend Song smiled at Livvy—"and her father." Then he turned to engage Livvy's dad in small talk.

Livvy worried that her father might clam up and make things awkward all evening. She honestly didn't know what to expect. As quiet and withdrawn as he was, Livvy could only hope that her dad would try to fit in. At least for this one evening.

"I understand you are the new pastor in town," her dad remarked as they sat at the elegant table.

Reverend Song nodded, his eyes squinting a smile. "Yes, and what a delight to know that by moving here, our daughters will be able to become better acquainted."

Livvy grinned at Jenna, sitting next to her. "I think our dads are getting along just fine," she whispered.

Jenna nodded. "They ought to . . . they have *us* in common."

When the hot tea was poured in each tiny cup, Mrs. Song sat down. Her husband bowed his head and began to bless the food. "Thank you, Father in heaven, for this evening together with new friends. I ask a special blessing on Livvy and her father as they put down roots in this small community. And I pray that you will lead and direct them. May they experience your divine love and wisdom." He went on to thank the Lord for the food and the hands that prepared it.

All the while, Livvy clasped her own hands in her lap, paying close attention to this kind and gracious man's prayer.

After a full-course Korean dinner, Jenna took Livvy upstairs to her room. They hung out together, laughing and talking, while Livvy's dad chatted with Jenna's parents in the living room.

———

Later, when she was alone in her own room, Livvy knelt beside her bed. "Dear Lord, I'm sorry about ignoring you for so long. I guess you know how angry I've been."

She sighed. "It wasn't easy losing Mom, especially when I wish you would've done something to stop it. But that doesn't mean I don't still have faith in you . . . with all of my heart. Please help Dad come to believe in you soon. Let him know your love and that you didn't let Mom die to punish him—just because he isn't a Christian yet."

At the end of her prayer, Livvy thanked God for bringing her to Alpine Lake, "even if it's the Podunkiest town on earth. Amen."

———————

Two days later, Grandma Hudson arrived. Livvy rode along with her dad to the Colorado Springs airport.

"There's my honeybunch," Grandma said, squeezing Livvy's cheek.

"Hi, Grandma. Welcome to Colorado." Livvy stepped forward as passengers walked past her.

Her dad kissed his mother, offering to carry the overnight case. "The altitude's much higher here than Illinois," he warned, "so you may have to take things slow and easy."

"Oh, I'll adjust in no time," Grandma said.

Livvy spoke up. "If you drink lots of water, it helps take away altitude sickness."

"But some folks never have any trouble," Dad said, hugging Grandma once again. "We're going to have a wonderful time together."

"How long can you stay?" Livvy asked. She was hoping for a four- or five-day response . . . maybe even a week. But not more than that.

Grandma raised her eyebrows and offered a broad smile. "Well, I'll just have to see about that. Looks to me like you could use a good dose of mothering, Olivia Kay. Are you eating three good meals a day?"

Livvy nodded reluctantly. She was eating just fine— and cooking for her dad, too!

All the way up the long concourse to the main terminal, she wondered what Grandma meant about "a good dose of mothering." The idea that her father's mother had come to take over the household worried Livvy. She noticed that her grandmother had packed very light. Maybe things would be super fine after all.

Livvy could only hope so.

Dreams on Ice
Chapter Eighteen

One week later, Livvy and Jenna were eating ice cream at the Oo-La-La Café. They'd chosen a table outside on the patio section of the tiny mall restaurant. The breezes were warm and gentle.

"September in the mountains isn't so bad," Livvy said.

"Sounds like Podunk is growing on you," said her friend.

"Oh, maybe . . ." Livvy's ice cream was melting fast. Licking it kept her from having to say more.

"My mom signed me up for ballet classes," Jenna said out of the blue.

"With Natalie Johnston?"

Jenna's mouth dropped open. "How'd you know?"

Livvy told her about meeting Natalie and her students

at the ice rink. "I see her working with her skaters several times a week. She seems really nice."

"My mom thought so, too. She interviewed her yesterday and toured her dance studio. I can't wait."

Livvy's heart sank. She wished *she* could say she was signing up. One thing at a time, her mother had always said.

"It'll be tough juggling gymnastics and ballet," Jenna told her. "But I have my goals. And I decided not to try out for cheerleading."

"Me neither."

Jenna spooned up her chocolate ice cream. "Gotta keep focused."

"Speaking of that, I have a date with an ice rink," Livvy said, grabbing a napkin out of the holder. She wiped up the melted mess off the table before excusing herself.

"I'll come by later," Jenna said. "We can walk to my house afterward."

"Okay. See ya." Livvy hurried the few yards through the café to the mall.

She wasn't too surprised to see Mr. Sterling again. He was wearing blue dress pants and a white long-sleeved shirt. He looked dashing, almost younger than his years. As usual, he sat on his favorite bench.

Someone else was there, too. Mrs. Newton, all decked out in bangles and bows.

"Ready for the show?" she asked, looking at both of them.

"Skate away," said Mrs. Newton. "That's why we're here."

Mr. Sterling inched up his shirt sleeve, studying his wrist watch. "Her Grace is right on time." He chuckled and settled back against the bench.

"I've learned my lesson about being late!" Livvy remembered the strange assignment she'd written for her homeroom teacher.

Taking her time, she pulled on her skates. She'd learned so much already right here at this mall rink. By herself. Yet, to be honest about it, she knew that most of her practice methods had come straight from Elena. All those years with such a super coach . . .

Livvy had come to accept the fact that she could only go so far on her own. Somehow, it seemed all right. Because today she would not daydream about performing for a huge audience. Today she would skate her heart out for two wonderful people. Two of her biggest fans.

Above all, she would enjoy her skate session for herself. *I'll just have fun,* she promised.

She took the ice with more energy and dash than she'd ever known. At least since her arrival here.

First one spin, then another. Fancy footwork across the width of the rink. Next, Livvy flew into the air, smiling as she practiced her jumps. She was having such a good time.

When forty minutes had come and gone, she could hardly believe it! And she wouldn't have known it if Mr. Sterling hadn't waved his hands in the air. "Time for a break," he called, motioning her to the sidelines.

She flew across the ice to him.

"Good, clean skating this afternoon." He leaned on the railing that circled the rink.

"Thanks." She was surprised to see that he'd abandoned his bench. And glancing back, she realized that half of her audience was missing. "Too bad Mrs. Newton couldn't stay around."

He nodded. "Oh, but she saw some splendid moves before she returned to work."

The playful flicker in his eye made Livvy wonder why Mrs. Newton had *really* come.

She took a quick drink from her water bottle.

"Olivia . . . I want to talk to you about something."

She couldn't help but chuckle. "Do you have some more suggestions for me?"

He pulled out his note pad, grinning. "What do you say I give you a few pointers?"

"That all depends on how much you charge."

He reached for his pen. "We'll settle that little issue later."

"You used to coach some of the very best skaters back east, didn't you?"

His eyebrows flew up and hovered over his pensive blue eyes. "You've done your homework on me, I see."

"I sure did. I called Elena, my former coach, and she told me all about you."

"Well, well. You've discovered my secret."

"So you *have* to charge me," she insisted. "As well-known as Coach Odell Sterling is—"

"Was," he said with a wink. "I'm hiding out in Podunk, remember?"

"Alpine Lake is the place to be."

"Thanks to you, Her Grace. Now . . . don't breathe a word, or I won't have much of a retirement, will I?"

"I *have* to tell my father. And my best friend and . . ."

He shook his head, chuckling. "Really, Livvy. I'm doing this for you. Only you."

"You're too good to be true, Mr. Sterling."

His eyes narrowed, and he put his hand on her shoulder. Just like Elena used to. "I believe in you, Olivia."

"My mother used to say that."

He was nodding. "She had every reason to."

Livvy's heart was full of joy.

———

Jenna stopped by later, and Livvy introduced her to Odell Sterling. "He's a famous skating coach," she said. "But we can't tell anyone."

"Coming out of retirement on behalf of a talented young lady," he added, flashing an endearing smile Livvy's way.

"Can you believe it?" She was jumping up and down. "I've finally got myself a coach."

"What'll your dad say?" Jenna asked.

"What *can* he say?" Livvy said, settling down. "He'll be surprised, but I think I can talk him into it. After all, my grandma's running the show now. She'll help convince him."

"She's staying?" Jenna asked.

"Hey, she makes a mean pasta casserole, so I'm not complaining."

There was laughter all around.

Livvy said good-bye to Coach Sterling and promised to be prompt for their first real practice.

Tomorrow!

The girls walked down Main Street together. "This is so cool, Livvy," her friend said. "I'm so happy for you!"

"Yes, and I have a funny feeling you're partly responsible."

Jenna's lips pinched into a weird, almost mysterious expression. "My secret is sealed!"

"Wait a minute . . . that's what Mrs. Newton said about

the cheerleading outfits." She stopped Jenna right there on the sidewalk. "She was in on this, wasn't she? She put a bug in Mr. Sterling's ear about me, didn't she?"

"What bug? And who are you talking about?" Jenna said ever so innocently.

"You talked to Mrs. Newton, and she told Mr. Sterling about my skating dreams. She must've known he was a retired skating coach—one of the best!"

"My lips are still sealed!" Jenna burst out laughing.

"See . . . I was right!"

But Jenna wouldn't admit it. "Mrs. Newton has some jazzy-looking patterns for skate costumes."

"You're changing the subject."

"Well, she *does*. And you'd better check them out."

Livvy flipped her hair. "I will when my grandma and I finish sewing Diane's cheerleading outfit."

"You must be kidding! *You're* sewing it?" Jenna slapped her forehead. "Does Diane know?"

"It's my secret . . . mine and Mrs. Newton's."

"I know another secret," Jenna piped up, halfway to her house. "It's about Diane Larson. How do you think she knows so much about everyone?"

Livvy was laughing now. "Must be the school secretary—something about her reminds me of Diane."

"She's Diane's nosy aunt, who gets the scoop on everyone at the beginning of the year, then yaks it to Diane."

"So . . . *that's* how Diane knew I was a skater," said Livvy.

"Among other things." Jenna smiled her sweet, forgiving smile. "I don't know about you, but it's really no big deal to me . . . the gossip and stuff."

"I'm not surprised. You overlook everything."

"I try."

"Tell me about it." Livvy linked arms with her best friend.

Dreams on Ice
Chapter Nineteen

Livvy's world was beginning to spin on its axis once again. She wouldn't be sitting alone at lunch anymore. Wouldn't be writing long, letter-type essays for Mrs. Smith. And she wouldn't be so grumpy to her parrot, either!

She was getting her confidence back, thanks to a lot of super folks. In a not-so-Podunk place!

———

"Do you think Mom has any idea about my new coach?" Livvy asked her dad before bedtime.

"Well, if she doesn't, I'd be surprised." He leaned down and kissed her forehead, tucking her in. "Good night, Livvy."

"I love you," she said. "Don't work too late."

"That's impossible." He shrugged helplessly.

"I know." She understood his motivation and drive. It was the same kind of energy that inspired her to beat the sun up every morning.

Before turning out the light, her dad said, "Grandma's planning a big breakfast tomorrow. Better set your alarm."

"Oh, I'll be up. Easy."

"So will I," he said.

"Daddy?" She sat up in bed, staring across the room. "Does this mean what I think it does?"

He leaned on the door, his eyes serious. "It's time I met my daughter's coach."

"You're kidding . . . really?"

"Most of all, I want to see you skate, kiddo. I've missed out on too much . . . for too long."

It was impossible to sleep. An invisible choir of crickets buzzed away. The moon played tag with the bedroom curtains as they drifted back and forth. And Livvy daydreamed of regional competitions and ice revues.

Soon to come. . . .

Lying in the stillness, she began to whisper to her mother about all the super things that had happened since she'd moved to Alpine Lake. Things like getting a free (for now) top-notch coach. Like having a true friend named Jenna Song.

But she stopped. "Sorry, Mom. I'm not so sure I'm talking to the right person."

Livvy turned her chatter into a long prayer—and felt super good about it.

Only the Best

AUTHOR'S NOTE

I would like to thank the International Federation of Gymnastics, the U.S. Olympic Committee, and Craig Bohnert, Public Relations Director at USA Gymnastics.

A special thank-you to Alissa Jones, a young gymnast with a bright future, and Amanda Hoffman, my cheerful "teen consultant." Smiles to Christy Friesen, who gave Jenna's cat the purrrfect name and personality to match!

Information about U.S. Olympic Gold medalist Dominique Moceanu was provided by her official homepage and her autobiography, *Dominique Moceanu, An American Champion*.

Only the Best
Chapter One

"You'll never guess who sent me a personal email last night," said Jenna Song as she opened her school locker.

Her best friend and locker partner, Olivia Hudson, scrunched her face into a silly frown. "Let me guess . . . someone famous?"

"Maybe."

"Someone like . . . Dominique Moceanu?"

Jenna spun around, her three-ring binder dangling from the top shelf. "That's it, Livvy! How'd you know?"

"You mean I'm *right*?" Livvy's green eyes sparkled. "I just guessed!"

Jenna rescued her sliding notebook with one hand and grabbed Livvy's arm with the other. "I'm so-o totally jazzed. See, I sent Dominique this really short email asking about her favorite gymnastics events and stuff like that."

"And she wrote you back?" Livvy asked.

"Domi adores the floor exercise and the balance beam. Just like me!"

"Domi?" Livvy eyed her curiously. "Sounds like you're on a first-name basis with one of the hottest gold medal gymnasts around."

Jenna shrugged. "Well, she signed off with her nickname—Domi. So . . . yeah, I guess I am!"

"Okay." Livvy looked a little suspicious.

Stepping aside, Jenna gave Livvy a chance to gather her books for morning classes. Their locker was major first-class—one of the coolest in Alpine Lake Middle School. At least Jenna thought so.

The top and bottom shelves were decorated in hot pink carpet, scraps left over from remodeling her attic bedroom. And with Christmas only five weeks away, they'd hung tiny green bows and gold bells on the door.

"So . . . when do I get a peek at your email?" Livvy asked, stacking up her books.

"Tonight after ballet class, maybe?"

"I'll have to check with my grandma first," Livvy said, looking a little worried. "She likes me to be prompt after ballet and skating sessions. 'It makes for a terribly late supper,' she always says."

"How's it going—her living with you and your

dad?" Jenna leaned against the locker next to hers and Livvy's.

"As long as she doesn't pretend she's my mother, things are fine," Livvy said softly, closing the locker door. "Nobody can ever take Mom's place."

Jenna wished with all her heart that Livvy's mom had somehow beaten the cancer last summer. More than anything!

"It's really not so bad having Grandma live with us," Livvy said. "For one thing, she's way better at cooking than Dad ever was."

They laughed about that, then discussed the possibility of Livvy actually going home with Jenna after ballet. "Mom can drive you to our house when she comes for me," Jenna offered.

Livvy fluffed her shoulder-length auburn hair. "Sounds super. Can't wait to read your email from . . . *Domi*!" The girls giggled into their locker. No way did they want to be seen acting too silly. Even though they *were* on the sixth-grade end of the middle-grade totem pole!

But Jenna felt like flying. She was very excited about her personal connection with the youngest U.S. gymnast ever to win Olympic gold! She could hardly wait to tell Cassie Peterson, one of her teammates.

Jenna pranced to the end of the hall, jostled by the pre-homeroom crowd. "See you in P.E.," she called to Livvy as they parted ways.

"Okay!" Livvy waved and disappeared down the hall.

Jenna slowed her pace as she made the turn toward Mr. Lowell's homeroom. She'd rather be in any other class these days. Even strict Mrs. Smith—Livvy's homeroom teacher—would be light-years better.

Two annoying boys had started bugging her. Chris Stephens and Jamey Something-or-other were forever pulling on their eyes, making them slant down the way her eyes were shaped naturally.

"What kind of last name is *Song*?" Chris had jeered one day.

"Sing along with Jenna Song," Jamey Something had joined in.

Some days she could easily ignore them. But other times Jenna wanted to march across the room and tackle them good. She didn't want to risk hurting herself, though. Not *this* year! She was poised to move to a Level Nine in gymnastics. Nothing, especially not two terribly rude boys, was going to stand in her way!

———

After ballet class—and after Livvy had called home— the girls settled into Jenna's cozy attic bedroom. The room was cooler than cool with three large dormer windows on one side. On the opposite wall, her father had installed a barre and a wide mirror where she could practice her ballet moves and stretches. Sasha, her golden-haired cat, slept on the high four-poster bed, curled up in a tuck position. At the far end of the room, a built-in desk was home to Jenna's new computer. And high over the desk, an Olympic rings flag was tacked to the wall.

"Are you ready to preview my email?" Jenna said, sitting at her desk.

Livvy grinned and slid a chair next to her in front of the monitor. "Just think what fun we could've had with email when I lived back in Chicago."

"No kidding. As much as we *both* love to write letters, we probably would've been emailing nonstop." Jenna moved the mouse and clicked on the last entry. "Instead of pen pals, we could've been email amigos, right?"

"Yeah, and probably kissed your gymnastic goals good-bye . . . my skating plans, too," Livvy added.

"Never. Nothing comes between me and gymnastics." Jenna leaned forward. "Here we go . . . I found Dominique's message."

Livvy pressed in next to Jenna, studying the screen. "Wow, she says she can't live without her personal computer."

Jenna scrolled farther down. "Check it out—Domi collects lots of stuffed animals. Especially elephants. And guardian angels, too."

"Super," whispered Livvy. "Can you believe she told you all this stuff about herself?"

"I know. It's one of the coolest things to happen this year . . . next to you and me moving to the same Colorado town," Jenna said.

Livvy grinned at her. "You can say that again."

They abandoned the computer after a while, practicing their *arabesque* and *pirouette* moves together. "It's great having you in ballet class with me," Jenna said, catching her breath.

"For a while I wasn't sure if Dad was going to sign me up or not," Livvy said. "But thanks to Grandma, I'm in!"

Just then the computer announced an incoming email. Quickly, Jenna rushed back to her desk. She clicked the mouse to access the message. Scanning the screen, she read the words silently. "Oh, this can't be," she groaned, noting the name of the Denver adoption agency.

"Something wrong?" Livvy asked, coming over.

"Listen to this." She read the message aloud. " 'Friday, November 20. To Reverend and Mrs. Song: A healthy Korean infant is available for adoption. A certified letter with pertinent information will be sent to you immediately. Congratulations, and thank you for your patience in this matter.' "

Livvy turned to face Jenna. "Sounds like you're about to become a sister. How's it feel?"

Jenna's throat felt lumpy. "I didn't think it was going

to happen so fast," she admitted, more to herself than to her friend.

Astonished, she went to sit in the soft, pillowed area under one of the dormer windows. Sasha came purring and made herself comfortable in Jenna's lap. Silently, Jenna stroked her cat's sleek coat.

"I don't get it. You seem upset," Livvy said, coming to sit on a floor pillow.

Reaching for her friend's hand, Jenna squeezed hard. "Oh, Livvy. I don't know how to say it, but I don't think I'm ready for this."

Only the Best
Chapter Two

First thing Saturday morning, Jenna headed for the gym—Alpine Aerials Gymnastics. AAG, for short. Padded safety mats were out everywhere when she arrived. Gymnasts in various levels practiced on the uneven parallel bars, balance beam, and the vault. Others worked individual floor routines. Graceful, fit bodies were flying, swinging, or tumbling all over.

Cool stuff, she thought. The gym was pure heaven on earth.

For as long as Jenna could remember, she had been testing her balancing ability on the narrow curbs in her neighborhood. Or on the lines of a checkered kitchen floor. As a preschooler, she'd posed on a step stool in front of the TV, pretending to be an Olympic medalist. And in her imagination, the crowd was always cheering. For her!

When she was three, her mother had enrolled her in a preschool gymnastics group called Tumble Tots. Jenna caught on quickly, and by the time she was in kindergarten, she was showing other tiny gymnasts how to tuck their knees for a forward or backward somersault. "Teacher's little helper," her coaches used to say.

She was still the shortest girl on her team. But Jenna didn't mind being petite. The closer a gymnast was to the ground, the better advantage in overall performance. At eleven, she was more than confident with her moves. Stunts like the back handspring, walkover, and the straddle split. She could perform her entire floor, vault, and balance beam routines without help from Coach Kim or his Russian-born wife, Tasya.

Today she focused her attention on a long, hard workout. In two short weeks, the eight-member All-Around Team would compete in downtown Colorado Springs—at the Olympic Training Center!

"Think we're ready?" she asked Cassie as they changed clothes in the locker room.

"We have to iron the small things," the tall, slender girl said, grinning with thumbs up.

"Right!" But Jenna wasn't so sure. She couldn't concentrate today. Her thoughts were on the baby who was coming to upset her house. Would she get her required sleep? Or would the baby howl and fuss all night? Babies made lots of racket, she knew. Her aunt and uncle had just had a new baby. Most of the time they looked wiped out. Being sleep deprived was *not* an option for a gymnast!

Worried, Jenna taped her hands, then began her stretching exercises and aerobics with the team. After forty minutes, her muscles felt pliable, like warm honey. She started work on her individual routine, aware of the soft-crash pads beneath her bare feet. Waiting for the musical cue, she practiced her salute for the judge, who today happened to be her coach, Benjamin Kim.

"Push . . . push to perfection," Coach Kim called, his hands high in the air.

Jenna focused her attention on her tumbling moves, especially the salto, front pike somersault, and aerial walk-over. "Okay, time to show your stuff," she whispered to herself.

Impatiently, she bounced on her toes, anxious to start. She waited . . . and waited. But she heard no music floating through the speakers. Coach went to investigate.

While she waited, Jenna performed several back walk-overs. All the while, she thought of the startling email. The one from the Denver adoption agency. The one that might change the outcome of her entire gymnastics future!

She'd made an attempt to talk to her parents last night—after Livvy Hudson left. But by the time Jenna printed out the important email, her dad was already busy with Sunday sermon notes. And her mother was talking on the phone to a sick church member.

Jenna had gone to bed without saying a word to either of them. As long as it was her secret, maybe it might not happen, she reasoned. Feeling terribly left out, she'd tried to tell God about her worries but didn't get very far before falling into a nightmarish sleep.

Now, as she anticipated the jazz melody to her floor routine, she knew she couldn't put off talking to her parents. She'd go right home and tell them about the baby. If she waited too long, the certified letter would arrive anyway. It was do or die!

Finally the musical selection began with the smooth, clear sound of the saxophone. Though Jenna had practiced the routine hundreds of times, she hesitated at the take-off point, arms out, chin up, toes pointed.

"You can do it, Jen!" shouted Coach Kim from the outside edge of the mat.

"We're rooting for you!" her teammates cheered and clapped.

"Go, girl!" shouted Cassie.

But hard as she tried, Jenna froze up on her tumbling pass and didn't go far enough on her somi-and-a-half. Her back handsprings were sloppy, and she tilted the landing on her aerial cartwheel.

All Jenna wanted to do was cry.

Only the Best
Chapter Three

Jenna confessed to her parents about the information she'd kept secret. "An email for Dad came through from the adoption agency," she said at supper, glancing at each of them. "You're getting a baby . . . very soon."

Her mother's eyes were wide with delight. And when she tried to talk, she nearly blubbered. "Oh, we had no idea . . . no idea at all that something would happen this quickly. My goodness! What wonderful news!"

Yeah, wonderful, thought Jenna.

Her father spoke up. "The caseworker told us we were in for a fairly long wait. So far, it's only been ten months since the initial application was approved."

"I'll call the agency first thing Monday," her mom added quickly. "They'll tell us if the baby is a boy or girl."

"We requested a *boy*," Dad spoke up. His face was actually glowing, like it was Christmas Eve or something.

Jenna couldn't stand it any longer. She stared down at her plate, a lump growing in her throat.

"What's wrong, honey?" asked her mother. "Are you all right?"

She could hardly speak. "I . . . I thought you were happy with just me." Her words came out all squeaky.

"Oh, honey, we *are* . . . we're very happy." Dad reached across the table for her hand. "Mom and I have plenty of love to go around . . . enough for the new baby, too. We talked this over with you and the caseworker months ago. Remember?"

Jenna held in the sobs that threatened to burst out. Months ago? Back then she figured adopting a baby was probably years away for them. Maybe even never.

Dad continued. "And about using your computer . . . well, I knew you wouldn't mind. It was a handy way to keep in touch with our caseworker now and then," he said almost apologetically.

She nodded. Borrowing her computer wasn't the problem.

"We love you dearly, Jenna. And your mother and I want to give an orphaned child a chance. Make a difference somehow."

His words made Jenna feel even worse. "What about

gymnastics and ballet? What will happen with that?" She couldn't continue. If she did, she might cry. And that would mean she was a selfish little brat. She certainly didn't want her parents to think *that* of her!

"Life will go on, same as always," Dad said, refolding his napkin. "You'll still attend gymnastics and ballet and school and church."

She hoped he was right, but it was hard to believe. Everything was going to change. She was sure of it!

Mom got up to clear the table. "We'll all travel together to greet our new baby," she said, looking suddenly younger than her years.

All of us?

"When?" Jenna asked.

"The certified letter will surely tell us," Dad said. He sat tall at the head of the table, his regular place. But tonight he looked more handsome than usual. His black hair shone in the soft luster of the dining room chandelier. His face was determined but compassionate.

Mom reread the email printout. "Sounds like we'll be hearing any day now."

Jenna wouldn't hold her breath for it. As long as the letter hadn't arrived, she could focus on the gymnastics meet. And something else, too. She had a feeling Coach Kim was going to make her captain of the team.

"I wish you would've told me we might be getting a baby this year," she said at last. "It's hard to think of someone that tiny . . . and noisy fitting in around here. With the three of us."

Mom placed a dessert dish of peach cobbler on the table. "Adopting a baby will take some getting used to," she said.

Dad smiled. "But we're willing to do whatever it takes to welcome a precious homeless child into our hearts."

Mom sat down and began dishing up the dessert. Her eyes twinkled with anticipation, and Jenna couldn't remember ever seeing her this excited.

"I can hardly believe it," Mom said. "We're going to have a brand-new baby in the house. Very soon!"

"Yes, and we're going to give him or her lots of love," Dad said, accepting a generous serving of cobbler with a smile.

Jenna listened, staring at her dessert. They could go right ahead and shower plenty of love on their new baby, she decided. But what about *her?* Would they forget about their firstborn and her gymnastic goals?

Only the Best
Chapter Four

Sunday afternoon, Jenna sat cross-legged on her bed and picked up the telephone. She punched the buttons to call Livvy.

"Hudson residence" came the delicate voice of Livvy's grandmother.

"Oh, hi," she said. "May I speak to Livvy, please? This is Jenna Song."

"Just one moment."

When Livvy answered, Jenna told her the latest. "My parents are so thrilled about the baby. They're dying to get some more details. Mom's calling the agency tomorrow."

"So they really *are* adopting a baby," Livvy said cheerfully. "Congratulations."

"Yeah, well, guess again."

"What's *that* supposed to mean?" asked Livvy. "Are you really that upset about it?"

Jenna clammed up. A long pause followed.

"Well?" Livvy was pushing. "Are you gonna talk to me or not?"

Sighing, Jenna asked, "Whose side are you on?"

"What are you talking about?" Livvy sounded puzzled. "Do you really think I'm against you?"

"You mean you aren't?"

" 'Course not," Livvy said. "I just think you sound, uh, insanely jealous."

She felt hideous. Livvy had no right! "Look, this conversation's going nowhere," Jenna said, the anger creeping into her cheeks.

"Well, you called *me*," Livvy replied. "So I guess you have the right to hang up whenever you want."

"Oh, is *that* how you feel?"

Click!

Jenna hung up on her friend. She dropped the receiver back into the cradle and just stared at it. "What's wrong with me?" she whispered, fighting back tears.

Livvy would be terribly hurt. She didn't deserve this sort of treatment. Not after losing her mom to cancer and having to move away from her Chicago hometown all in the space of a few months. Not after just moving here to Alpine Lake, Colorado—same as Jenna's family.

"Ohhh!" she groaned, lying there in her pajamas. "My whole life is falling apart!"

She could see it now. Her mom would want to rush out and start shopping for baby things. Years ago, they'd given away Jenna's old crib and high chair, so they were starting over from scratch. Starting over in more ways than one!

And there was the nursery. Her parents would expect her to help them fix up the old guest room—turn the small room into something special.

On top of everything else, there probably wouldn't be time for anyone to drive her to gymnastics anymore. Mom would be too busy planning and preparing for the blessed baby event.

She sighed, worrying over every possible detail. *Once the baby arrives, what then?* she wondered.

Jenna skipped reading her Bible and her devotional book. She didn't bother to pray even the shortest prayer. Crawling into bed, she curled up in a ball. Hot tears slid down her face and onto the pillow. "Why me?" she cried. "Why *now?*"

Only the Best
Chapter Five

"Our big day is Saturday, December fifth," Jenna's mother announced at breakfast two days later. She held the certified letter in her hand.

Jenna felt her heart thumping hard. "December fifth? No way!" she said, her spoon in midair.

"What do you mean?" Dad said, looking aghast.

"That's the day of my gymnastics meet at the Olympic Training Center," Jenna blurted.

Dad was silent, and Mom was beginning to look mortified. "We'll just have to work something out," she said.

"No! I can't skip this event, Mom!" Jenna insisted. "I've been working forever to compete with the team."

Her mother nodded, brushing a loose strand of hair from her face. "I didn't mean that you'd have to miss the meet. Of course we want you to attend . . . and to do your very best."

Jenna had always been one to overlook things, including conflict with friends at school and church. She had a way of just wanting to forgive and forget. But today she struggled with her stressful feelings and felt physically sick.

Excusing herself, she scooted away from the kitchen table. She trembled as she leaned against the archway to the dining room, unable to speak.

Dad's voice filled the awkward silence. "Jenna, dear, no other child can possibly change our love for you, if that's what's troubling you."

She felt tiny and weak, wishing he'd stop talking about how much they loved her.

"We've been asking God for another child for a long, long time," he was saying. "We wanted to adopt a Korean baby boy . . . to match our nationality."

Jenna spun around. "So . . . what you really want is a *son*?"

"Only because we already have a wonderful daughter!" His eyes were gentle, his face solemn. "We hoped you'd be as delighted as we are."

She voiced what she was thinking. "Just so this kid won't intrude on my life," she muttered.

But her mother had heard the cutting remark, and her look was stern. "What a selfish thing to say, Jenna."

Mom's right, she thought. *But I can't ignore the way I feel.*

———

"Hey, turtle eyes," Jamey Something whispered in homeroom.

Jenna looked the other way. She refused to give him the time of day.

"Yo, Swan Song," sneered Chris Stephens.

Get a life, she thought. One way to keep from losing her cool was to dream up a put-down in her head. She was the Queen of silent put-downs. And getting better at it every day!

During math period, Chris sat directly behind her. He kept whispering to her when the teacher wasn't looking. "Olive face," he taunted.

Her hair prickled on the back of her neck. Her father would say to ignore the boy. Better yet, turn the other cheek—the Bible way.

"Almond eyes," he scoffed.

She took a deep breath. In her imagination, she turned around and slapped him silly. Somehow, just thinking that way really helped. It was the same way she was able to focus on her gymnastic moves. Think it through, *see it,* then make it happen.

The only difference between imagining that she'd

bopped the jerk a good one and actually doing it was the leftover feeling of frustration. And knowing it was the *wrong* thing to do—imagination or not.

Had she laid into him for real, he might never make fun of her again. And she'd feel better . . . maybe. But hitting him was not her style. Still, it was all Jenna could do to keep her attention on the math assignment.

When the teacher called on Chris, she had to stifle a laugh. *He's toast now,* she thought, watching him drag his feet to the chalkboard. Anybody could see he wasn't prepared. Probably hadn't even done his homework. Probably hadn't for a long time.

Secretly, she was glad. Maybe now he'd back off and give her some peace. Till English class, anyway.

She wished Livvy was in more of her classes. But two out of seven was better than none. She wondered how Livvy would act toward her today. Yesterday she had been thoroughly ticked off—didn't even eat lunch with Jenna. Didn't hang around the locker much, either.

Jenna couldn't blame her friend. After all, it was Jenna's own fault for hanging up.

Would Livvy ever forgive her?

Only the Best
Chapter Six

During P.E., Jenna tried to strike up a conversation with Livvy. But Livvy didn't seem too interested in hearing about Chris and Jamey and their racist remarks. She kept leaning into her gym locker, away from Jenna.

"Did you hear anything I just said?" Jenna demanded. "Do you even know who I'm talking about?"

Livvy cast a painful look her way. "Oh, so *today* you're talking to me?"

Jenna nodded. "I know you're probably furious about the other night, and I don't blame you."

Livvy slammed her P.E. locker. "What was wrong with you, anyhow? You seemed so . . . so out of it. So angry."

"Yeah, I was." She didn't want to get into it. Not here in the middle of gossip city. "I'm sorry, Livvy. Can we talk later?"

Livvy stared at her feet, then slowly nodded. "I'll save a table at lunch," she said without looking up.

"Thanks, Livvy. I'll see ya." She hurried back to her own locker to towel dry her hair, thankful that she'd had it cut chin length before school started this year. Waist-length hair had become a major problem with all the extra hours at the gym.

Quickly, she pulled on her jeans and a soft blue sweater for her next class—science. Unfortunately, Chris and Jamey were in the class, too! She tried not to think about their insults. But she was more upset than she wanted to admit.

After brushing her damp hair, she hurried off to science just as the bell rang. The best part about show-ing up nearly late was getting to sit at the back of the classroom—far removed from the likes of Chris and Jamey.

She got seated at the desk and took out her folder. When she settled back to look at the teacher, the boys did that ridiculous slanty thing with their eyes. Two girls behind them poked them good, and they turned around.

Jenna congratulated herself on arriving almost late to science. Maybe she should do that in every class from now on. For the rest of the year!

She listened to every word Mr. Rahn was saying. All about plant phyla—species—and boring stuff like that.

She doodled on a clean sheet of paper, mostly drawing symbols for the different gymnastic elements. Like the double salto forward—two loops moving to the right.

When the teacher called on her, she hadn't exactly heard what he'd asked. "I'm sorry," she sputtered. "Can you repeat the question?"

"Please see me after class, Jenna."

Her heart sank. She couldn't afford to get herself in trouble at school. She'd always gotten pretty good grades—high *B*s and some *A*s—all through grade school. And now this year, too.

When the bell rang, Chris and Jamey walked past her desk and whispered, "Sing a sad, sad song, Jenna Song."

"Stay away from me," she said not so softly.

They kept strutting by, pretending they hadn't heard.

When everyone had cleared out of the room, Mr. Rahn motioned for her to come to his desk. "May I see your class notes?" he asked.

She swallowed hard. "My notes?"

He nodded, standing behind his desk. "You were taking some during class, weren't you?"

She was caught. "Uh, no, I wasn't, Mr. Rahn. But I *was* listening."

"Very well, but next time, it might be a good idea to sit closer to the front," he pointed out. "It seems you were a bit distracted today."

There was a good reason for that. And she almost told him about Chris and Jamey's constant insults. She was that close to blowing the whistle on them when in walked Livvy Hudson.

"Oh, sorry," Livvy said when she saw her friend and the science teacher talking.

"No . . . no," said Mr. Rahn. "Come on in, Livvy."

Her face turned instantly white. "I didn't mean to interrupt."

"We're almost finished here," the teacher replied. Then he turned back to Jenna. "Is it possible you're preoccupied with news of the baby . . . the one your parents are hoping to adopt?"

His question took her off guard. How could he possibly know?

"I . . . I don't understand," she muttered.

Mr. Rahn was actually looking like a proud father himself. "Well, if you ask me, I think it's terrific," he said, his arms folded across his chest. "Your dad and I keep running into each other at the library. Both of us are doing research on different things, of course. But we got to talking about your parents' plans to adopt a Korean baby. It's something my wife and I have discussed for years."

"Oh," was all Jenna could say. How many other people knew about the adoption?

The bell rang for lunch, and Mr. Rahn waved Jenna and Livvy out the door.

"Wow, that was weird," she told Livvy when they arrived at their locker.

"What was?"

"Mr. Rahn made me stay after class so he could tell me he knows about my parents' plan to adopt a baby."

"That *is* weird," said Livvy, piling her books into the lower section of their locker.

"I came that close to telling him about Chris and Jamey," Jenna said, lowering her voice.

"Why didn't you?" Livvy popped up to check her hair in the mirror attached to the locker door.

"If they keep it up, I'm going to the principal. Mr. Seeley can handle them," she said. "But don't tell anyone. I don't want it to get around."

"Like the news of the baby your parents want to adopt?" Livvy piped up.

Jenna shrugged. She couldn't deal with any of this. Not here, not now, and not with her best friend!

The whole idea bugged her—especially the possibility of having to miss out on the gymnastics meet. She *had* to attend the event in Colorado Springs. There was just no way she'd let an alternate gymnast take her place! Not so she could go off to some child-placement agency. Not for *anything* linked to a baby brother!

Only the Best
Chapter Seven

Jenna wasn't surprised when Tasya asked her to work in front of the mirrors. She scurried over to the far end of the gym. "I'm not smiling today . . . right?" she said.

"You are not smiling, yes," replied Tasya. "Why do you look completely miserable?"

Because I am, she thought.

"Things are not all right with you?" asked Tasya, who wore a white shorts set and a concerned frown.

Jenna shrugged. She wouldn't lie. "Let's put it this way—my life's never been so messed up."

"Well, we cannot have that." Tasya squatted on the floor next to her. "Do you want to tell me about the mess?"

"Not really, but thanks," she said, turning and forcing a fake grin at the mirror. "I'll get over it."

If I can, she thought.

"Well, remember, if you do need someone to talk with, I'm here . . . Coach Kim, too."

"Thanks. That means a lot." Jenna turned and finished her stretches at the barre. As best as she could, she centered her thoughts on the work at hand. The attitude of a gymnast had a lot to do with getting high marks. She knew she'd have to work very hard at pulling up her confidence level. It was important not to crumble under the pressure of the upcoming meet.

Cassie and two other teammates worked the uneven parallel bars at the other end of the gym with Coach Kim. Jenna headed toward them, watching Lara Swenson, the youngest girl on the team. Lara's dismount was a perfect twist and clean stick. Not the slightest bobble.

She breathed deeply, wondering how *she* would do today.

Coach called to her, "Jenna, come! Let's work your floor routine first thing." He motioned her over to the large floor mat. "I want you to focus on composition today— each individual skill is a building block. Remember that. Let's start with your tumbling pass."

She felt like a beginner all over again. It was so humiliating. Especially in front of her teammates, some younger and more advanced. "My aerial cartwheel was lousy last time," she admitted, taking her artistic stance at the edge of the mat.

"Now . . . Jenna, you must focus on what you came here to do," he stated. "And never, never give in to distraction. Push . . . push for perfection!"

Push for perfection. One of his favorite expressions.

She pushed, all right, hard as she could. Focusing, pointing, twisting, rolling, tucking, springing . . . flying through her routine. But on the aerial cartwheel, she lost her momentum and landed poorly.

Again and again she worked the move, always off on either her timing, height, or landing. Frustrated and concerned about her status on the team, Jenna was given a time-out.

Coach Kim strolled over to her at the drinking fountain. "Something's not working for you, Jenna," he said softly.

She couldn't deny it. "I'm freaking out."

"I can see that."

Still, she held back, not telling the reason for her frustration and lack of concentration. She recited aloud the key words to her floor routine just as Coach Kim had taught her and his girls to do. "Pose, speed, leap, twist, pike, double back."

When her ten-minute break was up, her coach led her to the vault area instead of the floor mat. "A change of apparatus might do you good," he said with an encouraging smile. "Just enjoy yourself, Jenna. Can you do that for me?"

She nodded. "I'll give it my best shot."

"That-a girl!"

Gripping her hands together, she stood at the end of the mat. She made a mental note of the masking tape mark on the floor, the springboard, and the horse beyond.

"Just have fun," she said to herself and ran hard down the runway. But her feet overshot the springboard by a fraction of an inch. Hardly any bounce. She toppled clumsily onto the soft pile of safety mats. So much for the first vault.

"Try again," Coach Kim called to her.

The second attempt was even worse. She didn't have enough speed, and the bounce wasn't high enough. A limp front handspring on the vault led to an imperfect stick, not straight and clean with both feet firmly planted on the mat.

———

Discouraged after practice, Jenna hurried home to shower and change clothes for supper. Her mother was picky about her coming to the table all sweaty or wearing a leotard. Jenna wondered what it would be like to have a laid-back mom. From the time she'd started gymnastics, Mom had expected only the best from her. Nothing less.

"If it's not worth doing one-hundred-and-ten percent, it's not worth doing at all," her mother would often say.

Only the best . . .

Jenna had adopted that standard for her life—ballet and gymnastics, especially. And Coach Kim and Tasya definitely promoted the vigorous approach. She wondered if they were thinking of dropping her from the team. After today's pitiful workout, she wouldn't be surprised.

"How was practice today?" her father asked as they were seated in the dining room.

"Pathetic." She fingered the lace table covering and stared at the cloth napkin under both forks.

"Well, tomorrow's another day," he replied. "Things will improve, you'll see."

Her mother carried a tray of serving dishes—rice, chicken, *kimchi,* and bean sprouts sautéed in sesame oil. "Did you tell Coach Kim and his wife about our baby?"

"Not yet." She thought of her science teacher but didn't offer to share the story. Jenna wasn't up to being scolded for doodling in class.

"Your father and I have discussed the upcoming meet," Mom said, still standing near her chair. "You've never missed a single competition, Jenna. Not even for illness." She sighed. "Not since your preschool classes began years ago."

Jenna knew what was coming. "But, Mom—"

"Just listen, please, Jenna," her father cut in.

Mom continued. "Even though it isn't a good idea

to cancel so close to competition, we feel you can miss, just this once."

"I told you how I feel!" Jenna blurted. "I won't skip out on the team . . . just so you can go off and adopt somebody's baby!"

"Jenna Lynn Song!" Her father stood up. His napkin fell to the floor. "That is quite enough."

She felt the stain of shame on her face. But nothing more was said about her outburst or her poor posture at the table. She picked at the soggy rice and the garlic-flavored kimchi.

When will Mom start cooking like an American? she wondered, overflowing with anger.

———

After supper, Jenna slipped away to her room with Sasha, who seemed *purrr*fectly delighted to see her. "Hello, prissy kitty," she said, burying her face in the soft, golden coat. "I missed my sassy girl today."

Mew.

Sasha wasn't one for being fussed over. She liked to be petted and stroked, sure. But all this cooing and baby talk, well, enough already!

"Wanna help me write in my diary?" Jenna kissed her cat on the top of her soft head. "Do you?"

The cat blinked her eyes, uncaring.

"You curl up here, and I'll write." She positioned the cat in her lap, but Sasha didn't stay put. She bounded down off Jenna's lap and over to the bed.

"Okay, be that way." Unlocking her secret diary, Jenna was ready to record the events of her disastrous day.

Tuesday, November 24
    Dear Diary,
    Thanksgiving is only two days away. But I don't feel very thankful this year. My parents can't understand why I don't care about getting a baby brother. I guess they have no clue. Things are perfectly fine the way they are . . . just the three of us.
    On top of everything else, I'm having trouble with my aerial cartwheel, something I've never flubbed before—not since I first learned how. It's gotta be the baby thing. I just can't concentrate very well! But I won't give up, and I won't let Coach Kim and Tasya down.
    What am I going to do?

Only the Best
Chapter Eight

Thanksgiving Day was filled up with relatives and friends at her father's Korean church. The coolest thing to happen was Livvy's arrival, just in time for supper. The girls sat with other teenagers, eating noodles and kimchi leftovers, talking and laughing together.

Jenna introduced Livvy to her Korean pals as her "best all-American friend. She's an incredible figure skater . . . headed for the Olympics."

"Someday," whispered Livvy, tugging on Jenna's shirt.

"Yes, *someday* we'll watch her on TV and say 'we knew her when.' " She turned to Livvy. "Are you totally embarrassed yet?"

Livvy's face was growing redder by the second. "Did you have to say all that?"

"Don't be ashamed of your skating talent, girl. God gave it to you for a reason," Jenna said.

"I'm not ashamed. Just modest, I guess."

"That's cool. So . . . *I'll* brag on you," Jenna said, laughing.

When the dishes were cleared away, the group games began. The kids and the grown-ups played for more than an hour.

Darkness soon settled over Alpine Lake, and church members began offering testimonies of thanksgiving.

Jenna's uncle Nam, a new father, stood tall and held up his tiny son. "We are very grateful to God for a healthy child this year," he said, grinning.

Another man stood and thanked the church for helping him through hard times. His wife stood at his side, smiling and nodding, giving thanks in Korean.

Next, Jenna's mother stood and told everyone about the baby they were going to adopt. From that moment on, Pastor Song's soon-to-be-adopted son was the topic of conversation. Talk of a baby shower hummed in the air, and the church ladies chattered in Korean, smiling and planning.

Oh great, thought Jenna. She was sure she'd have to attend all the hoopla for her adopted brother. The whole thing was getting out of hand!

———

A light snow was falling as Jenna and her friend headed for the church parking lot. She was glad she'd worn her warmest jacket and scarf. Winter in the Colorado Rockies meant skiing, snowboarding, and other exciting activities. Best of all for her was working out in a heated gym!

On the way to the car, Livvy commented, "Your church is really super. So friendly and connected, like a community."

"Asian-Americans stick together. And one of the best things about going to a Korean church is getting to hear the sermons in my first language."

"Thanks for inviting me. I like the unique culture—especially the noodles." Livvy pulled on her mittens. "I'll have to get your mom's recipe. They're super good."

"Nothing to it," explained Jenna. "Just tell your grandma to sauté them in sesame oil. It gives that yummy flavor."

The girls waited beside the Songs' family car. "Do you ever speak Korean around the house—you know, with your parents?" asked Livvy, leaning against the car door.

"Lots of times. And even sometimes at gymnastics because my coach is Korean, too."

"And Tasya is Russian," Livvy added. "I wonder how that works out at their house?"

Jenna chuckled. "Their kids probably speak three different languages."

"Really? They have kids?"

Jenna honestly didn't know. She'd never heard either of them talk about children. Come to think of it, they probably didn't. Their "kids" were all the girls who trained at their gym.

Nothing more was said about the upcoming adoption. And Jenna was relieved. She'd heard more than enough talk of a new brother at church for one day.

Only the Best
Chapter Nine

For as long as she could remember, Jenna had preferred home meets. Even though AAG was smaller than a big-city gym, it was easier doing routines on familiar apparatuses where she trained three times a week. And there were the usual ceiling marks she liked to watch when she did her aerials. The spots helped keep her position when she was in the air.

But all the girls on the team were jazzed about going to the Olympic Training Center headquarters. Especially Cassie Peterson, the tallest sixth grader. "I've heard all kinds of awesome stuff about OTC," she said, her blue eyes shining.

"Like what?" Jenna asked as they dressed in leotards in the locker room.

"For one thing, the equipment is state-of-the-art."

Cassie seemed pretty sure of herself. "A first-class place."

"It oughta be."

"OTC oozes with excellence and professionalism," said Cassie, her face beaming. "I can't wait to go again."

"Me neither, except this'll be my *first* time."

"You'll love it, trust me." Cassie sighed, looking a bit discouraged. She looked almost sad.

"What's wrong?" Jenna asked.

"It's just that . . . oh, I'm not really sure about gymnastics anymore."

Jenna sat on the bench beside her. "What're you saying?"

Cassie straightened. "It's a good thing we're going, I guess. This'll probably be my last year at AAG," she said suddenly.

"You're kidding!" Jenna was shocked. "You've been involved with gymnastics since you were in preschool. I thought you were in this forever. Like me . . ."

"I thought so, too, but I just don't know anymore." Cassie pulled on her white warm-up pants, her gaze directed toward Jenna. "It's such a big commitment. You know what I'm talking about."

Jenna knew. She knew as well as anyone at AAG. To achieve Elite level—which had been both Cassie's and Jenna's dream—required an exhausting training schedule.

Thirty hours a week, at least, just to maintain Elite status. And there were always injuries just waiting to happen. With that much pressure, a gymnast was often subject to broken bones, sprains, or worse.

She watched Cassie twist her long, blond locks into a knot at the back of her head. For a single moment, Jenna almost missed her own waist-length hair. Then she spoke up. "You won't quit without thinking it through, will you?"

Cassie closed the door to her locker. "That's just it. I've been thinking nonstop ever since the qualifying meet last spring. If I keep testing up—to Level Nine and finally to Elite level—I'll have to drop out of public school. Probably have to be homeschooled."

"So what's wrong with that?"

Cassie shrugged. "I really like going to regular school. Besides, my parents don't have time to school me at home."

Jenna didn't know what to say. She couldn't imagine Cassie quitting gymnastics. "I guess we'd better get going," said Jenna, removing her watch and earrings. Jewelry was not allowed during practice or competitive sessions. It was one of the many safety rules Coach Kim and Tasya insisted on for *every* gymnast.

"Coach'll wonder where we are," Cassie said with a sigh.

"Yeah, probably," was all Jenna said.

Cassie stayed behind in the locker room. "I'll see you later . . . at warm-ups."

"Better hurry," Jenna advised, rushing out of the locker room.

More than ever, she was determined to attend the meet in Colorado Springs. Not because Cassie was so up in the air about gymnastics. It wasn't that. Jenna just could never think of turning her back on the sport.

Lost in thought, she zoomed out the girls' locker room door.

Crrrunch!

She plowed straight into Coach Kim. "Oh, I'm sorry." Her hand flew out to steady him. "I didn't see you, Coach. Are you all right?"

He caught his balance and chuckled, towering over her. "I'm quite fine . . . but what about *you,* young lady?"

"A little startled, that's all." And she turned toward the hallway, leading to the gym. "See you at the balance beam."

"Jenna . . . wait," he called to her. "There's something I want to ask you."

She whirled around, wondering what was on his mind. "Yes?"

"I want you to be team captain for the rest of the school year. What do you say?" His face was very serious. He meant business.

"Sure, I'll do it."

He clapped his hands twice. "Done! Now, get going . . . lead the stretches today."

"You got it!"

He was smiling his big polar bear grin. "I'll be in for tumbling warm-ups."

"Okay, Coach. See ya!" She couldn't remember feeling so terrific. Coach Kim really believed in her, even though she'd had some trouble with her floor routine. He knew what kind of stuff Jenna Song was made of.

Head high and shoulders back, she hurried through the doors and into the gym.

———

Friday, November 27

Dear Diary,

It felt great not having school today—the day after Thanksgiving. Mom and Dad hit the mall for the start of the Christmas shopping season—for baby furniture (what else!)—while I worked out at the gym.

Being team captain is so cool. I think it's actually going to help me with my routines. My aerial cartwheels are improving, too. Yes!

I wrote another email to Dominique Moceanu. Even if she never answers again, I'm thrilled about getting her first reply. If only I could perform under pressure the way SHE does! Wow!

Cassie's got me worried about our team. She's definitely losing interest . . . or something's happening. I wish I knew what to do to help. Maybe I'll give her a call on the weekend. Maybe I'll pray for her, too.

Only the Best
Chapter Ten

"I'm so glad it's almost Christmas," Jenna said, steadying the tabletop Christmas tree in the waiting area at Alpine Aerials Gymnastics.

"Me too," said Lara Swenson, the youngest girl on their team. "What're you getting this year?"

"I haven't asked for anything," Jenna said, bending each artificial branch carefully. "What do *you* want for Christmas?"

"A new warm-up suit and a bigger gym bag would be great," Lara spoke up.

She glanced at the petite girl. "A new water bottle might fit in my stocking." She laughed.

"That's *all* you want?" Lara's big brown eyes got even bigger.

"Well . . . maybe I'll ask for another Olympic rings flag

for my room. I already have the small one." She couldn't honestly think of anything she needed or wanted. Unless it was some new church clothes. Her parents had already forked out a lot of money for her birthday present at the end of the summer—a classy new computer. Besides, she figured most of her dad's salary would go toward the new baby.

One by one, Jenna hung little wooden ornaments on the tree. The decorations were tiny gymnastics apparatuses or figurines of boys and girls performing various stunts. She and Lara had volunteered to decorate the tree yesterday when Tasya mentioned it after class. Jenna had jumped right up, saying she'd help. Anything to get her mind off the upcoming adoption. But she hadn't told Tasya the reason for her eagerness. Not Lara, either. So far, no one at the gym knew about the baby.

"Oh, look . . . how clever!" Lara had discovered a garland of wooden beads mixed in with Olympic rings and flags.

"Hey, cool," Jenna said, inspecting it. "I wonder where Tasya found this."

"They travel all over the world," Lara said, winding the garland around the tree. "Could've come from almost anywhere."

"Looks like something from Germany." Jenna had seen similar holiday trimmings in the catalogs that sometimes arrived in the mailbox. "There's only one way to know," she observed.

"Ask Tasya, right?" Lara giggled as she spun around the room, pointing her toes and posing.

Jenna stepped back and examined the tree. "So . . . what do you think?" she asked. "Are we good at this or what?"

"Oops, I see an empty spot." Lara rushed over to fill it with two additional ornaments. "There, how's that?"

"The best," Jenna said, studying the tree again.

Lara stood against the wall, staring at her. "You do everything that way, don't you?"

"What do you mean?"

"You never miss a chance for perfection." The younger girl wore a curious expression. "Am I right?"

Jenna had to laugh. "You didn't see my floor routine last Saturday, did you?"

Lara frowned. "You're kidding. You mean you actually flubbed?"

"Not only that, I wiped out!"

"I must've been working on bars," Lara said. "I totally missed it."

Jenna shook her head. "I'm surprised none of the girls said anything. I had an all-around lousy practice," she confessed.

"Well, I never heard about it."

Jenna wandered over to the vending machines, where

only healthy foods were available. She selected a can of pure carrot juice. "That's one of the cool things about our team," she said, pulling the flap off the can. "We support each other."

"Like Coach always says—we're family around here. We work together." Lara selected an apple juice from the juice machine and a fruit yogurt from the snack machine. "Want some of this?"

"No, thanks. I better work out a little before I go home," she said, glancing at her watch. "I'll see you later, Lara."

"Thanks for helping with the tree."

"We'll do it again next year, okay?" Jenna called over her shoulder.

Anxious to work on the uneven bars, she hurried to the locker room, changed clothes, and got herself focused. Several other girls from the team were working their floor routines.

Jenna did all her warm-ups—running, sit-ups, jumps, and her drills. When she was ready, she asked Tasya to spot her.

Tasya came willingly, as always. "You seem happier, yes?"

Jenna nodded. "I'm trying."

"Good, then. Let's hit everything today."

Hitting everything was a gymnast's single goal. "I'll do my best." She placed grips over her palms and wrist supports. Next, she applied some chalk and water to keep her fingers from slipping on the bars. Saluting, she raised one arm over her head, even though there was no judge in sight. Not today, but very soon . . .

Jenna felt totally confident about this routine. Because she loved bars. Since the days of Tumble Tots, she had practiced her technique thousands of times. It took courage and confidence, above all.

Mounting the lower bar, she felt the smoothness beneath her grip. *Hit everything.*

Tasya backed away slowly. "Remember now, Jenna: Always, *always* focus on your body. Know precisely where you are up there," she told her. "You *know* just where your toes end and where your fingertips begin, yes? Feel . . . know . . . *own* the weight of your body."

Jenna began with a gentle swing up to a handstand on the lower bar. *Smooth, stretch, pike, handstand, catch, back salto . . .* The key words for each second of her routine, combined with muscle memory, carried her through to the most difficult part of her bars routine. The Geinger. She released the bar and caught it again as she circled around in midair.

Big swing, stretch, twist, smooth, double swings . . . The dismount was a layout with a full twist. Her feet pounded the safety mat, jarring her body.

"Clean stick! Very good!" shouted Tasya, her face beaming.

201

Jenna couldn't help grinning as she threw her arms high over her head. There was no question in her mind. She had performed only her best.

She left the gym with one thought buzzing around in her head. *I have to work on a stronger floor routine . . . especially my aerial cartwheels!*

Only the Best
Chapter Eleven

At church the next day, Jenna bowed her head silently during prayer time. She prayed for Cassie and for herself—about the aerial cartwheels and the upcoming meet.

Jenna had no interest in doing the same for little Jonathan—the name her father had already chosen for the baby. If she *did* bring the matter up, God wouldn't understand her uncaring attitude.

After the sermon was given and the benediction sung, the women went to cook in the fellowship hall. Every Sunday they served up a feast. And every Sunday the church members—visitors, too—gathered downstairs and ate kimchi and noodles and other Korean specialties to their hearts' content.

This Sunday was no different, except that Jenna sat off by herself. Several young people tried to coax her to join them, but she refused. She was miserable, just like Tasya Kim had said five days ago. Miserable and stuck with the pain of jealousy.

———

That afternoon, Jenna called Livvy from her portable bedroom phone. Livvy answered on the second ring. "Hi, it's me," Jenna said. "I'm glad you're home. I need some company. Can you come over?"

"I have a few more pages of homework, but maybe I can. Wait a minute, I'll ask my dad." Livvy wasn't gone for more than a few seconds. "Sure, my dad said he'll drive me over."

"Cool! I'll be waiting." She nuzzled her face against Sasha's furry body. "Bye!"

Jenna hung up and went to turn on her computer. When she checked her email, she was surprised to see another message from Domi . . . or probably someone representing the Dominique Moceanu Homepage. With thousands of messages pouring in, there was no way America's little sweetheart gymnast could possibly keep up. No way!

The email began: *Hi, Jenna! I hope you do well at your meet in Colorado Springs. You'll love OTC. It's a great place to "show your stuff." Have fun!*
Domi M.

Jenna hurried downstairs to tell her parents. But Mom was taking a nap, and Dad was brushing up on his notes for the evening vespers.

Sitting on the sofa, Jenna watched for Livvy. On the coffee table, she noticed a brochure of an adoption agency. She studied the front and discovered that it was the one her parents were working with.

Casually, she thumbed through the pages, surprised at how many children and infants were featured. Most of them had lived their short, needy lives in overseas orphanages. Without the love of a permanent family. Their tiny faces touched her, made her feel sorry for them. Each one.

Sighing, she wondered how she might've felt about an adopted brother if she hadn't spent the last nearly twelve years as an only child. *Would I care more about baby Jonathan then?*

She turned the pages more slowly, studying the ethnic children. Indian, Chinese, Korean, Filipino. Many of them had already been approved for adoption. They were just waiting for loving parents. So many children . . .

The doorbell startled her.

Quickly, she opened the front door to Livvy. "Come in," she said, greeting her friend. "Glad you came over. Want some pop or something?"

"Super." Livvy removed her jacket and wool hat. She

wore a tan turtleneck and brown corduroy jeans. "It's starting to snow again," she said, shaking her hair a bit. "My dad said he'll pick me up in a couple of hours."

"That's good." Jenna hung up Livvy's coat and hat in the hall closet. Then she led her into the kitchen. "Wanna make root beer floats? Or are you too cold for ice cream?"

"Whatever you like." Livvy was perched on the edge of a chair.

Jenna laughed. "Hey, I think we've switched roles."

"Like how?"

"You're the relaxed one these days," she said, dipping ice cream into two tall glasses.

"So why're *you* uptight?" Livvy asked, leaning back in her chair. "You've got one of the best gymnastic coaches around, a fabulous ballet instructor, and two terrific parents."

Jenna noticed the obvious absence. Livvy hadn't said one word about Jonathan, the soon-to-be baby brother. "So you think I should be perfectly calm and relaxed? My world's totally together, right?"

Grinning, Livvy waved her hand. "Oh, whatever."

"Yeah, right. Whatever." Jenna set about pouring the root beer over the ice cream. It foamed up, threatening to spill over the sides.

"You've got everything a girl could possibly want," Livvy continued. Then she paused, staring out the window.

"You know, I'd give almost anything to have my mom back. But that's selfish of me. I know that."

Selfish . . .

Jenna didn't want to touch that topic. She didn't need to feel guilty today, on top of everything else. "Your mom was always involved with your skating, wasn't she?" Jenna asked.

Livvy's eyes glistened suddenly, and she turned from the window. "Mom took me to every skating event from the time I was in preschool on. She went along to cheer for me, but she was never uptight about competitions. Not like some moms on the sidelines."

"Like *my* mom," Jenna said softly. She carried the root beer floats over to the table and sat down. "My mother is so strict . . . expects way too much. Especially in gymnastics."

"But that's a good thing, isn't it?" Livvy spoke up.

Jenna dipped a straw into her float. "It all depends, I guess."

"On what?"

She wasn't sure how to explain what she felt. "It's just that my mom wants me to achieve—keep pushing myself—because she knows I can reach my goals."

Livvy was nodding her head. "What's so bad about that?"

"She's stuck on me being the best."

"Lots of moms want that for their kids." Livvy was staring at her now.

Jenna shrugged, feeling almost sad. "But it sounds like your mom was different . . . didn't push so hard."

"Oh, she did, but in a gentle way. But best of all, my mom accepted me. That was always number one with her." Livvy leaned down to sip her soda.

Jenna thought it over. "That's the kind of mom I want to be someday. The ideal mom—someone like your mother."

"You know what I think?" Livvy said.

Jenna shrugged.

"Better be thankful for what you have," Livvy offered.

Jenna ignored the comment. She didn't need another sermon. That wasn't why she'd invited Livvy over. The truth was she felt lonely—needed a listening ear. She honestly wished she could talk to her own mother like this. But Mom was too busy arranging baby furniture and sewing nursery curtains to listen to the child she already had.

Only the Best
Chapter Twelve

Monday, November 30

Dear Diary,

The meet at OTC is this Saturday! I talked to Cassie at school today, trying to get her psyched up for the event. But she seems so wiped out. Even after volleyball in P.E. I wonder if she's pushed herself for too long.

Will that happen to me? I really hope not because my goal to qualify for the Junior National Team someday is still VERY strong. If Cassie drops out at the end of the year, her decision might bring the rest of the team down (so to speak).

I wonder what Coach Kim and Tasya would say if they knew Cassie was struggling? Maybe they could help boost her spirits. . . .

Jenna finished writing her diary entry, then reached for the phone. She dialed Cassie's phone number. "Hey, Cass," she said when her friend answered. "Busy?"

"Doing homework. What's up?"

"I was wondering," she began. "Have you talked to Coach and Tasya about what you told me last week?"

Cassie gasped. "Are you kidding? They're professional coaches, Jenna. They'd never understand what I'm dealing with."

"I think you're wrong. Why not give them a try? They might help."

Cassie was silent.

"Look, I don't mean to get on your case, but I hate to see you feeling like this about gymnastics. Someday soon you and I are going to the qualifying meet for Elite gymnasts . . . aren't we?"

"Well, maybe."

"So you haven't decided for sure?" Jenna's fingers were crossed.

"I won't give up without a fight—my own personal battle, that is."

Jenna understood. "I know, Cassie, and I'm praying for you, okay?"

"That's probably a good thing." Cassie chuckled a little. "I need all the help I can get."

"Hang in there, girl," Jenna said, glad she'd called.

"Thanks, I will."

"See ya at practice tomorrow."

"Okay, bye."

Jenna hung up the phone. She leaned back on her bed, staring at the ceiling. Sasha came over and settled down next to her. "Something's really bugging Cassie," Jenna told her cat. "I hope she snaps out of it before Saturday."

Sasha's purring rose to a gentle roar. And Jenna closed her eyes and began to pray.

———

After supper, Jenna made herself cozy near the fireplace with Sasha in her lap. Dad sat on the sofa next to Mom as he read the Bible and the family devotional. Jenna stared into the orange and gold flames as she listened.

The reading was about changes and learning to trust God through them. She wondered if her father had searched the book just to find this topic. But she didn't shut out the message because of it. She didn't feel upset about the things her dad was reading. Not the way she might have a week ago.

Gazing into the fire, she remembered the images of orphaned babies and children from the agency pamphlet. She remembered how stirred up she'd felt the first time she'd seen it. Maybe because the pages represented the caseworkers that had located baby Jonathan for her parents. And for her. . . .

The longer she sat there, the worse she felt. In a few days, a baby was coming to Alpine Lake. *Her* parents would become *his*. And she would become Jonathan Song's big sister!

She knew she ought to be getting ready for the special day. But how?

Only the Best
Chapter Thirteen

Jenna met Livvy at their locker first thing Tuesday. "How'd skating go this morning?" she asked.

"Really super," Livvy replied, carrying her skate bag over her green parka.

"That's the stuff!" Jenna put both thumbs up and waved them in Livvy's face. "You can brag on yourself once in a while, especially to your friends. How's it feel?"

Livvy laughed, depositing her jacket and the books for her afternoon classes inside the locker. "No comment," she said.

Jenna watched her stack up her math and English books. The little Christmas bells taped to the locker door jingled as the girls took turns primping at the mirror.

"I've been thinking about your gymnastics event—the one coming up," Livvy said, turning to face her. "I've got a brainwave about it."

Oh, great. Jenna braced herself. She had a feeling she knew what Livvy was going to say. Something about traveling to Denver with her parents to bring the baby home. "Uh . . . if this is about skipping the meet, I can't do it." She closed the locker door so hard the tiny bells kept jingling inside.

"You mean you *won't* do it," Livvy shot back. "Anybody knows your coach'll let you off. That's what alternates are for."

"Livvy, stop!"

"Look, I'm not on your case, Jen. I just think you should change your mind."

Change . . .

There it was again.

Jenna stood her ground. "I'm not a horrible person, really. I just can't let my coach or the team down."

Livvy got right in her face. "Listen, I have an idea . . . but only if you really want to go with your parents to get your baby brother."

"It's not possible!" Jenna spun away on her heels, not wanting to hear more. She tore off toward homeroom. And to the face-making weirdoes, Chris and Jamey.

Sitting at her regular desk, she pulled her notebook out of her book bag. She found her assignment book and double-checked her homework. All the while, Chris and Jamey were yanking on their eyes.

Any other day, she might've overlooked them—put up with their antics one more time. But now she'd had enough.

Up! Her hand flew high.

Chris and Jamey blinked their eyes and jerked their heads at attention. They shuffled around in their desks, probably looking for a book . . . something to make them look busy.

Jenna held her hand even higher, hoping Mr. Lowell would hurry and look her way before she lost her nerve. She sat as tall as she could in her seat. Filled with confidence, she was reaching for the uneven parallel bars in her mind. She was doing her best to "see" her routine, while Mr. Lowell paid absolutely no attention.

Stretch, catch, swing, kick . . .

Mr. Lowell looked up. "Yes, Jenna?"

"Uh . . ." She glanced over at Chris and Jamey. Could she follow through?

Beat the nerves, Coach Kim was always saying.

She took a deep breath. "I need to see you after class, please," she said.

"That will be fine," her homeroom teacher said.

Chris and Jamey wilted like old lettuce. And they didn't look her way even once with a rude or racist gesture the entire period.

Despite her worries, things went okay with Mr. Lowell. "I'm glad you told me, Jenna. I won't tolerate that sort of behavior in my homeroom," he insisted when she'd spilled out the whole story.

"I really didn't want to get anyone in trouble," she was quick to say. "It's just that . . . well, I'm sick and tired of their faces and constant slurs."

"You shouldn't have to put up with that nonsense." He smiled at her. "I'll handle things."

Before she left the classroom, he thanked her.

"I hope I did the right thing," she said.

"You did the *best* thing for Chris and Jamey. Mr. Seeley will want to know about this."

Mr. Seeley—her principal—would come down hard on the boys. She was sure of it.

Rounding the corner to math, she spied Chris and Jamey. Their drooping faces gave them away. "We don't like snitches," Chris said, mustering up some courage.

She kept walking, ignoring them.

"Why'd ya have to go and tell?" Jamey whined, following close behind her.

She stopped. "Why'd you have to keep bugging me?"

Their mouths dropped open.

"You've had your warped fun, now leave me alone!" With that, she turned and escaped into her math class.

Relieved to be in a class without the boys, she chose a desk close to the front. Taking a deep breath, she opened her homework.

Out flew the adoption pamphlet. "What's this doing here?" she whispered and leaned down to rescue it from the floor.

"Hey, what's that?" someone said.

Jenna sat up to see Cassie sliding into the desk across the aisle. "Oh, it's . . ." She almost said "nothing."

"Let's see it." And before Jenna could stop her, Cassie reached for the brochure.

Jenna's heart was pounding. She didn't want *everyone* to know about her parents' plans for adoption. It wasn't anyone else's business!

"Where'd you get this?" Cassie persisted, turning the pages.

Jenna felt her face burning. "I . . . uh, can we talk about this later?"

Cassie glanced around. "How come?"

"Just because." Jenna's embarrassment was turning to anger.

"Is somebody in your family going to adopt a baby?" asked Cassie, leaning over and handing the pamphlet back.

Jenna didn't want to admit it. But she felt almost helpless, afraid of what Cassie might think. Especially if her friend knew how selfish Jenna had been.

Cassie crouched on the floor beside her. "Listen, Jenna, not too many people know this, but *I'm* adopted. And it's the greatest thing . . . really."

Surprised, Jenna looked—*really* looked—at her friend. "I never knew that."

"Well, it's true. Just ask my parents." Cassie's eyes sparkled with her smile.

"That's amazing."

"My big sister thought so, too, way back when," Cassie said as she looked inside her book bag. Out came her wallet, and the next thing Jenna saw was a snapshot of Cassie and her older sister. "Stacy's nearly ten years older, but that never kept us from being close."

"But . . . I thought Stacy was your *real* sister. She looks so much like you," Jenna managed to say.

"She's a real sis, all right. In every way that counts. And about looking alike, well, my parents just happened to hook up with an agency that matched ethnic backgrounds."

"Cool," Jenna said. And she meant it. What Cassie had just said *was* really cool. In fact, the same thing was going to happen to her and her new baby brother.

In every way that counts . . .

Jenna couldn't get the words out of her head!

———

When the bell rang at the end of first hour, Jenna could hardly wait to find her best friend. What *did* Livvy have in mind for this Saturday?

Dashing back to their locker, she hoped to find Livvy there. No sign of her friend in the hall. She'd have to wait till P.E.

Frustrated, she trudged off to a gigantic English test. *How will I ever survive this day?* she wondered.

Only the Best
Chapter Fourteen

There was no time to grab a conversation with Livvy during or after P.E. So Jenna headed off to gymnastics without hearing her best friend's plan.

Things actually went well with the team. All eight of them. Jenna led warm-ups—twelve long stretches and several tumbling passes for each girl.

Then Coach Kim came over and gave them a solid pep talk. He was known for his short but straight-to-the-point approach. His talks made his gymnasts think and remember long afterward.

"We're here to do our best," he said. "Only our best."

Jenna glanced at Cassie, sitting next to her on the bench. She wondered how the zip in Coach Kim's voice might affect Cassie's final decision.

Coach continued. "Are we a team? Are we in this together? Do we breathe, see, and taste victory?"

The girls nodded, some clapping after each question.

Jenna saw the enthusiasm on Coach's face and the energy in his step as he paced back and forth. His words made her feel as if she were born to do the sport. More than anything, she wanted to compete. More than anywhere else, she could be herself inside the walls of a gym. She was at home here. At Alpine Aerials Gymnastics!

And things would go just fine in Colorado Springs, too. She was sure of it. They were a team. Like family.

We're in this together. . . .

————

On the drive home, Jenna kept sneaking glances at her mom. "You should've heard Coach Kim today," she said as they waited at a red light. "He was really pounding nails."

Her mother seemed dazed, out of it. "I'm sorry, what did you say, Jen?"

"Coach Kim . . ." She stopped. No sense repeating herself. Mom was in nursery land somewhere. Jenna knew by the dreamy look in her eyes. And even though Mom seemed to be paying attention to traffic, her mind was probably on Jonathan—a gift from God. That's what his name meant in the book of names Dad had purchased.

Jenna had sneaked a peek at the name book. She'd looked up the baby's name. Hers too. Jenna meant "God is gracious." Seeing those words after her name made her feel special.

"You must see the darling nursery lamp I bought today," Mom was saying.

Jenna was right. Her mom *was* daydreaming about the new baby.

"It's the cutest thing. A white sliver of a moon with a cow jumping over it." Mom pulled into the parking spot at the curb in front of their three-story brick house. "I almost bought the lamp with the Humpty Dumpty design on it, but there was just something wonderful about that cow. . . ."

Jenna didn't attempt a comment. Nothing she might've said or asked would have been heard or answered anyway. Honestly, she'd never seen her mother like this. Not even the day Jenna placed first at State on beams and bars two years ago!

"Let's head right upstairs," her mom said, pulling the parking brake. "I want to show you something."

Jenna got out on the street side and waited for her mother to come around. The sidewalk was slushy now from yesterday's snow. All day long, the sun had warmed things up, making the first day of December almost a no-jacket day.

"God's smiling down on us," Mom said as they walked up the steps to the house.

"You mean because of the mild weather?" Jenna thought she'd laugh but held it in. Mom wasn't her normal self. Not one bit!

———

Upstairs in the nursery, Jenna checked out the cow-jumping-over-the-moon lamp. It really *was* different. And cute. "I've never seen anything like this," she told her mom.

"Neither have I." Turning toward the closet, Mom went in search of something. "I want you to have a look at this, Jenna," she said, her body halfway into the closet.

Jenna waited, not too eagerly, in the white wicker rocker. It was a good choice for the green-and-yellow nursery.

"I bought a baby book for our Jonathan," Mom said, carrying the book to Jenna. "Just look at all the different things we can write in your brother's book."

"We? You don't mean *me,* do you?" She looked up at her mother.

"I certainly do. Dad and I . . . and you are going to write in this beautiful book. For the new baby."

Jenna held the book on her lap, hesitating to open the pages. "I wouldn't know what to write," she said softly.

"Well, let me give you an idea." Mom scurried off down the hall to the front of the house, to the master suite.

Jenna had no idea what her mom was searching for. And she didn't exactly care. But she sat quietly, looking around the room at all the new stuff. The cow lamp, the changing table, and the white crib with a green-and-yellow ruffled quilt and tiny sham to match. On the wall, a matching fabric collage was framed in white wicker—to match the rocking chair, Jenna guessed.

Once or twice, she'd poked her head in here since the certified letter had shown up in the mail. But never had she entered the room or allowed herself to get too close to any of the baby furniture.

"Here we are," Mom said as she returned to the nursery, holding a white-and-pink book. "Do you remember this?"

Jenna remembered but hadn't seen *her* baby book for the longest time.

"Look through it, honey. You'll see the wonderful words Daddy and I wrote for you. Notice all the different stages in your infancy, toddlerhood, and up through your preschool years and beyond."

Jenna read with great interest. There were pictures, too. Color snapshots of her parents taking turns holding their tiny daughter—Jenna Lynn Song.

She looked closer, and sure enough! The very same goofy look was on her mother's face in these pictures. The same glazed, almost spaced-out look she'd seen in the car today.

"We fell instantly in love with you," her mom said, kneeling beside the rocking chair. "Look there, how Daddy and I fussed over you."

The picture showed her parents leaning over a crib, on either side, cooing into Jenna's baby face.

"Who took the picture?" she asked.

Mom grinned. "Your father had an automatic camera back then, all set up on a tripod. It was one of his grown-up toys."

Jenna couldn't help herself. She laughed out loud.

"What's so funny?" asked Mom.

"Nothing really . . . and everything, too." She was making at least as much sense as her mom. Or anyone else waiting to adopt a baby, she guessed.

Only the Best
Chapter Fifteen

"Guess what I did after I got home from gymnastics yesterday?" Jenna asked Livvy on the phone the next day.

"Beats me."

"C'mon, guess!"

"Honestly, Jenna, I don't know. Just tell me, will ya?"

She heard the impatience in her friend's voice. "Okay, okay. I checked out my old baby book."

"What's the big deal?"

Jenna was quiet. She wasn't sure how to say this. "I'm . . . uh, having second thoughts."

"About what?"

Sighing, Jenna told her. "About being okay with—"

"Your brother's adoption?" Livvy interrupted.

"Uh-huh." She wondered what her friend would say now.

"Well, I think it's about time!" Livvy was laughing. "Are you saying what I think you are?"

"Well, not exactly."

"So . . . are you *still* going to the meet this Saturday?" Livvy asked, her breathing filling up the silence.

"You don't have to ask. You know I'm going." She didn't want to argue this subject anymore. But it was clear Livvy wasn't giving up. Her friend had some weird plan, but it was a waste of time. Jenna was sure of it.

"I've gotta run," Livvy said.

"Yeah, me too."

They hung up, and Jenna hurried to change clothes for the midweek church service.

———

After church, Uncle Nam motioned to her. He was carrying his baby boy—Jenna's new cousin—showing him off. "You haven't said hello to Kyung yet." Her uncle leaned down so she could have a close-up look.

Jenna peered down into the face of the tiny bundle. "Oh, he's cute," she whispered, touching the tiny cheek with her pointer finger.

"Kyung's *handsome*—the handiwork of God," crowed Uncle Nam.

"You're right," she said.

Unexpectedly, Baby Kyung wrapped his teeny fingers around her own, and her heart did a double salto with a full twist. "How sweet," she whispered, surprised at her reaction.

Uncle Nam was more than a proud father. He was generous, too. "Would you like to hold him?" he asked.

"Uh . . . I better not." Jenna hadn't been one to baby-sit or take care of little ones through the years. In fact, she had never baby-sat like many of her girlfriends. Every free moment was spent at the gym.

"He won't break," Uncle Nam persisted.

If I hold him, he might, she thought.

But before she could voice her concern, the cuddly young cousin was in her arms. The baby made adorable squeaky sounds, almost happy sounds, Jenna thought. And nearly without thinking, she began to rock him gently.

Why was I so afraid? she wondered. *Babies aren't so bad.*

Just then her aunt came down the aisle. "It's getting late," she said, a denim baby bag slung over her shoulders. "We must head home . . . tuck our baby into his cradle."

Reluctantly, Jenna returned her cousin to his father. "Bye-bye, handsome baby," she said softly.

Uncle Nam nodded, wearing a big smile. "Remember . . . he's God's creation." Then he turned and headed for the foyer area, talking in Korean to his sleeping son, then to his wife.

Jenna's brain buzzed with unexpected thoughts. She sat on the last pew in the sanctuary, thinking about tiny Kyung. Uncle Nam was right. There was something very precious about the baby. Something belonging to God.

The chapel was soon empty of people, except for her parents and one other church member. She could hear sounds of the branches brushing against the building outside. A white half-moon peeked through one of the stained-glass windows.

Leaning back against the wooden pew, Jenna wondered if the baby boy from Korea would affect her this way. Would she miss holding him the way she missed her new little cousin right now?

She thought more about the idea of a baby brother. And when she tried to picture what he might look like, she started to feel the tiniest shiver of excitement. Until yesterday, sitting in the nursery at home, she'd had no interest in being a big sister to an orphaned infant. But now? She could hardly wait to meet her new brother, Jonathan Song.

Most of all, she wondered how she would tell Coach Kim and Tasya. She'd have to forfeit the meet after all. But how would Coach and Tasya take it? Giving them only three days' notice wasn't very sportsmanlike. Not fair at all. She worried about that. But she knew it was her fault for waiting this long—for disobeying her parents.

Looking into the dear little face of cousin Kyung—God's creation—had touched her. It had begun to change things.

Maybe everything.

Only the Best
Chapter Sixteen

Thursday morning, Jenna hurried downstairs to breakfast. She was still wearing her pajamas and bathrobe. "Good morning, everybody," she said, sitting at the kitchen table.

"Well, aren't *you* the cheerful one?" Dad said, putting the paper aside.

Her mother did a double take. "Your hair looks like it woke up on the wrong side of the bed!"

Laughing, Jenna reached her hand up to her head. She felt the hairs sticking out. "Hey, you're right," she said, giggling.

"Maybe this is a new hairstyle," Dad said, reaching for his cup of coffee.

"Could be," she said. "I'll have to see what Livvy thinks."

"By the way, Livvy called here earlier," Mom said. "She asked if you can meet her at the mall skating rink before school."

Jenna glanced at the wall clock above the sink. "If I hurry, maybe I can."

"I'll drive you, if that helps," offered Dad.

"Thanks." She wondered what her best friend was up to.

Quickly, she went upstairs to shower and dress. Before heading to her room, she crept away to the yellow-and-green nursery at the end of the hall. Standing beside the crib, she looked down. She touched the ruffled crib sham and quilted coverlet. It was easy to imagine a baby sleeping there. A baby as adorable as her very own cousin.

———

On the way to the rink, Jenna asked her dad about the Saturday plans. "What time is the appointment at the adoption agency?" she asked.

"Eleven o'clock sharp," he replied without glancing her way. "Why do you ask?"

She didn't tell him why. Not yet. "I just wondered" was all she said. She figured they'd leave for Denver around seven-thirty. Because, knowing her parents, they'd want to be as prompt as possible.

"Your mother and I expect that you already made arrangements with Coach Kim . . . to inform the alternate." He pulled up to the curb.

"Don't worry, Dad," she said before getting out.

He stopped the car near the entrance to the mini shopping center. "I'm not worried, Jenna, and you mustn't be, either. Trust the Lord for His plan for your future. For our family's, too."

He seemed almost ready to step behind a pulpit. For as long as she remembered, her dad was always eager to get a word in for God. "Thanks for the ride," she said, opening the door.

"Any time!" He smiled and waved.

Jenna watched him pull away from the curb. "What a really cool father," she whispered before heading into the mall to find Livvy.

———

The skating rink was situated in the center of the small emporium. There were live trees decorated with giant red bows and white lights for the holidays. Quaint benches scattered the area.

Tired of lugging her gym bag, Jenna sat on one of the benches and waited for Livvy to finish up her session. There were several other advanced skaters on the ice. Two ice dancers caught her eye. They looked like twins—a boy and girl about Jenna's age.

Who are they? she wondered, her eyes glued to the incredible blond twosome.

Livvy soon spotted her and motioned for her to come to the edge of the rink. "Your mom must've told you I called," she said, catching her breath.

"Yep, that's why I'm here. What's up?"

Glancing over her shoulder, Livvy said, "See those ice dancers?"

"How could I miss them? I can't take my eyes off them . . . especially the boy." Jenna smothered a giggle. "Who are they?"

"Heather and Kevin Bock. And they're really super skaters."

"I noticed." Jenna watched the pair circle past. "They must be twins—they look so much alike."

"They're twenty months apart. Best friends, too!" Livvy turned and watched them for a moment.

"I've never seen them at school," Jenna said.

"That's because they're homeschooled."

"Really?" Jenna was dying to meet them. Especially Kevin. "So when are you gonna introduce me?"

"As soon as they take their break," Livvy said, grinning. "I really wanted you to meet Heather because she's starting ballet after Christmas."

"With *us*?"

Livvy nodded, facing her now. "And there's another reason why I want you to meet Heather and Kevin." Her merry face had turned serious.

"Why?" asked Jenna.

"They have a younger brother and sister . . . both adopted."

Jenna should have known. "That's interesting," she said, playing along.

"Wait here," Livvy said, skating off toward center ice.

Jenna watched as Livvy chatted with the Bock kids. Being new to the mountain town, she was glad to meet more young athletes. Kids with similar goals . . . and kids with adopted siblings. She wondered how many *more* adopted people she was going to meet in one week!

Only the Best
Chapter Seventeen

Jenna went looking for Coach Kim as soon as she arrived at the gym. It was one of her off days, so she knew he wouldn't be expecting to see her.

She found him positioning heavy safety mats under and around the balance beam. "Jenna, what a nice surprise!" His big voice bounced across the gym.

"Uh, excuse me, Coach." She wished she could hide under the largest floor mat. "I need to talk to you."

His usually jovial face turned to a frown. "Is something wrong?"

"No . . . actually, everything's *right*." Suddenly, she felt more confident. "I should've told you this two weeks ago. I'm sorry I waited so long." She explained about the baby her parents were going to adopt. That she would have to miss the meet and go to Denver instead.

"I haven't been much of a team member," she confessed. "You always say we're a family here at AAG—that we work together. But I haven't acted like a part of this family."

Coach Kim's face broke into a big smile. "On the contrary, Jenna. What you're doing with your parents is far more important than any gymnastics meet. You mustn't forget that. Only the best kind of person would do what you're doing." He touched her head gently. "You are one of those people, Jenna. You will make the new baby a very good sister."

She thought she might cry. "I hope the team won't hate me for this . . . for backing out so late."

He put his finger to her lips. "Hate never built a strong family . . . or a team. Nobody's going to say a word about this. I promise you."

She hugged him and said good-bye, then hurried outside. On the long walk home, she thought of Cassie and Lara and the others. How would the All-Around Team score without her? How would the competition play out? Who would they pick for the alternate?

Her heart sank as she thought again of missing out. But she knew she'd made the right choice. It was the best choice for her family—and for her new brother.

———

When she arrived home, her mother met her at the door. "Livvy's on the phone. She sounds very excited."

Jenna rushed into the house and picked up the living room phone. "Livvy? Hi, what's up?"

"I've been thinking."

"Better be careful, that could be dangerous," she said, laughing.

"No, seriously. Let's start a club. For girls only."

"With *two* members?"

"Well, no. Actually, I was thinking about including Heather Bock. If it's all right with you," Livvy said. "What do you think?"

"Of the club or Heather?"

"Both."

Jenna really liked the idea. "Sure, why not? Heather's really cool. What's *she* think of your idea?"

"I haven't said anything because I wanted to talk to my best friend about it first." Livvy was laughing. "You *are* my best friend, you know!"

"Sounds like we might be expanding to three." She wondered how long it would take to get to know Heather Bock. *Really* know her the way she and Livvy knew each other.

"When should we have our first club meeting?" Livvy asked.

Jenna was ready now! "How about right away?"

"You're kidding."

Jenna chuckled. "Come over in a half hour. Let's start by practicing our ballet stretches and moves at the barre in my bedroom. Isn't my attic room the perfect place?"

Livvy agreed. "I'll call Heather. See ya!"

Jenna hung up the phone and went searching for her mom. "We've got company coming . . . Livvy and Heather. Hope it's all right with you." She told her mother all about Livvy's club idea. And about Heather and Kevin.

Mom's face brightened as she sat at the kitchen table. "Sounds like fun."

"We won't bother you if we work out in my room, will we?"

"That's fine," Mom said. "And when you're finished with your meeting, maybe the girls can stay and help us put up the Christmas tree."

Jenna was pleased. Mom was bending over backward to be agreeable. "I'm getting to be a pro at decorating trees," she said.

"Oh?"

She described how she and Lara had put up the little tree at the gym. "And this afternoon, I talked to Coach Kim . . . finally. Everything's set. I'll miss this one meet, but he understood." Saying the words brought a twinge of pain, but Jenna didn't regret her decision.

"*I* talked to Coach Kim today, too," her mother said. "What a fine coach you have."

"We all knew he was from the start."

Mom smiled knowingly. "It's even more obvious to me now."

Jenna didn't pry. She didn't ask her mom about the conversation with Coach Kim. "I'm sorry for dragging my feet about canceling the meet," she said. "I really wanted to go."

"I know, honey. It was a difficult thing for you to do. I'm very proud of you. Both Dad and I are."

Jenna hugged her mom and held on tight. "I can't wait to meet our baby," she said, pulling away at last. "And I mean that."

"Would you like a sneak preview?" Mom asked, getting up and heading for the dining room.

"What do you mean?" She followed Mom to the buffet.

There, between two china candleholders, was a tiny face with the cutest nose and the sweetest eyes.

Mom picked up the framed picture. "This is Jonathan. The photo came in the mail today."

"And you framed it already?" Jenna gazed at the adorable face.

"I couldn't help myself," Mom said.

"I think I know how you feel," Jenna replied.

Only the Best
Chapter Eighteen

Jenna chose one of her favorite classical CDs—*Peer Gynt Suite*. "Wait'll you hear this," she said as the *Girls Only* Club members prepared to do their ballet warm-ups.

"Heather's a classical music nut, too," Livvy said, smiling. "Just like me."

The blond ice dancer nodded. She wore a pale blue jogging outfit that brought out the blue of her eyes. "I like all different kinds of music," she said. "Music brings out the zip and pizzazz in me . . . in my brother, too. We always talk over what music we like best for our ice-dancing routines."

Jenna wondered what it would be like to have a partnership with an older brother. "Do you ever blame Kevin for flubs or getting marked down at competitions?" she asked.

Heather shook her head. "No . . . never. We've worked as a team since I was in second grade and Kevin in third."

"That long? Wow," Jenna said. "So you really know what to expect from each other?"

"Always." Heather went to sit next to Livvy on the floor, under the barre. "This is really some special place," she said, glancing around the room.

"Thanks," Jenna said. "You should've seen it before we put in the new carpet and the wallpaper. It was such a mess."

Livvy nodded. "It sure was. But then, so was the old Victorian house my dad bought on Main Street. Remodeling is the thing—for ancient houses, at least."

The girls chatted about their homes, parents, and school. Heather showed off a wallet picture of her grade-school-age adopted brother and sister. "It's just like they were born into the family—no difference," she said.

Jenna wondered how that could be. She guessed she'd find out sooner or later.

The girls began discussing the club name. "Is *Girls Only* okay with you two?" Livvy asked.

Jenna pulled up her knees, leaning her chin on them. "I don't know about either of you, but I think it's a really cool name for our club," she said. "It's got a lot of class."

"Yeah, and the initials spell *GO*—which describes each of us exactly," Livvy said.

Heather nodded. "Because we're always so active, right?"

The girls agreed, grinning at each other.

Jenna went to her desk and changed the CD. "Who's ready for some Christmas tunes?" she asked.

Livvy and Heather definitely were. And within seconds, the strains of "Greensleeves" floated through the attic room. "Hey, let's work up a ballet routine to this!" Heather said, getting up and twirling on her toes.

"Super!" Livvy said, mimicking Heather.

Jenna liked the idea but stopped to look out one of the dormer windows near her desk. A light snow had begun to fall again, just since Livvy and Heather had arrived. The tops of the neighbors' houses were already dusted white.

She didn't tell Livvy or Heather that her thoughts were on the All-Around Team. *Her* team was going to Colorado Springs without their captain!

Putting on a smile, Jenna did her best to count off the dance steps. She followed Heather's lead. With every move, she focused on *GO!*—a cool club for a super three-some.

Thursday, December 3

Dear Diary,

I can't believe it's almost Saturday! Mom's got everything ready for the baby—diapers, bottles, blankets, clothes, and the tiniest bibs. Dad's still trying out middle names to go with Jonathan.

Me? I'm getting used to the idea of sharing my parents with somebody else. Somebody new!

Heather Bock's really cool. Livvy and I had a great time getting better acquainted with her. (She doesn't know it, but we both think her brother Kevin is VERY cute!)

Our first official GO! Club activity was to memorize a ballet routine—which Heather helped create. We're really good at it, for only just working it up. Maybe we can perform it during Christmas—for our parents.

Livvy and Heather stayed to help decorate our living room tree—just like Mom had hoped. We all got along so well together. (Even Dad was impressed with Heather's good attitude and helpful nature. He says there's something special about homeschooled kids!)

The girls think the nursery is darling. Livvy said it was "super sweet." Heather doesn't have any favorite word to describe things. At least, I haven't noticed one yet.

Tomorrow Mom and I are going to Uncle Nam's to see baby Kyung again. Mom wants to ask more questions about baby care—Korean style. I know it's because she wants to be the best mother for Jonathan. But knowing my mom, she'll do just fine. After all, look how I'm turning out!

I finally heard Livvy's "plan" for my Saturday. Her uncle's got a private pilot's license, from what she said. She had this crazy idea that if I could work things out, I could go with the team to the meet at the Olympic Training Center. Her Chicago uncle would fly in and take me to Denver just in time to meet my parents and the baby.

It was an interesting thought while it lasted. . . .

Only the Best
Chapter Nineteen

Early Saturday morning, Jenna stared up at the Olympic rings flag above her computer desk. "Go, team," she said, stretching in her bed. "Hit everything at the meet. Do it for me."

Heading down the hall, she turned on the shower and let the water run. She peered into the mirror over the sink. A sleepy-eyed, All-Around Team captain in a pink-flannel nightgown stared back at her. A girl with high goals and lofty dreams.

She drank a glass of water. Looking in the mirror again, she saw a Korean pastor's daughter. An only child about to become a sister.

———

The ride to Denver seemed never-ending. Dad rehearsed a hundred different middle names for the baby. Mom read aloud from a baby-care book.

Jenna had to smile at her parents' approach to all of this. "You act like you've never done this before," she said.

Mom looked back over the front seat at her. "In case you've forgotten, it's been eleven years since we've had a baby in the house."

"It'll come back quickly," Dad said, offering Mom a reassuring smile. "You're a natural with little ones, dear."

The comment seemed to help. Mom shrugged her shoulders and returned to her reading.

Jenna stared out the car window, watching the mountains blur past. *This is my first day as a sister,* she thought, deciding to be the best one Jonathan could possibly have. More than that, she wanted to make her parents glad they'd given birth to her.

"I think I'm ready to write in the baby book," she spoke up. "Did you bring it along?"

Her mom pointed to a canvas bag next to Jenna on the backseat. "It's in that bag right there."

Opening the bag, Jenna looked inside. Her pink leotard, palm protectors, wrist guards, and beam slippers were in the bag, too. "I wondered where these were," she said, reaching for the baby book instead.

Mom stopped reading. "There's a page close to the

front," she said. "You'll see the heading—*The Day You Came to Live With Us.*"

Jenna scanned the baby book. She hadn't realized that it was a book for adopted children. Totally different from the one her mother had kept for her.

She read the words her parents had written, wondering how her brother would feel reading them, too, when he was much older. Finding a pen in her purse, she clicked it on and began to write.

To my brother, Jonathan:

You don't know me yet, but I know something about you. Your eyes and your cute little face in our first picture of you made me feel happy all over. I hope you like being a member of our "team."

Love,
Your big sister, Jenna

She read through the entire book, understanding how each page related to an adopted child. By the time she was finished, they were coming into the busy outskirts of the big city of Denver.

Mom double-checked the map and gave Dad directions to the adoption agency. Jenna felt the first butterflies in her stomach. She thought about Cassie—how proud she was to be adopted. And Heather's wallet picture of her little brother and sister. So many happy "adoptive" families . . .

———

At least five different times, Jenna checked to make sure tiny Jonathan was snug and secure in his infant car seat next to her. She wished she could hold him all the way back to Alpine Lake, but he was much safer where he was.

"Jonathan Bryan is the cutest baby on earth," Jenna said, using the middle name her parents had finally chosen.

She settled back in the seat, staring at him. Jonathan was as olive-skinned as she was but with darker hair. His fingers and hands were perfectly formed, and when he sighed, she knew she wanted to protect him forever.

"How fast do babies grow?" she asked, leaning forward.

"Oh, he'll be walking in six or seven months from now," her mom said.

"How old was I when I took my first steps?" she asked.

Dad chuckled. "You were an early one, Jenna. We always knew we had a gymnast in the family."

"Tell me again." She'd heard the story many times but wanted to hear it again. Just for fun.

"Well, you liked to somersault and balance your feet on anything that resembled a straight line," Mom said.

"And always with your arms out and your head tilted up," Dad said. "You were moving constantly."

Jenna watched her sleeping four-month-old brother. *Will Jonathan be a gymnast, too?* she wondered.

Her mother was rattling the map in the front seat. But Jenna noticed that the sound didn't startle her brother at all. "Looks like he's a sound sleeper."

Mom turned around. "The caseworker said he sleeps straight through five hours at night."

"And then he wants to be fed, right?" she said.

Her dad glanced over at her mom. "We'll take turns getting up with him," he offered, reaching his arm around Mom.

"I'll help, too," Jenna said.

"But gymnasts need a full night of sleep," Mom said, handing the map back to her. "Here, see if you can find the turnoff for Interstate 25."

"What for?" she asked, opening the map.

"We need to help Dad find the way to Colorado Springs," said her mother.

Her mom's words didn't quite register in her brain, but she started looking for the highway. Suddenly, she realized what Mom had said. "Why are we going to Colorado Springs?" she asked, her heart thumping hard.

Mom was smiling the most curious smile. "You have a gymnastics meet to attend this afternoon," she said.

"I *what?*" Jenna could hardly believe her ears.

Dad was nodding his head and looking at her in his rearview mirror. "Coach Kim said if we could get you to the Olympic Training Center by two o'clock, you could compete with the team."

"Oh, you're kidding! This is so cool!" And she leaned over and whispered to the baby, "You're going to your first gymnastics competition, Jonathan Bryan Song."

Then she leaned back against the seat and began psyching herself up for competition. She thought through each of her routines. When she came to the floor routines in her mind, she visualized a perfect aerial cartwheel. She'd do her very best to hit everything. For the team . . . and for baby Jonathan.

Only the Best
Chapter Twenty

"Jenna, you're here!" Cassie said, clapping and smiling.

All the girls circled her, calling out encouragement to each other and to Jenna.

"Where were you?" Cassie asked. "Why didn't you ride along with the team?"

"It's a long story . . . but a very cool one," she said.

Cassie frowned. "I have no idea what you're talking about."

"Don't worry, I'll tell you later." She almost said *I'll show you* but didn't want to draw the focus off the competition. After the meet, there'd be plenty of time for introductions to her baby brother.

Coach Kim and Tasya helped the girls pep up with words like "We can do it!" and "We're going to hit everything . . . everything!"

The atmosphere was electric. Cassie was right, the place was totally amazing and buzzing with the crowd and the competitors.

Jenna had plenty of time for some short warm-ups with the rest of the team. She felt so good, like the confidence might burst right out of her.

"I feel so ready for this," she said to Cassie. "How are you doing?"

A smile broke over Cassie's face. "I thought I wanted to do other things," she said softly. "Things that I was maybe kind of good at without having to work so hard . . . you know, the way we do in gymnastics. But I've made a decision."

"You're staying in?" asked Jenna, reaching to hug Cassie. "You're not quitting, are you?"

"Things that come easy aren't worth doing, are they?" Cassie replied, her eyes glistening.

"Yes!" shouted Jenna.

The girls danced around, hugging and laughing. "I'm going to nail every single routine today," Cassie said. "I promised myself."

"Me too," Jenna said. She glanced up in the stands and saw her dad waving a banner. On the bench sat her mom, holding Jonathan. Tears threatened to spill over, but Jenna waved at the three of them instead. "I love you," she whispered.

The girls were chanting behind her. "Hit it . . . hit

it. . . ." Over and over they said the words, until there was so much energy around them, Jenna was dying to get started. They all were.

Finally the All-Around Team from Alpine Aerials Gymnastics marched into the arena. Jenna was first in the line of eight girls because they were arranged in stairsteps—shortest to tallest. Each girl was so pumped up and ready.

They warmed up some more and then started the competition on the uneven parallel bars. Jenna was up third, right after Cassie and Lara. She prayed silently before the judges gave her the green light to begin. All three girls nailed one routine after another. So did the rest of the team.

The vault was next, followed by the balance beam. Jenna remembered everything Coach Kim and Tasya had told her. She flew through her routines, hitting every single one!

They went to the floor mats, trailing another team from Grand Junction, Colorado. But that gave Jenna and the others all the more courage to do their best.

"Only the best . . ."

She could hear her mother's words in her ears as she saluted the judges. Jenna focused on her tumbling run, took a deep breath, and hit every element with complete confidence. Even the aerial cartwheel—crisp and clean!

The crowd was cheering as she raised her hands high over her head. *Yes! I did it. I did it. . . .*

When her score—9.820—flashed on the scoreboard, she thought she heard her parents cheering. She strained her ears to sort out the sounds, and she was sure now. Because their shouts of glee were in Korean.

And then she heard a baby's cry. Jonathan? Was her baby brother "cheering" for her, too? In his own unique way, she knew he was.

It was one of the best days of her life.

———

That night, after she helped her mom tuck Jonathan into his crib, she sat down to her computer. She keyed in the email address for Dominique Moceanu and began her message.

Hi again, Domi,

I had my first meet at OTC in Colorado Springs. You said I'd love it, and I did.

Guess what! My parents adopted a baby boy today. Actually, the adoption will be finalized several months from now. But I thought you'd enjoy this, especially since your little sister is eight years younger than you are.

My new brother's name is Jonathan Bryan. Does that sound like the name of a famous gymnast???

I'm so excited about how well our team did today. We

aren't Elite gymnasts yet, but we're on our way. Our team placed fifth in the state. Not bad for small-town girls!

I feel so pepped up tonight. I wish I could send an email to Shannon Miller and Amy Chow, too. Their performances at the Olympics, along with yours, gave me the heart to keep trying to HIT EVERYTHING in all my workouts and competitions.

Thanks for your friendship, Domi. I hope you make it to the 2000 Olympics.

Bye for now,
Jenna Song

She read her message quickly before sending it, then called for Sasha. "Come here, little girl. I haven't seen you all day," she said, coaxing the drowsy feline onto the bed. "You're not the only baby around here anymore. You're gonna share my attention with a real baby. How do you like that?"

Sasha opened her eyes, then blinked slowly and was soon snoozing again.

"Sweet dreams," Jenna whispered and turned out the light.

She thanked God for working things out for her and her family and for the team. Her mother came in and tucked her in for the night.

"Thanks for everything, Mom," she said. "You're the best."

"Well, I don't know about that, but it's nice of you to

say it." And she sat on the edge of the bed and kissed Jenna's forehead.

After her mom left, Jenna could see the dim hall light through the crack under her bedroom door. Tempted to get up and sneak to the nursery, she lay still, thinking about the day. Her parents had arranged for her to attend the meet. She still could hardly believe it. What a surprise!

If she were to think of the key words for the day's events, she would have to start by saying, "baby brother" and end with "just too cool."

Only the Best
Chapter Twenty-One

Girls Only—the club—met again on Monday afternoon. Jenna, Livvy, and Heather rehearsed their ballet routine for their Christmas show. They listened to other CDs, too, deciding on additional music.

Later, while sipping apple juice, Jenna told the girls about the incredible gymnastics meet. Then she took them into the nursery, and they each held her brother. "I got what I wanted for Christmas already," she said, stroking Jonathan's little fist.

"Hey, you're right," Livvy said, getting her face up close to the baby's. "Not fair. Santa came early to your house."

They laughed at that, but Jenna knew better. God had brought this baby here. And into her own heart.

Livvy handed the bundle back to Jenna. "I almost

forgot to tell you what I heard about Chris and Jamey," she said with a strange look on her face.

"Do we *have* to talk about them at a time like this?" Jenna asked, staring down into her brother's face.

Livvy continued. "The principal gave them a very interesting assignment."

"For a punishment?" asked Jenna, surprised to hear it.

"They have to do a big research paper on Korea . . . all about the geography, capital, population, history. The works."

"You're kidding," she said, wondering if the boys would focus in on the people and their unique looks. The way they had on her these miserable weeks.

"And get this," Livvy said, her face glowing. "They're talking about visiting your father's church on Sunday."

"Are you sure?" Jenna asked, laying the baby down in the crib.

Livvy was giggling now. "Chris says he wants to interview a Korean pastor. He thinks he'll get extra credit for it or something."

"Well, if he interviews my dad, he could end up talking to God, too. You know how my dad is," Jenna said, feeling better about the whole thing.

Livvy nodded. "Sounds like the assignment might not be such a bad thing for them, after all."

"God works things out for good," Jenna said, remembering the Scripture.

"Yeah, in more ways than one, right?" said Livvy.

Heather was smiling, too.

Jenna and the girls tiptoed out of the nursery. She was excited about the future. Her future as a gymnast— and as a sister.

Girls Only!

A Perfect Match

AUTHOR'S NOTE

Great, big thank-yous to Justin and Heidi Koleto—brother/sister ice dancers who happen to be homeschoolers!—and their mother, Michelle, for answering so many questions about the sport.

I am also grateful to the U.S. Figure Skating Association and the helpful folks at the World Arena in Colorado Springs, Colorado. My appreciation for the research assistance received from the IOC (International Olympic Committee).

For readers interested in learning more about skating news, tips, and the Stars on Ice tour, check out the Kristi Yamaguchi Web site.

For

Heidi Koleto,

*who ice-dances with her
brother, Justin,
and has high hopes for the
Olympics.*

A Perfect Match
Chapter One

"It seems like forever since our last club meeting," said Heather Bock. She sat cross-legged on the floor in Jenna Song's attic bedroom, holding the "minutes" notebook.

"I know what you're saying," agreed Jenna, residing president of the exclusive *Girls Only* Club. "Christmas break was just too long this year."

Olivia Hudson—vice-president—spoke up. "Two weeks and two days, to be exact."

Jenna snickered. "Leave it to Livvy to count the days."

"Want the hours and minutes, too?" Livvy teased.

"No, thanks," replied Heather, grinning at both girls.

"It's been nearly a month since we presented the ballet show for our parents, don't forget," Jenna said.

Heather hadn't forgotten the dance extravaganza. How

could she? The *Girls Only* show was one of the absolute best things all year. At least the most creative thing she'd done with her girl friends, including some awesome choreography, blocking, narration, and, of course—the music!

Every other spare minute was spent ice-dancing with her older brother and partner, Kevin. Often they practiced three to four hours a day, four days a week. And every other weekend they spent Saturdays in Colorado Springs, less than an hour away.

"So . . . are you going to tell us about *your* Christmas break, Heather?" asked Livvy. Her auburn hair was pulled back in an emerald green clip that brought out the color of her eyes.

"Kevin and I worked on our compulsory dances," Heather explained. "Business as usual, I guess you could say."

"You two are so-o-o *perfect* on the ice," Livvy cooed. "I've watched you guys skate and, I'm not kidding, you're really good."

Jenna nodded, her black hair brushing her chin. "Livvy's right. You and your brother are a total class act."

"With synchronized steps that are absolutely super," Livvy said, her eyes sparkling. "I don't know how you do it."

Heather forced a smile. "The same way Jenna does her incredible gymnastic routines." She glanced at her petite Korean friend, then back at Livvy. "And the way *you* show your stuff as a free skater."

Opening her spiral notebook, Heather wrote the date in the upper right-hand corner. *Friday afternoon, January 8*. Then, in the center of the page: *Girls Only—Club Minutes*.

"Are we all set to begin?" asked Livvy, leaning her back against the side of Jenna's bed.

"Hold on a minute," said Jenna, wearing a curious frown. "I'm dying to know something."

Livvy giggled. "Uh-oh, watch out."

Heather had no idea what was going on but waited till Jenna scooted closer and began to whisper. "Do you mind if I ask you something personal?"

Shrugging her shoulders, Heather felt awkward all of a sudden. "I . . . guess not. What's up?"

"Well, it's like this." Jenna looked at Livvy and hesitated, turning terribly shy.

"C'mon, spill it," Livvy said, grinning from ear to ear, like she knew exactly what Jenna was thinking.

Jenna took a deep breath, looking right at Heather. "What's it like working so closely . . . you know, with your brother?"

Heather couldn't help herself. She had to laugh. "What do you mean?" she ribbed her friend. But she knew what Jenna was getting at. She was pretty sure, anyway.

"It's just that Kevin's so cute." Instantly, Jenna's olive skin darkened. Livvy, too, looked a bit sunburned.

"So is it safe to say that *both* of you have a huge crush on my brother?" Heather looked first at Jenna, then at Livvy.

"Well, he *is* drop-dead gorgeous," Jenna admitted.

Livvy wasn't quite as bold. "Yeah, he's real . . . uh, fine."

Sighing, Heather understood. Kevin was as handsome as the girls said. Even better, he was a positively awesome Christian—eager to follow God.

"Okay, now back to the question," Jenna insisted.

Heather chuckled. "Do you wanna know what it's *really* like ice dancing with Kevin?" she repeated.

Livvy and Jenna nodded their heads, eyes wide with anticipation.

"Well, to begin with, my brother's very careful with me on the ice. We practice the hardest moves very slowly at first. He'd feel horrible if he ever dropped me."

Livvy gasped. "Oh yeah . . . I forgot about the lifts and stuff."

"Accidents happen if you're not careful," Heather explained. "I've seen lots of skaters land on their heads and have to get tons of stitches. Even miss a whole season for injuries."

"So it's a dangerous sport?" Jenna said.

"It's like gymnastics or any other sport, I guess. You

just have to be careful. But when I'm on the ice, I like to think more about having fun . . . and working hard toward our next medal," Heather said.

She thought back to a practice last week. Kevin and their coach had "walked" her through some new and difficult moves. Because Kevin was taller—and almost two years older—Heather felt completely safe on the ice with her brother. And he never was bossy or pretended to know more because he was older. Never.

"Kevin and I have been skating together since I was five and he was seven," she told the girls.

"Wow, that long?" Livvy said.

Heather nodded. "I can hardly remember *not* skating with a partner. I guess you could say my brother and I are like two bicycle wheels—where one goes, the other follows."

"I'd be more than happy to be a bike wheel for Kevin Bock," cooed Jenna, her deep brown eyes staring off into space.

Picking up her pen, Heather ignored Jenna's comment and began writing in the club notebook. "So, have we discussed my brother adequately?"

Livvy was giggling, but Jenna pushed her face into the "minutes" notebook. "Hey, what're you writing?" Jenna asked, looking completely aghast.

Playfully, Heather jostled Jenna away and began to read the entry. " 'The very first order of business on Friday,

January eighth, was a discussion about Kevin Bock, the secretary/treasurer's thirteen-year-old brother.' "

Jenna and Livvy screeched in unison.

"No . . . no! You can't put *that* in the club notes," Jenna said, eyes wide.

"And why not?" Heather replied, stifling a laugh.

"Because it's just so . . . uncool," answered Jenna.

"Besides, what if an outsider reads the notes?" said Livvy. "What then?"

"Or what if *Kevin* reads them?" Jenna asked, covering her mouth with her hand. "That would be the uncoolest thing!"

Smiling at both of them, Heather closed the notebook. "Okay, then, maybe we should say the talk about my brother was simply off the record."

Jenna and Livvy leaned back against the bed, their eyes rolling around in their heads. Heather knew she'd closed the door on the Kevin thing.

For today, at least.

They went on to discuss other things, but not a word about boys. Instead, they talked about what to do to raise money for their next show—and when it should be. "How about a Spring Dance Festival?" Livvy suggested.

"We could invite Kevin to perform," Jenna piped up, eyes sincere.

Heather shook her head. "Our club is for girls only, in case you forgot."

"Oh . . . for a second, I guess I did." Jenna's face did the weird greenish purple thing again.

"Actually, I could ice dance alone," said Heather. "Just this once." She was surprised how easily she could say those words—*dance alone*—even though it would seem very strange to perform her fancy footwork and moves without her partner. She was thrilled to offer a solo dance because deep inside she had a secret longing. And tonight, she planned to talk to Kevin about it.

If she had enough courage, that is.

A Perfect Match
Chapter Two

Where's Kevin hiding out? Heather wondered.

She scraped the supper dishes and loaded them into the dishwasher. Quickly, she wiped the table clean and shook the place mat over the sink. Then she hurried upstairs to look for her older brother.

Stopping in the hallway outside his bedroom door, she could see Kevin sitting at his desk. Probably doing homework. When he was off the ice, he usually had his nose in a book.

"Knock, knock," Heather said softly.

"Door's open," Kevin said without turning a-round.

She smiled. "You probably knew I was standing out here, right?"

"Before you ever said a word." He turned and grinned.

"That's what happens when you skate, breathe, and think like your little sister for six years."

She smiled. "Doing geometry?"

"Always."

"Just wondered if you want to take a walk," she said, hoping she could keep up her nerve.

"Now?"

"Sure, why not?" She hoped he wouldn't refuse.

Closing his math book, he got up. "It's dark out . . . and snowy. You sure about this?"

"We could walk down to the Oo-La-La Café and get some ice cream," she suggested. "I'm buying."

Kevin's face broke into a wide smile. "Well, if that's the case, we're outta here. Let's see . . . I'll have a double banana split with extra ice cream and triple—"

"Hey, slow down. Who said anything about pigging out?"

"Aw, c'mon." He pretended to sulk, playing along.

"You know what Coach says about eating bad stuff," she reminded him. "Ice cream once in a while, and then only in moderation."

"Hey, it's one thing to get lectured from Coach, but do I have to hear this from my skating *partner,* too?" From his emphasis of the word *partner,* she wondered if he suspected something.

"Better ask Mom and Dad if we can go out," Heather

said as they hurried down the stairs. They stopped by the coat closet in the entryway.

"Dad's working with Tommy on his rocket project," Kevin said, reaching for his jacket.

"In the garage?" she asked.

Kevin nodded. "I think Mom and Joanne are out there, too. Last time I checked, they were."

Heather followed him out to the garage, where they found the rest of the family wearing coats and scarves, helping Tommy with his homeschool project. A giant red rocket.

"Is it okay if Heather and I walk down to the mall for some ice cream?" Kevin asked their dad.

"Isn't it kind of late?" Dad said, glancing at his watch. He was a tall, thin man with the same blond hair as Heather and Kevin.

"We'll be home by eight," Heather volunteered.

Dad looked at Mom, who was nodding her head that it was all right. "Okay, but don't be gone long."

"And go easy on the sweets," Mom said as they headed outside. "Remember, you have practice tomorrow."

"Four-thirty comes so early," Heather muttered.

Kevin chuckled. She could see his breath as they walked toward the sidewalk. "You'd think after all these years, getting up before the chickens would be easy," he said.

Heather watched the glow from the streetlights. They

dotted the narrow street, three to a block, and the effect against the snow reminded her of their recent trip to Colorado Springs. On the city's West Side, there was an enchanting section of quaint shops and eateries not far from the World Arena—called Old Colorado City.

She wasn't sure why she thought of the place just now as she and Kevin walked in perfect stride. Maybe it was the memory of a ceramic doll in one of the shop windows—a skater dressed in a flowing white dress with silver beads sewn on the bodice, sleeves, and hem. A girl without a partner, soaking up all the limelight. Sharing the applause with no one.

What would that be like? she wondered.

The stillness was awkward and brought her back to Alpine Lake. She sensed that Kevin knew why she wanted to walk with him along the quiet, narrow street on a cold January evening.

Kevin was in tune with her that way. He seemed to know her mood better than most anyone. Even their homeschool friends—and their relatives—said the two-some were as close as twins. If that was actually true, Heather decided there was only one reason for it. All the skating—the lessons, the practicing. Constant to-getherness.

For the longest time, she and her brother had been the only two children in the Bock family. Then one day, their parents sat them down and discussed the possibility of adoption. Heather could still hear her father's words, even though she was just a tiny girl at the time. *"A little boy and girl need a home,"* he'd said with glistening blue eyes.

Dad had held Mom's hand as they told of two youngsters orphaned by a fatal car accident. *"Their names are Tommy and Joanne, and they're darling little ones,"* Mom had said excitedly. *"You're going to have a new brother and sister."*

Heather remembered the brightness on her parents' faces. She also remembered the love she felt from them and *for* them. So changing from just the two of them—Heather and Kevin—to the four of them wasn't terribly difficult. For one thing, Mom and Dad were eager to make the transition a smooth one. They worked hard at blending the family; even gave little Tommy and Joanne skating lessons for several years. Heather remembered how much fun it was to have a new brother—a younger one—and a little sister.

But changing from ice dancing with a partner to free skating by herself would require a lot of dedication and effort. Much more work on her part—a complete regimen of off-ice training, too. After all, Livvy Hudson was one of the best skaters in all of Alpine Lake, and she did many different types of training off the ice. Things like cycling on a stationary bike, lifting small weights several times a week, and skating in the church parking lot on in-line skates. Beside that, she trained with her coach three times a week and practiced on her own every day . . . even on Saturdays!

So Heather knew what was ahead of her. That is, *if* Kevin would agree to let her go it alone. If . . .

———

"Uh, Kevin," she began when they were within sight of the restaurant. "I need to ask you something."

He sighed, his breath turning to a wispy cloud of ice crystals. "You're not happy with the way we're doing the fish lift?"

She almost laughed. Of course he'd think of something like that. Something related to one of their skating positions. "No," she said softly, "nothing's wrong with the fish lift."

"Are you sure, because if there is . . . we can work on your spiral some more and the preparation and—"

"It's not about that," she said emphatically.

He was quiet for a moment. Then, "What's wrong, Heather?"

Just the way he said it made her feel sick in the pit of her stomach. She was hesitant to tell her brother the truth. Afraid what her new goal—her incredibly exciting ambition—might do to him. So she was silent, too unsure of herself to say what was on her mind.

"Heather?"

"It's nothing to worry about," she said, furious with herself for not having the grit to follow through. She scrambled for something to discuss and remembered that their dad's fortieth birthday was coming up. "We should have an over-the-hill party. Dad would get a kick out of it, don't you think?"

Kevin seemed relieved. "Sure. Let's talk to Tommy and Joanne and see how much each of us want to chip in."

"We get our allowance tomorrow," she said, feeling like an icicle, walking through a daze of mist and snow. And wishing she'd never invited her brother out into the frosty night.

Bottom line: She was a coward, too scared to tell her skating partner the truth. But how could she without hurting him?

This is horrible! What am I going to do? she wondered.

A Perfect Match
Chapter Three

The three of them—Heather, Livvy, and Jenna—were doing their warm-up stretches at the barre on Monday after school. In the far corner of the ballet studio, Natalie Johnston, the dance instructor, was giving the pianist some final instructions.

"Better limber up in a hurry," Heather told her friends as she watched them in the mirror above the barre. "Natalie will be calling us to center stage any minute."

"I still have some kinks in my legs," Jenna complained, shaking her right leg. Then she leaned forward, stretching it again.

Heather nodded, wishing *her* problems consisted of only a few leg kinks and tight tendons. She'd tried again to talk to Kevin before they took the ice during their early-morning practice session. Right before Coach

McDonald arrived all fired up about their straight arm lift. He'd called it brilliant—said something about it being positively perfect.

But she'd gotten exactly nowhere with Kevin, partly because he was preoccupied with their dad's fortieth birthday plans. "Mom's all for a big party," he'd said as they laced their skates. "We'll do the black streamers, black everything, over-the-hill party hats—you name it."

Heather had forced a smile and a chuckle, trying to conceal her true colors. Things would be bad enough when she finally came out with it and told Kevin that she didn't want to partner with him anymore. That she wanted to try something brand-new.

Livvy was calling, "Hey, Heather. Time to line up."

The opening measures of Beethoven's haunting "Moonlight Sonata" were the cue for center practice—the slow, sustained exercises to improve balance and graceful movement. But for Heather, everything was a big, fat blur. Like a puppet, she followed Miranda Garcia, her tall Hispanic friend—fabulous dancer and Alpine skier. Miranda, too, had high hopes for the Olympics. Someday.

"Hey, Heather. How's it going?" Miranda flashed a big smile.

"Okay," she said, but her thoughts were elsewhere. Sighing, she felt completely frustrated with her lack of heart. She needed to pull herself together enough to talk to Kevin. Had to!

———

"Something bothering you?" Jenna asked after class.

Heather didn't dare mention her wish to become a free skater. She couldn't without raising a lot of eyebrows, especially around Jenna and Livvy. They'd never understand—not in a quadrillion years. Mostly because they'd made up their minds (and probably their hearts, too) that Kevin was something extraordinary. A boy to make the heart beat faster, and all that jazz. Which was probably quite true—if you weren't related to him.

For that reason, it would be next to impossible to convince her girl friends that her new mission in life was an excellent choice. For *her*, Heather Elayne Bock. But they would never understand.

She could hear it now. *How can you possibly think of giving up all those years of skating with Kevin?*

And . . .

Are you out of your mind? Your brother's so-o-o adorable.

Or . . .

What I'd give for a skating partner like Kevin!

Livvy followed her into the dressing room. "You upset?"

Unsure about what to say, Heather shrugged off the question. "I'm just thinking, that's all."

Livvy's face drooped. "This isn't about our Spring

Dance Festival, is it? You're not backing out on us, are you?"

"No, it's nothing like that," she replied, wondering what had caused Livvy to think of their festival plans.

"Then what *is* it? What's got you in a blue funk?" Livvy insisted.

Digging through her sport bag, Heather located her hairbrush and began brushing vigorously, ignoring Livvy.

"C'mon. Something's wrong, Heather. I can see it in your eyes. They're blazing blue."

Heather snorted accidentally. "Sounds like lyrics to a song or something." With that, she walked toward the dressing-room cubicle and pulled the blue curtain across the rod. Grateful for a little privacy, she changed out of her simple practice clothes into jeans and a sweat shirt.

When she opened the curtain again, Livvy and Jenna were staring at her, still wearing their bell-like skirts and tight-fitting pink bodices.

"What's with you two?" she muttered.

Jenna's face sagged. "Maybe we should ask *you* that."

"You're right. . . ." She didn't know what else to say.

"Hey, we're best friends, remember?" Livvy said, sporting her crowd-pleasing smile.

"Yeah, so lighten up." Jenna poked her in the ribs.

Heather wondered how long she could hold out on her friends. "Maybe we oughta have a club meeting," she said at last.

"We just did," Livvy piped up.

"But that was *last* week," Heather said, hoping they'd give it some thought. She just might be able to share her top-secret longing in a secluded setting. Somewhere like Jenna's attic bedroom. The dressing room here at Natalie's ballet studio wasn't the best place for a heart-to-heart talk about her athletic future.

"I think we oughta have a midweek club meeting." This time there was a sense of urgency in her voice. She knew it came through loud and clear because the girls started to nod their heads.

"Sure. We can get together before Friday's regular meeting if you want," Jenna said, glancing at Livvy. "No problem."

Livvy, too, was very agreeable. In fact, she reached out and slipped her arm around Heather's shoulders. "Is this an emergency meeting?" she whispered.

Suddenly, Heather felt like crying. "I . . . I guess you could say that."

"That's all we need to know," Jenna said, taking her place on the other side of Heather. "*Girls Only* Club is calling a zero-hour meeting this Wednesday after school."

Livvy looked confused. "What's zero hour?"

"It means, my dear club member, that we've got

ourselves a crisis," Jenna answered. "Any time one of us is freaking out, we're gonna alter bylaws and make some changes in the club schedule. And that's all there is to it!"

Heather felt a smile coming. No . . . it was actually a giggle. Jenna Song had a way of making things seem all right.

The threesome walked out of the dressing room and down the hall to the main doors, arm in arm, past Miranda and several other girls. But Heather didn't care anymore. She let the tears drip down her face. All the while, her smile struggled to be strong.

A Perfect Match
Chapter Four

Early the next morning, Heather took a deep breath as she stared at the Alpine Lake mall skating rink. The place looked ten times smaller than she'd remembered since she and Kevin last practiced here. She was definitely spoiled by the beautiful Olympic-sized rink at the World Arena.

Today, the ice looked exceptionally dazzling and new, like it did right after the Zamboni made its clean sweep. Leaning against the barrier, she waited for her brother to lace up, wondering how to tell him. It wasn't the least bit fair to skate halfheartedly as an intermediate ice dancer. No, it would only be right to tell her brother as soon as possible.

By tomorrow afternoon, she would know precisely what to do. Livvy and Jenna could help her dream up a good way to break the news to Kevin. That is, *after* they got over the initial shock. She sincerely hoped they wouldn't try to talk her out of her new goal. Surely they'd understand.

Why does this have to be so hard? she wondered.

———

"Straighter, straighter . . . arms must be completely straight for this lift," Coach McDonald instructed. "Careful, now, not too high." He cautioned Kevin not to lift Heather higher than his shoulders. The rule about the height of lifts was a strict one and had to be followed closely.

Still, she enjoyed the feeling of elevation—even if only a few feet off the ice. How exciting it would be to jump high into the air and whirl and spin the way Livvy Hudson did as a novice-level free skater.

Kevin brought her down slowly. He set her gently on the ice, the blade of her right skate making contact with the surface.

"Wonderful, simply wonderful," Coach said, applauding them. "Now, let's do it again."

"Five more times," Heather grumbled.

"What's wrong?" Kevin asked as they skated in unison around the rink.

"Later," she said, wimping out once again.

He reached for her hand as they prepared for the lift. "Ready?" he whispered.

"I'm counting the beats," she said, knowing that she must keep her arms straight for the difficult move.

"One . . . two . . . three!" Kevin reached out, keeping his arms stiff, too, as he lifted her off the ice.

This time the lift was excellent. But they continued to repeat the practice, making their footwork accurately match the meter of the music. Working through the preparation and the actual move with Kevin, she thought back to the first time she'd laced up the boots on her rental ice skates. She was a tiny preschooler, just turned four years old. The feel of the ice beneath her feet was like nothing she'd ever encountered. From that moment on, she knew she wanted to be an ice skater.

Ice-dancing lessons came a year later, after Heather had learned a few skating basics. At that time, she and her brother were so close in size that their parents (and their coach) decided they should train as ice dancers instead of pairs skaters.

At first, neither Kevin nor Heather had understood the difference between pairs skating and ice dancing. So Coach McDonald made an attempt to explain. "In pairs skating, there are side-by-side jumps, spins, and other dangerous moves."

"What kind of dangerous?" little Heather had asked.

"The death-spiral, for one . . . and the hand-to-hand lasso lifts are risky," her coach said.

Back then, Heather had thought pairs skating was much too hard. But she was only five and still tripping on the front porch steps. The idea of skating like a unit of one seemed almost impossible. Especially with her energetic older brother!

"What's ice dancing all about?" was Kevin's question.

"Ice dancing is fancy footwork performed in time with dance rhythms like the cha-cha or the fox-trot. As partners, skaters must demonstrate different styles of music," Coach had told him. "It's like ballroom dancing on ice. And they have to mirror each other, just like in pairs skating."

Later, they learned that there were special holds and positions—all part of the ice-dancing technique. But each partner had to keep at least one skate on the ice at all times. The only exception was allowed during certain lifts and jumps.

After six years of spending many hours each week, perfecting complicated steps and arm positions, Heather was ready to make a change. Maybe the biggest risk of her life!

———

"Where was your head today?" Kevin asked later as they stepped off the ice. He seemed upset with her, but she had it coming. After all, they were in training for the Summer Ice Spectacular—only six months away. She couldn't fault Kevin for asking.

"You know how it is. Off days and on days . . ." A ridiculous reply, but she wasn't ready to blurt out her plans. Not here at the rink. Not with Coach within earshot.

"No, I really *don't* know, Heather. Maybe you better explain." Frowning now, her brother stood near the barrier and stared. Like he was trying to put things together without a single puzzle piece. "Maybe we should finish that talk we started the other night."

Heather felt trapped. Besides that, Coach McDonald was coming toward them. "Later," she said quickly. "We'll talk some other time."

"So . . . there *was* something on your mind last Friday night. You bribed me away from my math homework for ice cream, but you didn't finish what you started."

He knew her so well!

She took a deep breath and put on her skate guards. "Well, if you know so much, why don't you tell *me* what I was thinking!"

Kevin shook his head and turned on his heels. He went to sit on one of the wooden benches surrounding the rink. Heather watched him, her heart sinking. They rarely had harsh words between them. Almost immediately, she was sorry about the outburst.

Oh great, she thought. *Now he knows there's something bugging me.*

Yet she didn't know how to smooth things over. They would walk home together, sit across from each other at the dining room table—for homeschool lessons—and eat lunch together, too.

Togetherness was the thing that was beginning to gnaw at her, almost more than anything. She wanted to become something on her own. If only she could break free of the skating partnership. If only she could go it alone!

Coach had a few suggestions for them off the ice, and then they headed for the mall doors. Together. During most of the long walk home, they were silent. They carried their sport bags over their shoulders and tromped down the snowy sidewalk. Occasionally, a brave bird flew overhead, twittering a wintry song.

At the intersection of Main and Cascade Streets, Heather exhaled, letting the arctic air carry her frustration on wings of white frost. Two more blocks to go.

Kevin finally broke the silence. "We were stunning today . . . had the same great line and terrific action going on in our feet. Coach thinks we have a good chance at a medal next summer."

Summer Ice Spectacular! What an incredible thrill it would be to take first place. Heather had literally dreamed of the beautiful medal. And it wouldn't be just for her and

Kevin to enjoy. They'd share the delight and the honor with their close-knit family.

She could imagine little Joanne wearing it, the medal hanging down to her chubby knees. And Tommy? She knew he'd want to run off with Kevin's and show the neighbor kids on the block.

As for Kevin, he would value the win as much as either of them. After all these years, he was still devoted to working hard. He had perfected his half of their partnership. She was sure *he* had no secret plan to run off and pursue a new skating goal! Kevin was focused on being the best ice-dancing partner ever.

Wishing for an easy solution to her problem, Heather listened as Kevin recounted Coach's approval of their morning workout. She watched his expressive blue eyes and the determination set into his chin. His hair was every bit as blond as hers, cropped short on the sides and fuller on the top. Though a boy, he was almost a reflection of herself—only taller.

Most of all, she knew Kevin's heart. He was a compassionate but highly driven sort of guy. And at thirteen, he seemed to know exactly what he wanted in life. At least when it came to his ice-dancing career. He was headed for Junior Olympics and far beyond. And he was taking his partner with him. Whether she liked it or not!

Unless she jumped off *his* bandwagon and got on

board her own, she'd be stuck ice-dancing through her teens and who knows how far into her twenties. She had to change course. As soon as possible!

Groaning silently, she could hardly wait for the *Girls Only* Club meeting. By tomorrow afternoon, Livvy and Jenna would have an amazing plan for her to follow.

Surely they would!

A Perfect Match
Chapter Five

"The zero-hour club meeting will come to order," said Jenna, waiting as Heather and Livvy gathered onto her four-poster bed. Sasha, her golden-haired cat, was curled up near the pillows, oblivious to the trio of girls.

"Any old business?" Livvy asked, leaning forward on her elbows. Her stockinged feet waved in the air.

"Let's just get on with it," the president spouted. Jenna's comment made Heather feel nervous. Especially because both Jenna and Livvy were gawking at her, probably eager to hear what was so important. They had every right to know.

Struggling with her feelings, she realized there was only one reason they'd agreed to this special meeting. Only one. It was because of her tears after ballet class. They felt sorry for her.

She studied her friends under the recessed lighting of the newly remodeled attic room. Livvy was as pretty as a picture with deep auburn hair and the greenest eyes ever. Her skating history (awards and competitions) would make anyone proud to say she was her friend. Livvy also loved to write letters, especially the snail-mail kind, because she enjoyed writing in cursive. The feel of a smooth ballpoint pen on fine stationery, she always said, reminded her of ice skating on a perfect ice surface.

Livvy's grandmother had recently moved to Alpine Lake to give her granddaughter "a good dose of mothering." At least, that's the way Livvy described it. Heather knew that Livvy often fought the sorrow in her heart; losing her mother to cancer at such a young age had made Livvy a very private person. Heather and Jenna never pushed for more than Livvy felt comfortable sharing.

Jenna, on the other hand, was as chatty and warm as Livvy was thoughtful and dreamy. An advanced gymnast and ballet dancer, Jen was the only daughter of the village's Korean pastor and his wife. She wore her black hair in a short, perky style, and when she smiled, her dark eyes squeezed shut.

The joy of her life was tiny Jonathan—her newly adopted baby brother. In fact, Jenna was always showing him off to the *Girls Only* Club members.

Heather always felt terrific when she visited Jenna, knowing there was a sweet baby just down the hall.

Baby Jonathan reminded her of the day her parents had adopted Tommy and Joanne.

"Earth to Heather!" Livvy was waving her hand in Heather's face.

"Oh, sorry," she blubbered.

"You're not sick, are you?" Livvy said, her own face turning a bit pale.

"No . . . I'm fine. It's just that I'm having a tough time these days."

Jenna scooted closer to her. "That's one of the reasons why we have this club, you know. We're your friends, Heather. You can tell us anything."

Anything? Heather wondered about that.

"Maybe we should pray," Livvy suggested.

"Sure, let's," Jenna agreed, touching Heather's arm.

"I *have* been talking to God about things," Heather told them. "But I'm not being selfish or anything. If that's what you think."

Livvy's eyes widened. "About what?"

Taking a deep breath, Heather knew the time had come. It was now or never. "I can't keep this to myself any longer," she said, gazing at one of the dormer windows. The light from the sky gave her courage somehow. "I've decided to quit ice dancing. I want to train with a free-skating coach. Go it alone."

The room was still, except for a little gasp from Jenna. Livvy, however, wore a timid smile, almost as if she was offering encouragement. *She* would know what sort of challenge Heather was up against, switching to figure skating.

"Are you sure about this?" Jenna whispered.

"Definitely," Heather answered, feeling an unexpected surge of confidence. She turned her gaze to Livvy. "Do you think I can make the switch? I mean, do I have what it takes?"

Livvy's face lit up. "I think you'll do super fine."

Heather waited for the question that was sure to come. Jenna was the one to bring it up. "What about your brother? Does Kevin know about this?"

She felt the weight of the world on her. "That's the hardest part," Heather admitted. "I thought maybe you could help me with that. Help me know how to tell him."

Jenna's face was serious. "What can *we* say?"

"Just give me some ideas—how to break it to him," she said, reaching over and petting Jenna's cat.

"Why don't you come right out and tell him?" Jenna suggested.

Livvy didn't seem as sure of that approach. "Maybe it would be better to tell him in phases," she said.

"Like how?"

"You know, uh, bring him to one of my coaching sessions, maybe," Livvy said, her eyes filled with concern.

"I'm sure that would get him thinking about what *you're* thinking."

Heather was amazed. "You mean you two aren't gonna try to talk me out of this?"

"Why should we?" Livvy said. "It's your athletic future we're talking here."

"Your choice, too," added Jenna.

Heather was quiet for a moment. "Do you know what I actually thought you guys might say?"

Jenna's dark brown eyes turned curious. "Something about being out of your mind to abandon your skating partner?"

Heather nodded.

"Well, to tell you the truth, I think you must be," agreed Jenna, putting on a silly smile.

"Yeah, to give up ice dancing with someone so *adorable?*" Heather teased.

Livvy shook her head. "No, seriously, just because a guy is cute—or your brother—doesn't mean you should stick with a partner . . . or your old goal."

"I know. And I'm not."

"But," Livvy added, "you should know that when skating couples split up, they really do mess up their relationship. And usually get off course for a while."

Heather had given that plenty of thought. She hated the idea of setting Kevin back, away from his goals.

"It takes lots of time to develop a solid relationship with a new skating partner," Livvy said.

"Or . . . maybe Kevin will go solo," offered Jenna. "Ever think of that?"

Heather didn't know what to think. For one thing, her idea sounded outright selfish in some ways. And whether Kevin would believe it or not, selfish was the last thing she wanted to be!

"Oh, I wish I didn't have to do this to him," she groaned. "It's gonna hurt so bad."

"Poor Kevin," whispered Jenna.

"No kidding," replied Heather. But she felt much better having shared her dream—and now her dilemma—with Jenna and Livvy. "You guys are the best."

Livvy grinned and rolled over on the bed. "We know."

"We're the *Girls Only* Club," said Jenna. "What do you expect?"

Getting up and stretching her legs at the barre across the long wall, Heather was glad for Jenna's terrific bedroom/workout room. "Let's practice ballet," she said.

"You're on!" Livvy said, hopping up.

"What's your style?" Jenna hurried to the CD player.

"Something slow and sad," Heather replied. Which was exactly how she felt.

"Something zippy and bright will cheer you up," replied Jenna.

"Probably not," Heather said softly.

A Perfect Match
Chapter Six

First thing Thursday morning, the phone rang. Heather hurried to get it. "Hello?" she answered.

"It's Livvy. Are you awake?"

"Definitely. It's almost time to leave for skating practice."

"I know . . . for me, too," Livvy said. "I was just wondering if you told your brother anything about . . . well, you know."

"Not yet."

"Oh." There was a short pause, then, "I have an idea. Why don't you talk to my coach before you decide anything."

Heather had actually thought of doing that. And she told Livvy so. "It's just that I'm so sure of myself now. Know what I mean?"

Livvy chuckled into the phone. "But it's such a major switch. You've been programmed to be an ice dancer . . . with a partner. There's a huge difference between that and free skating."

Heather felt hurt. "I guess you just don't understand where I'm coming from."

"Honestly, I'm trying. It's only that you've spent all these years training a certain way—a very *specific* way. Free skating is totally different."

"Please don't try to change my mind, Liv. I need your support, not a lecture." She sighed. "I'm telling my brother right after practice."

"What about your parents?" asked Livvy.

"I'll tell my mom the minute we get back," she replied.

"Oh, Heather, I really hope everything goes super well for you." Livvy's voice was quivering a little.

"Thanks. That means a lot."

"Well, I guess I'll see you at ballet," Livvy said before hanging up.

"Okay, see ya later." She was still holding the receiver in her hand when Kevin came up behind her.

"What's with the phone?" he asked.

Quickly, she hung up, hoping he hadn't heard her end of the conversation. "Just Livvy."

"Ready to go?" asked Kevin, wearing his red-and-blue stocking cap.

She looked up at it and grinned. "You must think it's going to be cold outside."

"I'm prepared," he said, his eyes searching hers, "for anything."

Her heart sank as she headed for the entryway closet. Reaching for her down jacket, scarf, and warmest gloves, she wondered if she would actually be able to go through with it and tell Kevin.

"Better take a pair of dry socks along," their mother called down from the top of the stairs.

"I always carry an extra pair," Heather replied.

Kevin said he did, too. "We'll be home in time for school at eight-thirty," he said, throwing Mom a kiss.

"From what Coach McDonald says, you two are going to snatch up that first-place medal next summer," Mom said, looking quite radiant in her white terry cloth robe.

"We've got a lot of work to do before then," he said, waving.

It was the way Kevin glanced down at her that made Heather worry.

"Give Daddy a hug for me," Heather said, turning to go.

"Bye, kids. Have a great skate," Mom called softly.

A great skate.

Heather honestly wished it *were* possible for her to

change her mind about her goal—about being a free skater. But there was no turning back.

Today was the day!

———

Thin flakes of snow seemed to hang in the air, teasing the ground. Kevin pointed it out to her, laughing good-naturedly as they walked toward the village mall.

Heather didn't see the humor in it. Nothing was funny about the snow looking stuck in midair. "There's just no breeze. That's all," she said flatly.

"But it looks like the flakes are standing still," he said, reaching out to touch the snow.

Standing still—stuck—just like my skating future, she thought.

The rest of the way, they talked about one of their cool homeschool projects—a model of a medieval castle. They were constructing it with the help of detailed blueprints, according to historical data, with Tommy and Joanne and several other homeschool families. Actually, Kevin did most of the talking. Heather was trying to muster the nerve to share her new goal with her brother.

"You daydream a lot lately," said Kevin as they headed toward the mall entrance.

"I do?"

"Sure seems like it."

"Well, maybe there's a reason." She paused, wondering what he'd think if she came out with something a little weird. "People who daydream are thinking momentous thoughts."

Kevin opened the door for her. "Life-changing thoughts?"

The question fairly knocked the breath out of her. *Does he know what I'm thinking?* she wondered.

"Well?" he persisted. "Are they . . . life-changing?" His eyes were fixed on her, blinking rapidly. Like he was determined to have an answer.

She felt awkward, standing there at the entrance of the miniature mall. But Kevin wasn't budging. "We better get going," she said at last. "Coach wants us to be prompt."

"Yes, and Olivia Hudson will be showing up soon—for *her* practice session," Kevin said out of the blue.

Heather felt her cheeks grow warm as he turned away. What was he getting at? What did he know?

The area of the mall rink was smaller than the World Arena, by far. But it had a cozy, familiar feel to it. Tall trees were scattered outside the ice rink, strung with little white lights the year round.

Kevin's remark about Livvy made Heather wonder. Maybe he had overheard the one-sided phone conversation, though he would never have eavesdropped purposely. The Bock kids—including Tommy and Joanne—had been taught in their character-building studies that snooping was wrong. She honestly couldn't imagine Kevin standing behind her, or even dawdling around the corner, listening in on her phone call with Livvy. There was just no way!

Yet just now he'd mentioned Livvy Hudson—Alpine Lake's Olympic free-skating hope for the future.

Why?

What *was* he thinking?

A Perfect Match
Chapter Seven

The ice was her enemy. Heather fell more times during warm-ups than she ever remembered. She did some high-speed skating on her own, with lots of hard stroking around the rink.

When she and Kevin came together and did two back-to-back run-throughs of their original dance routine, the cha-cha, Heather kept tripping and falling.

Even Coach McDonald seemed concerned. "Must be one of those bad practice days," he muttered, shaking his head as he watched from the sidelines.

"Sorry," she said again and again. But her heart wasn't in it. She just wasn't trying.

"What's happening?" Kevin asked as they continued their warm-up step sequence.

Heather couldn't tell him. Not here, on the ice. Not

when they were supposed to be polishing their dance patterns. It would be cruel.

"Are you tired?" he probed.

She felt helpless to answer.

"Should we stop and talk with Coach?"

That would never do. "I'll be all right," she replied, but she knew today's practice was pretty much toast. In her mind, it was their last session together. And she could hardly wait for it to end.

"Have a great skate," Mom had said.

The words stayed with her as she separated from Kevin for some more solo stroking. Coach always had them drill their individual step sequences and turns. So she worked on the bracket—a one-foot turn that often tripped her up. Especially if she wasn't focused. Today was a disaster. She kept at it until Coach turned his full attention to Kevin.

Switching moves, she practiced the rocker—another difficult one-foot turn. The skate blade edge changed at the V-shaped tracing called the cusp, where the skate reversed direction.

All the while, her thoughts were on Kevin. What would her decision do to his Olympic dreams? And what would Mom and Dad say?

She was pretty sure Mom would hit the roof. Well, at first, anyway. But after the notion settled into reality, both Mom and Dad would come around—understand where she was coming from. At least, she hoped so. Heather was counting on their support. She needed them to understand and cheer her on.

In spite of all that, she couldn't seem to give this skating session her best shot. She was finished with ice dancing. Done!

Pretending to be a free skater was the only way to get through the next two hours. So she swirled across the ice, connecting the blades of her skates in clean, silent strokes against the surface.

Kevin's encouraging smile actually defeated her. She wished she had the courage to tell both her brother *and* their coach after practice. That would be the right thing to do.

After what seemed like an eternity, the skating session was over. Kevin was about to put on his skate guards when Heather spoke up. "Can we talk . . . just real quick?"

Coach hovered near, and she heard him take a deep breath. But he nodded to her, as if waiting for an explanation about her lousy performance on the ice. Kevin, on the other hand, was quiet, standing near the railing that circled the rink.

"I've been thinking about something for a long time," she began, hoping this was the right time to say what she'd been planning. "Neither of you will probably understand this. And that's okay."

Kevin's face was terribly sober and his eyes blinked rapidly. "I think I know what you're going to say, Heather," he said suddenly. "And it's all right with me."

She could hardly believe her ears. "You *know*?"

"I've sensed this coming for a while," he told her, glancing quickly at Coach. "Guess we're just too close, huh?"

She didn't know what to say. Kevin's comment was startling, and Coach seemed as baffled as Heather. She hesitated, then blurted the truth. "I want to be a free skater."

Coach McDonald's eyebrows had always been thick, but now they seemed too bushy, nearly hiding his almost stern gray eyes. "No . . . no, I think it would be unwise to try something so different just now, Heather. It would not be in your best interest to change horses in midstream. And certainly not a wise choice, considering your brother's goals."

She figured he'd say something sensible like that. He wouldn't be Coach McDonald if he didn't.

But what puzzled her even more was the way Kevin had stepped back a bit—away from her—studying her now, almost from a distance. He was silent and seemed perfectly content with her decision. This was strangest of all.

"So you don't mind?" she asked Kevin.

A fleeting smile crossed his face. "You're not looking for a debate, are you? Your mind's made up, right?"

She was quiet. He knew better than to quiz her this way.

He raked his fingers through his thick hair. "I'll have to look for another partner. That's the end of it, I guess."

She shivered slightly, wondering how her brother could be so confident. Had he already thought this through? Had he heard about her decision from someone?

Not wanting to make a scene—and with Livvy Hudson showing up just then for her lesson—Heather thanked Coach McDonald. "It's definitely been fun. You're a great coach," she said. "I'm sure Mom and Dad will want you to keep working with Kevin."

"And my new partner, don't forget," her brother added. "Maybe Coach has some ideas about who that might be."

Heather didn't feel the slightest twinge of regret when her coach reached down and gave her a bear hug. "You have no idea what you're up against, young lady. This is not a good athletic move for you. But I'm on your side— keep your chin up, kiddo."

When she stepped back, she noticed the corner of his eyes glistened. "I'm sorry, Coach, I really am. But I have to be honest with myself, don't I?"

He agreed with her, nodding his head up and down slowly. "I can help you with that, if you'll let me."

She couldn't stand here and listen to someone try to talk her out of what she knew she must do. Besides, Livvy Hudson was sitting on the bench within earshot, lacing up.

Kevin was the one to wrap things up. "We'll talk again, Coach . . . later."

"Yes, and I'll be phoning you tomorrow, Kevin," Coach said, his face too solemn.

I have to be honest with myself. . . .

Heather felt numb inside. She knew she'd been the cause. Still, only half of the ordeal was over. Now she had to tell her parents, starting with Mom.

In spite of everything, she felt freer than she had in months. "I was shocked when you said you knew what I was going to say," she told Kevin as they walked home.

He glanced at her. "It's easy to read you. Your eyes give you away."

"Since when?" She didn't like how this conversation was going.

He chuckled. "You should see yourself sometimes. You're a dead giveaway . . . about your feelings."

"I am?"

"Everything shows on your face," he said. "It's there for the world to see."

Well, she certainly didn't like the sound of this! Surely he was just making small talk. He couldn't mean it. Besides, whoever heard of reading someone's face?

"I think you must be getting strange ideas from your sci-fi novels," she lashed out at him.

Their boots *clunking* on the snow-packed sidewalk was the only sound she heard for several paces. Then Kevin said softly, "I won't make this a problem for you with Mom and Dad."

"Thanks."

"I know the sort of girl you are, Heather. You don't change your mind very often. This free-skating thing must be real important to you."

His words warmed her heart, and for a good half a block, she was glad again that he was her brother.

"I'll be doing some serious looking this Saturday when we go to Colorado Springs, though," he said as they turned the corner onto Cascade Avenue—their street. There was eagerness in his voice.

"I know you want to get on with your skating goals," she said as they headed up the front steps to the porch. "And I understand."

Stopping, Kevin turned to face her. "No, I don't think you do," he retorted. "Because if you did, you'd think long and hard about your decision. Bottom line: You just wouldn't do it."

"So . . . you're mad? That's the real truth, isn't it?"

He leaned his hand high against the storm door, looking down at her. "I'll never stoop to anger about this, Heather. God will provide a skating partner for me. You'll see."

"And He'll help me with my free skating, too."

Kevin offered a comforting smile. "Don't worry about telling Mom and Dad. Everything will work out."

Heather patted her brother on the back and went inside. She hoped her former skating partner was right. More than anything.

A Perfect Match
Chapter Eight

Kevin's face was everywhere! Even when Heather closed her eyes in the shower and shampooed her hair, she could see the disappointment in his eyes. His jawline had practically sagged as they'd stood on the ice with Coach McDonald after their skating lesson. Now she couldn't get the image out of her mind.

She knew he was hurt. Let him say what he wanted about sensing her intention ahead of time and all that— even sounding so sure of himself about finding another partner. But she knew better. No matter what Kevin had said on the porch this morning, she knew it was her decision that had bruised his ego.

After showering, she dried her hair and went to her bedroom to dress. Mom had always insisted that they wear clean clothes and look presentable even though *their* schoolroom consisted mostly of the dining room table, where they read the Bible together, wrote individual book reports and essays, and worked math problems. The kitchen area was used for science experiments, spreading out historical timelines, and a twice-a-week cooking class. The family room was large enough to build a model Gothic castle and put together an occasional three-dimensional puzzle. Still, Mom was a stickler for neatness. And honesty.

Heather smoothed the wrinkles out of her bedspread and stuffed her dirty clothes in the hamper in the closet. Glancing around the room, her eyes fell on the poster of Jayne Torvill and Christopher Dean, called the greatest ice-dancing team in history so far. The enthusiastic, bright faces of Torvill and Dean had spurred her on many mornings as she dressed for skating lessons or sessions with Kevin on their own.

"I won't be needing this anymore," she said, removing the poster from the wall. Then she carefully pulled off the adhesive from each corner and rolled up the colorful poster. Way in the back of her closet, she stood it on end, out of sight.

The wall looked bare now. Definitely exposed. Just like her dreams and goals had been laid bare to her brother and Coach McDonald this morning. But all of that would have to be worked out.

Sighing, she stared at the empty spot where the

poster had been. If her dad's birthday wasn't so close, she might've wanted to spend part of her allowance to purchase something new. A full-length poster of Kristi Yamaguchi—her current inspiration—would be the perfect replacement. Slender and light-footed, Kristi was strong enough to consistently land triple everything. Triple toe loops, triple flips, triple Salchows, and triple Lutzes. Unbelievable!

How many years till I can catch up? she thought of her free-skating dreams. *Am I too late?*

She gathered up her English homework. Along with history, science, and math, her parents were big on grammar. So she and Kevin and their younger brother and sister were reviewing correct sentence structure and usage of verb tenses. They even diagramed long sentences sometimes.

"I want to make sure you know how," Mom would say whenever Tommy whined about it.

Heather didn't mind doing things Mom's way, especially when it came to homeschool. But skating? That was another thing altogether. Would her parents be upset about the money they'd already spent on lessons, ice time, costumes, and everything else?

Nothing's been wasted, Heather reasoned as she headed downstairs for school. She would transfer all her ice-dancing knowledge into free skating. Easy as one . . . two . . . three.

On the living room bookshelf, she located her Bible and hurried to the dining room. Glancing at her watch, she saw that she was nearly late.

"It's about time," Tommy teased, his brown hair sticking out in the back.

"Did you primp real nice?" Joanne asked, sitting next to Heather at the long table.

"Not much." Heather ruffled her sister's ponytail. "Did you?" She tightened her sister's hair bobble, admiring the shine of the long brunette hair.

Tommy scowled. "Primping's yucky."

"Is not," Joanne said with a frown. "Heather's pretty . . . as pretty as any ice princess who ever lived!"

Quickly, she took her place at the table next to her sister. "What's this about an ice princess?" she asked.

"That's *you* I'm talking about," replied the little girl, offering a grin.

Heather noticed an empty space in Joanne's mouth where a front tooth had been. "Looks like somebody just lost something," she said.

"I sure did," Joanne said, her brown eyes shining.

"Did you save it?" asked Tommy.

Joanne pulled a tiny white tooth out of her pocket. "It's right here. But I'm hiding it from Mommy . . . for a surprise."

"Then you'd better smile with your mouth shut," advised Heather.

Joanne's eyes widened. "How do I do that?"

"Just keep your lips together. Like this." Heather showed her sister how.

"Yeah, but Joanne's got *another* loose tooth," Tommy whispered, pointing to her.

Smooshing her lips together, Joanne let out a peep. "That one's a secret, too."

Overhead, they heard a commotion. It was Kevin, rushing toward the stairs. He flew down them, landing on both feet. "Am I late?" he asked.

"Fifteen seconds!" Tommy hollered, studying his watch.

Kevin pulled out a chair across from Heather. "What's this about a secret?"

"Shh! You mustn't tell," said Joanne and quickly covered her mouth with her hands.

Kevin's forehead wrinkled into a frown. "There are too many secrets in this family."

Tommy and Joanne looked confused. "What're you talking about?" Tommy asked, staring first at Kevin, then Heather.

"Never mind," said Heather. "Mom's coming."

She couldn't help but think Kevin was going to blurt out *her* not-so-secret plan the minute Mom showed up. She even held her breath, but her fears were unfounded. Kevin opened his Bible and seemed to forget.

"Thank the Lord for a beautiful winter day," Mom said,

greeting each of them. Fortunately, she didn't inquire about their early-morning skating lesson. Instead, she had them bow their heads and pray about the day's studies.

When their prayers were finished, Mom asked, "Who'd like to read the Bible first?"

Tommy raised his hand. "I will," he said, eyeing Joanne. Her lips were still smashed together, hiding the missing tooth.

"Wait just a minute, Tommy," Mom said, looking at Joanne. "Is something wrong with your mouth, sweetie?"

Heather figured her sister's tooth secret was history. She wondered if now was a good time to bring up her own news. Toying with the idea, she shot a curious look at Kevin. But he was paying no attention to her. His nose was already buried in his Bible.

"My tooth fell out when I bit into my toast," Joanne was explaining to Mom.

"And—gross—she almost swallowed it!" Tommy said, clutching his own neck and pretending to gag.

Mom leaned down and kissed the top of Joanne's head. "Sounds to me like your brother's worried about you, little one."

Kevin must've heard what he thought was a reference to himself. "*Who* am I worried about?" he asked from the opposite end of the table.

Tommy saw his chance and ran with it. "Yeah, you're

worried. You said this family has too many secrets. I heard you!"

Slumping down a little, Heather knew what was coming. Her mother was no dummy; she'd taught school for a good number of years before Kevin and Heather were born. Mom knew the tricks kids liked to pull on one another.

"Family secrets, huh?" Mom's big blue eyes were firmly planted on Kevin.

He was nodding, looking a tad bit sheepish. "Better ask Heather about it" was all he said, which was enough to get the ball rolling.

Bible reading and grammar were both put on hold momentarily. And Heather was in the hot seat. Thanks to her big brother. She had no choice but to plow ahead. "I'm quitting ice dancing. I told Coach McDonald today." She stared down at the table. Didn't dare look at her mother.

"Uh-oh," Joanne said.

"Yikes," Tommy whispered.

"What's going on here?" Mom demanded of Kevin. "What's she talking about?"

Heather couldn't believe her ears—Mom was asking her brother instead of her!

"It's true," Kevin answered. "Heather wants to quit ice dancing and be a free skater."

Mom straightened to her full height. "You've got to

be joking! Am I dreaming?" Her voice sounded strange. Very weak.

Heather had her chance to speak up. "*I'm* the one dreaming, Mom. It's a fantastic dream, and I really want to do this."

"So . . . you're serious?"

"Definitely. I've never been so sure of anything in my whole life," she said, hoping her mother would understand. "Is it okay with you?"

"Well," said Mom, her face turning slightly pale, "I'll have to think about this." Mom promptly turned and headed into the kitchen.

Heather glanced across the table at Kevin and shrugged. "Now what?"

"She'll come around," Kevin assured her. "Just give her time."

"I hope so." But Heather wasn't so sure. Based on Mom's sickly expression, she decided to get the Bible reading started. Each of them took turns reading until the chapter was finished.

Mom was still in the kitchen when it was time for grammar. Kevin and Heather knew exactly what to do. They assisted their brother and sister with the elementary-level worksheets.

Mom's freaking out, thought Heather. *I'm in big trouble!*

A Perfect Match
Chapter Nine

"You and your brother are a perfect match," Mom insisted during a break in social studies.

"I know," Heather said. She couldn't disagree. Everyone who'd ever seen her and Kevin skate together always said the same thing. The truth was they *were* perfect together. But their partnering days were over. "I really want to free-skate, Mom."

"She's just bein' stubborn," Tommy said, waving his chubby finger at Heather.

"Now, Tommy, that's not for you to say," Mom intervened.

Relieved, Heather continued to state her cause. "It's so important to me, Mom. I *have* to try."

Mom shook her head, still frowning. "Is this about

the jumps . . . is that what you want?" She was clearly groping for reasonable answers.

Heather wondered how to make her mother understand. Taking a deep breath, Heather began again. "Yes, it's about jumping, and everything else that goes with free skating. I'll work hard, Mom. I'll do whatever it takes," she promised. Then she looked at Kevin. "I hope my former partner won't take this wrong, but I really want to skate on my own."

At that point, Mom cut off the discussion. She said they couldn't miss any more school time over the debate. Hoping Kevin truly did understand, Heather obeyed her mother and kept quiet about it.

———

"Girls'll be lining up for Kevin," Livvy told her on the phone that afternoon. "He won't have any trouble finding a new partner."

"Are you sure?" Heather had called to fill her friend in on the day's events.

"There are always girls waiting for skating partners. Especially for super-talented guys like your brother."

"You're right." She paused, thinking about what her next move would be *if* her parents gave permission to take free-skating lessons. "Mind if I watch you work with your coach tomorrow?" she asked hesitantly.

"Sure," Livvy said. "I'll even introduce you to him."

Heather could hardly hold the phone. "You're kidding! That would definitely be cool."

"You'll really like Coach Sterling. I can promise you that," Livvy said.

"Okay, but I'll double-check with my mom first."

"Super. I'll see you first thing in the morning."

"Hope so. Bye, Livvy."

"Hang in there, girl," Livvy said.

Heather hung up the phone. *This is definitely what I want!* she thought and scurried off to the kitchen. There she found Mom cooking supper. The expression on her mother's face was as close to dismal as she'd ever seen.

"I'll help make the salad," she volunteered. "And set the table."

Mom glanced at her, nodding, as though deep in thought. "Thanks, honey."

"I understand if you're upset with me," Heather said softly. "I didn't expect you to be thrilled."

"No, I suppose not." Mom's voice sounded hollow. "But if you're determined—and committed—I'll make a deal with you."

"Really?" She felt breathless. "You'll let me get a new coach and—"

"Listen, Heather. I've already talked to Dad, and he agrees with me on this." Mom paused for a moment, and it was then that Heather saw the hope begin to rise in her mother's eyes. "If it can be worked out with Livvy's coach, I'll pay him to give you one lesson. We'll see how you do with some jumps. Like the axel, maybe."

"You will?"

"I'll give Mr. Sterling a call tonight." Mom turned on the oven light, bending over to peek in at the meat loaf. "But there's a catch to all this," she said, straightening.

"Anything. Whatever you say." Heather meant it.

Mom's eyes were steady, fixed on her. "You must show Coach Sterling—and me—that you won't freeze up on your jumps. That you're not tense or hesitant going into them."

"Is *that* all?" She flung her arms around her mother's waist and squeezed. "Oh, thank you, thank you. I can't wait!"

"Let's see if Coach Sterling has some time this week . . . and if he wants to come out of retirement a little further," Mom said, heading into the dining room.

Heather had to smile because she knew the story behind Livvy and her famous, but retired, skating coach. The older gentleman had come to Alpine Lake to seek refuge from the Lake Placid skating crowd, among other things. He'd agreed to coach Livvy because she was new to the area, having lost her coach after she and her father moved to Colorado. Besides that, Livvy was on track for advanced-level competition. Maybe even the Olympics someday.

While her mother dialed the phone number, Heather went to the window in the breakfast nook. She stared out at the snowy landscape. The side yard between their house and the neighbor's was only a few yards wide, yet with a layer of new snow, the distance seemed more spacious.

Gazing out at the glittery whiteness, she was more than eager to have a lesson with Livvy's coach. But would Coach Sterling agree to give her a single lesson in jumping? If he did—and she could prove to herself *and* to Mom that she had the ability—she would definitely be on her way to a new and exciting career. More thrilling than ice dancing could ever be.

She sighed and sat down at the table. "This is almost too good to be true," she whispered. "But can I pull it off?"

A Perfect Match
Chapter Ten

By the time her mother was finished on the phone, Heather had devoured a whole apple, four carrot sticks, and a tall glass of milk.

"Oh, honey, you'll spoil your supper," Mom said, coming into the kitchen.

"Don't worry. I'll eat my share of your meat loaf. I'm starving." She took another bite of carrot, eager to hear about the conversation with Livvy's coach. "Does Mr. Sterling have time to help me?" she asked.

Mom pulled out a chair and sat down. "He's reluctant to commit to another student. Called himself an old man. Mr. Sterling wants to travel more, relax and enjoy life."

Heather's heart sank. "You mean he won't coach me just this once?"

"I don't know, honey. It might not work out," Mom said, her face showing signs of distress. "But on Saturday, when we go to Colorado Springs, I'll check around about a coach for you."

Heather slid down in her chair. "Maybe this isn't such a good idea after all."

"You're not giving up, are you?" Mom said, reaching over to pat Heather's hand.

"Well, no . . . but—"

"But, what? Heather, this may not be an easy situation," Mom reminded her. "If free skating is really what you want, you're going to have to fight for it. Hang in there with me."

Heather sat up straighter. "I know, and I will. It's just that I thought Mr. Sterling might have some time for me." She sighed. "Livvy invited me to watch her skating lesson tomorrow."

Mom smiled. "Livvy sounds like a good friend," she replied. "So many skaters have such a competitive attitude."

Having experienced the gossip and hateful back-biting among other athletes of this sport, Heather knew exactly what Mom meant. "You're right. Livvy's the perfect friend for me."

"So . . . you want to watch her work out with her coach?" asked Mom, a curious smile on her face.

"If it's okay with you."

"Sure, and I'll come along, if you'd like." Mom got up to check the oven.

"Any time." Then she thought of her brother. "What about Kevin? Who'll be his new partner?"

"I asked Livvy's coach about that," Mom said from the stove. "He knows of several skaters in the Colorado Springs area that may be good possibilities."

"That's great," she said. "I'm happy for him." And she meant it.

Definitely.

———

Heather was getting ready for bed when her little sister came into the room. Joanne closed the door and plopped down on the bed. "I've decided something," she said in her little-girl voice.

"Really? What did you decide?" Heather asked, trying to show some interest.

"I want you to keep my tooth—for the tooth fairy." Joanne handed over a small envelope with the obvious bump. "Here you go."

Heather looked at the envelope. "The tooth fairy might get confused about where to put the money."

"What do you mean?"

"Well, if your tooth is under *my* pillow," Heather said, "won't the tooth fairy get mixed up?"

Joanne paused, wrinkling her forehead into a frown. "I didn't think about that." She sighed. "And Mommy's the tooth fairy, right?"

Heather toyed with telling her sister the truth. "Think what you want."

"What's that supposed to mean?" The smaller girl put her hands on both hips.

"Mom's *not* the tooth fairy, Joanne."

"Then who is?"

Heather waited a moment. "Are you sure you really wanna know?"

"I'm sure."

"Okay, then . . . it's Daddy."

"*He's* our tooth fairy?" Joanne's eyes were round and growing wider by the second. "How can it be Daddy?"

"If you don't believe me, stay awake tonight. And watch with one eye," Heather advised.

"I will! But I'll need this, right?" Joanne snatched up her little envelope with the tiny tooth inside.

Closing her door behind her, Heather leaned against it. She thought back to when she was six years old—her little sister's present age. Back then, had she wanted to be a figure skater, doing fancy jumps and spins all over the ice? She tried to remember. For all her skating career, Kevin had been at her side. She'd never skated alone on the ice, except for solo stroking and working out her part of their dance programs.

"Tomorrow's just the beginning," she whispered, glancing at the empty spot on her bedroom wall. Ice dancers Torvill and Dean were gone now. It was time for a free skater to take their place. Tomorrow, after school, she'd go to the mall and buy a new poster.

Slowly, she walked to her dresser and picked up her hairbrush. She began her nightly routine. Twenty-five times on each side. Mom said vigorous brushing made her hair shine under the spotlights on the ice.

She thought of seeing Livvy tomorrow—and meeting her coach. She'd seen the old gentleman enough times to know who he was but had never been formally introduced.

Everything Livvy had told her about Odell Sterling was amazing. The man had coached many talented and dedicated skaters—including three World Champions. Two of his students had placed high at the Olympics and were now instructors themselves.

"If I could just get Mr. Sterling to help *me*," she said to the earnest face in the mirror. "Maybe then I'll have a chance. . . ."

Before she read her Bible and devotional book, Heather crept out of her room and down the hall. She knocked on the door of her parents' bedroom. Mom appeared, dressed in her white bathrobe. "Can you tell you-know-who that Joanne has a baby tooth under her pillow?" she whispered.

Mom grinned and hugged her good-night. "I'll tell Dad about it. Thanks, Heather. I completely forgot."

Tiptoeing back to her room, Heather wondered about her mother's remark. It was unlike Mom to forget important stuff. Heather hoped her plan to skate solo wasn't going to cause problems at home.

Before she fell into bed, she prayed. "Dear Lord, if I'm supposed to be a free skater, will you work things out for me? And since the whole family's affected by my decision, well . . . help all of us." She paused. "And, please, will you help Kevin find the perfect partner to replace me? Thanks for everything. Amen."

The light from her windows was soft and white. She was sure the moon must be full. But when she sat up in bed and looked for it, she saw only twinkling stars. High in the heavens.

It was at night that she always felt closest to God. She didn't know why. She just did.

A Perfect Match
Chapter Eleven

"Today's the day," Heather announced at breakfast, thinking of Livvy Hudson's invitation to watch her skating lesson.

"And it's *my* day, too!" Joanne showed off two quarters. "The tooth fairy found my tooth and gave me some money. Now I'm rich!"

Heather laughed as she observed the knowing exchange between her parents. "See, I told you to put your tooth under your own pillow," she said, pouring orange juice.

Joanne tilted her head, studying her father. "Are you really the one who left the quarters?"

Dad leaned back in his chair and inhaled slowly. "Well, now, are you sure you want to know?"

"Oh, Daddy, I *know* it was you," Joanne squealed. "I saw you!"

Dad was chuckling now. "You must've been dreaming, kiddo."

Joanne slid back her chair and ran to the head of the table. "You're the tooth fairy! Heather said so!"

Reaching down, Dad squeezed Joanne and gave her a kiss on the forehead. "Well, I guess I've been caught," he said, looking over at Mom. "Looks like our secret's out."

Mom folded her hands, her face bright. "It was fun while it lasted."

"Can't we still hide our teeth when they fall out?" Tommy pleaded. "Even if Joanne knows who the tooth fairy really is?"

"What do you think, Mommy?" Dad asked, wearing a mischievous smile.

Mom shrugged and nodded. "It's okay with me." Her response brought cheers from Tommy and Joanne.

Heather gave Kevin a sidelong look. He was smiling at their younger brother and sister. "Well, I'm glad that important issue's settled," teased Kevin.

When they bowed their heads, Dad began their short-sentence family prayer. Joanne was last because she was the youngest. "Thank you, God, for making my tooth come out with no pulling," she said. "And give Kevin a nice skating partner real soon."

After the prayer, Heather watched her older brother drink his juice. She picked up her spoon to eat the whole-

grain, sugarless granola, homemade by Mom. "What quali-
ties are you looking for in a partner?" she asked, almost
shyly.

Tommy spoke up. "Has to be a girl, right?"

"Of course," said Heather, cracking up. Mom and Dad
were laughing, too.

Joanne had an opinion. "Get someone real pretty. I
think that's real important."

Mom sighed audibly. "How about just someone who
skates well, has a good attitude, and is committed to
hard work?"

Kevin was nodding now and smiling across the table
at Heather. "A Christian partner would be nice."

Tommy looked over at Heather. "Are you really sure
you wanna quit skating with my brother?" he asked, wrinkling his nose.

Kevin leaned back against his chair the way their dad
often did. "To tell you the truth, Tommy, I hope to find
someone just like Heather."

Feeling a surge of sudden embarrassment, Heather
ate silently. Was Kevin saying that to make her feel guilty?
Yet, knowing her older brother as she did, she was pretty
sure he was just being nice. Nothing more.

"She's real special, our Heather." Dad winked at her
when she looked up. Mom, on the other hand, didn't say
a word. But her happy face spoke volumes.

"Thanks, Dad, but you really don't have to say that,"

Heather said. Then, turning to Kevin, she added, "And neither do you."

"I know, but I mean it," her former skating partner admitted.

She didn't quite know how to take his remark. Was he trying to get her to change her mind?

———

At the mall rink, there were eight other skaters besides Livvy on the ice when Heather and her mom arrived. Some were stroking around the rink for fun. Others were practicing spins and easy jumps.

And there was Kevin, going through his dance routine, then doing some hard stroking. Alone.

"Heather, over here!" called Livvy, motioning to them.

"C'mon," Heather said, pulling Mom along.

Livvy's coach was leaning on the rail circling the small rink. He wore a pair of gray dress slacks and a maroon-and-gray patterned sweater. Dashing as usual. He nodded politely when Heather and her mother approached.

In a flash, Livvy skated over to them. "Hey, Heather," she said. "Hello, Mrs. Bock. Heather said you might come along. It's nice to see you."

"Nice to see you, too," said Mom.

Livvy's coach perked up his ears. "So this must be

Heather Bock, the girl I've heard so much about," he said, eyes beaming.

"Yes, this is one of my best friends, Heather, and her mother, Mrs. Bock," Livvy said, introducing them.

Mr. Sterling extended his hand to each of them. "Delighted, I'm sure." Had he been wearing a hat, Heather was almost positive the man would have tipped it politely.

They sat down and watched Livvy run through her programs without a single break in between. She was obviously in good shape, Heather thought. And when Livvy did her jumps, Heather wished she were out on the ice with her, learning what to do.

"Let's see the double Lutz again," Mr. Sterling called to Livvy. His voice was calm and matter-of-fact. Not demanding like some coaches Heather had observed.

She watched as her friend worked up the momentum to do the jump. First came the long, powerful glide to set it up. Then, using the toe pick on her free foot, Livvy took off from the back, outside edge of her skating foot. Up . . . up she flew.

Heather held her breath as Livvy made two complete rotations and landed on the back, outside edge of her free foot.

"Perfect!" Heather said from the sidelines, recalling every aspect of the jump—the setup, the lift into the air, the revolutions, and the beautiful, clean landing.

"I can do that," she told her mom. "I just know it!"

Mom squeezed her hand and watched the rest of the session.

When Livvy's time was up, Mr. Sterling came over again. "You're welcome to stop by and visit anytime," he said.

"Thank you," Mom said, getting up. She was probably headed down to talk to Kevin, who was working out alone on the ice.

"Mr. Sterling, can you *please* teach me how to jump?" Heather asked. She surprised herself with her boldness.

Mom looked aghast. "Heather, I already discussed this with Mr. Sterling." Her words were pinched like she was talking through her teeth.

The older man's face seemed to light up. "Yes . . . yes, as a matter of fact, we *did* speak of a jump lesson, didn't we, Mrs. Bock?"

Heather's heart skipped a beat. "I'll work really hard, and I won't take up much of your time." She was pleading now, but she couldn't help it.

Livvy was standing behind her coach, nodding to Heather. She was grinning from ear to ear. Heather took that to mean she should keep it up, but her mom was actually glaring. "We don't want to impose on you, sir. You'll have to excuse my daughter's eagerness."

Worried that her mother's comments might hinder things, she began to pray silently. She hoped so hard she thought she might burst.

Mr. Sterling turned around, nearly bumping into Livvy. "You say Heather is your friend?"

"Yes, and she's one super cool skater," Livvy said, her hair bouncing against her face as she nodded.

"In that case, I'll see what I can do," the man replied.

Heather hugged her mom and Livvy both. And if Mr. Sterling hadn't stepped back a bit, she might've hugged him, too. "This is the most awesome day of my life," she said.

Mr. Sterling's cheeks turned an embarrassed pink. "Meet me here next Monday morning." He looked at his watch. "At say, eight-twenty. We'll have a jump lesson, Miss Heather—you and I."

"Oh, Mr. Sterling, thank you very much," she replied. "I'll be here, right on time."

"You're *very* welcome," Mr. Sterling said with a nod. Then he added, "I must say I do admire persistence."

Heather and her mom turned to go.

"Good-bye, Mrs. Bock," Livvy called.

"You're a wonderful skater," replied Heather's mother. "Keep up the good work."

"Bye, Heather," Livvy called. "See you at Jenna's this afternoon for our regular club meeting."

She waved at both of them—Livvy *and* her coach. And she could hardly wait till Monday morning!

A Perfect Match
Chapter Twelve

A ballot box—fashioned in tin foil—was balanced on the barre when Heather arrived. The *Girls Only* Club meeting was about to begin.

"Off the record, I have some exciting news," Heather said, settling down on the floor.

"Yes, and it's super cool news, too," said Livvy.

"Well, let's hear it," insisted Jenna. She was holding her cat in her lap. Sasha opened both eyes, blinked twice, then gave in to dreamland.

"Livvy's coach is going to give me a jump lesson!" Heather announced.

"Cool stuff," Jenna said, offering a high five. "What's next after the first lesson?"

Heather explained her mom's deal. "If I can actually jump, then Mom'll look for a coach for me."

"Maybe Coach Sterling will take you on," Livvy said.

"I won't move in on your territory," Heather assured her.

Livvy shrugged. "Coach Sterling doesn't belong to me."

The girls continued their bantering, talking about Jenna's "horrid" science project and Livvy's friend Mrs. Newton, the cheerleading coach.

Heather described her five-page handwritten report on Israel . . . *and* her little sister's tooth. "Joanne found out today that our dad's the tooth fairy," she said.

Jenna's eyes were big. "That's just cooler than cool. I mean, most dads aren't really all that involved in the fun stuff."

"Well, my dad is," Heather replied, feeling proud to say it. And it was true, too. Her father made it a point to hang out with all four of the Bock kids, taking them skiing in the winter, swimming near Twin Lakes in the summer, backpacking at Breckenridge in the autumn, and, of course, attending all the skating events throughout the year.

She wondered how much more hectic her parents' lives would be with Kevin and his new skating partner competing at all sorts of different times than Heather's solo performances. Her whole family would be busier than ever—running in all different directions, too!

"I think it's time we call our meeting to order," Jenna

said, lifting Sasha off her lap. She got up and went to the barre, carrying the foil-wrapped ballot box.

Jenna set it down in the middle of the circle. Smiling, she raised her eyebrows. "As president of the *Girls Only* Club, I'd like to propose that we expand our membership."

Livvy looked surprised. "By how many?"

"Four's a nice, even number," Jenna explained. "If we had four girls, we could practice ballet better. Maybe even double up on some dance projects."

"Partners, like in kindergarten?" Livvy teased.

Heather listened carefully, wondering why a threesome wasn't an okay number for their club.

"So . . . what does the vice-prez and the secretary/ treasurer think?" Jenna asked, sitting on the floor.

"Are we gonna campaign for members or what?" Livvy asked.

Heather stared at the Olympic Rings flag mounted high on the wall above the computer desk. "All three of us have athletic goals. If we added another member, she'd have to be a sports nut, too," she said at last. "Just like us."

"Yep," Jenna agreed. "That's the most important part of our bylaws."

Opening the "minutes" notebook, Heather found the rules for club membership. They'd written them on the first meeting, months ago. "Okay, here we go. 'The president, vice-president, and secretary/treasurer agree to encourage each other's athletic aspirations. We will uphold the goals and dreams of each of our members.' "

"It doesn't say a word about adding new members," Livvy pointed out. "But I think it's a super good idea. What do *you* think, Heather?"

"Shouldn't we just vote on it?" she replied, feeling pressured.

Jenna nodded. "I motion that we vote to add another member to the *Girls Only* Club. The coolest cool club ever!"

"I second it," said Livvy.

"Uh, before we do anything," Heather spoke up, "are we voting on four members total?"

"Could be," Jenna said, fidgeting. "Maybe more."

Livvy looked at Heather. "How do you feel about four?"

She felt funny being put on the spot. "I thought we were voting, *secret* ballot," she replied.

"Hold everything." Jenna scurried to her desk for some paper to make ballots.

"I think the prez has someone in mind," whispered Livvy.

Heather wondered who it might be. "Why don't we just talk about the new member instead of voting about how many?" she suggested when Jenna sat back in the circle.

The prez gave each of them a ballot and a pencil. "First things first," said Jenna. "Like the bylaws say."

Heather knew the bylaws weren't etched in stone. She'd read through the bylaws enough times to memorize them. There was nothing in there about additional members. "When we started this club, we never said anything about more than three members. What's wrong with just us?" she asked.

"Nothing," Jenna insisted.

"But maybe Jenna's idea is something to think about," Livvy added quickly.

They discussed the notion of four members instead of three. Then they voted. One by one, they stuffed their folded ballots into the big box.

"Drum roll!" Jenna shouted, turning the box over and fishing out the ballots. She turned her back and counted the ballots. "Two against one—two yesses and one no," she said in nothing flat.

Everyone knew, of course, who'd voted "no." And Heather definitely felt weird about it.

"Majority wins," Jenna announced, throwing away the ballots.

"The secretary/treasurer is supposed to count those, right?" Heather said, upset at Jenna's take-charge manner.

"What's it matter?" said the prez.

"It's in our bylaws who counts the ballots," explained Heather.

"Well, if it's in the bylaws, I guess we just messed up." Jenna marched across the room to the trash can and emptied it onto the floor.

"Jenna, *please* don't do this," Heather said. "Put the ballots back in the trash. It's okay."

"The secretary/treasurer must count the ballots," parroted Jenna.

"Don't be ridiculous," Heather replied, glancing at Livvy, who'd buried her head in two pink pillows.

Jenna sneered, "Well, if you thing *I'm* ridiculous, what about someone who changes her skating goals in the middle of her career. That's ridiculous, Heather Bock, and you know it!"

"Excuse me?" Heather was horrified.

"You wanna dump your partner and go for broke," Jenna said. "That's real stupid, if you ask me!"

Livvy's head was still hidden. She was staying out of it.

"Who said anything about dumping my partner?" Heather retorted.

"Well, that's exactly what you did!" Jenna's eyes bored into Heather.

"Look, I'm not gonna argue with you. What I did is between Kevin and me. He's cool with it, and so am I."

Jenna was quiet for a moment. Then she shoved the ballot box across the room, where it came to rest under her desk.

Livvy slowly emerged from the pillows. "Un, excuse me . . . may I say something?"

Jenna glared. "Whatever."

Livvy seemed hesitant to continue and started to cover her head again.

"Go ahead, Liv," encouraged Heather. She hoped maybe Livvy would talk some sense into the prez.

"I'm thinking about . . . well, maybe this thing about adding members oughta wait," Livvy said softly. "Let's make sure we can get along—just the three of us—before we add someone new."

"I'm with Liv," said Heather.

Livvy was tactful and kind. "We're a club of girls who care about each other, right?" She didn't wait for an answer. "We shouldn't have to argue to solve our problems."

Jenna was nodding her head. "We voted and the vote stands. Now I have a recommendation."

Heather wished she'd stayed home. Better yet, maybe someone else could take her place in this horrible club!

Jenna stroked her cat while she continued. "Miranda Garcia might be an excellent choice for our club," she said. "She's a fabulous downhill skier and ballet dancer. A Christian, too."

They already knew this info about Miranda. What was the big deal? Heather wondered. "So why not invite *all* our church girl friends who have Olympic dreams?" she said.

Jenna nodded. "Fine with me," she said. "What do you think, Livvy?"

"Personally, I like the idea of a small club. Don't forget, I'm an only child—not so used to lots of sisters."

Jenna seemed to understand. "Up until last year, I was the only kid in my family, too. I guess you might be right. Heather too."

Sighing, Heather was starting to feel better about this discussion. "Miranda *is* a good choice," she agreed. "Let's vote on including her."

Jenna began cutting more ballots. "I'm sorry, Heather, about what I said before. I shouldn't have gone off like that. Forgive me?"

Heather nodded. "I guess I just wasn't ready to change things in our club. It's real comfortable, like having two sisters my own age. Definitely cool."

Jenna and Livvy came over and hugged her. "Change is tough," Livvy said. "I should know."

Heather was pretty sure Liv wouldn't explain. Her mom's death and their recent move from Illinois had been difficult for Livvy and her father.

After more talk about the club, they voted on their mutual friend Miranda Garcia. "Does Miranda know about *Girls Only*?" asked Livvy.

"I've kept the club top-secret," said Jenna.

"Me, too," said Heather.

"Maybe Miranda won't wanna join," Livvy said, laughing.

Jenna's face broke into a broad smile. "I have a feeling she'll like the club. It's just her and her mom at home."

"Super good thinking," Livvy said.

"Who should invite Miranda to join?" Jenna asked.

Heather volunteered. "I will."

Jenna was all smiles. "Cool. The meeting's adjourned," she said. "Who wants to see my baby brother?"

Heather and Livvy both followed Jenna down the hall to the nursery. The room was aglow in sunlight, and Jonathan was just waking up.

"Oh, he's so sweet," cooed Heather, touching his tiny yellow bootie.

"He has undeveloped gymnastic ability," Jenna informed the girls. "Watch his left foot."

Sure enough! Heather noticed a jerking, forward motion. He nearly kicked off his little bootie. "I think you're right."

Just then Jenna's mother came smiling into the room. "Is my little fella ready for his supper?" she asked, reaching down to pick up the round bundle.

"Better hurry. He's not howling yet," Jenna said.

The girls followed Mrs. Song downstairs and watched her give the baby his bottle.

Jenna served up a lemon-lime concoction she made

in a blender, complete with crushed ice. "To our health!" she said, holding her glass high.

"To our Olympic futures!" Livvy added, doing the same.

"To our new club member!" said Heather, joining in.

A Perfect Match
Chapter Thirteen

When Heather was limber enough, she stepped onto the ice at the World Arena Ice Hall. Kevin had come to look for prospective skating partners. Mom too.

Heather would simply enjoy the ice time, practicing old moves and a few easy spins. For fun. The mall rink in Alpine Lake seemed to be shrinking by the day. An hour stint on the Olympic-sized rink was definitely a nice change.

"What do you think of the skater with the jazzy purple outfit?" Kevin asked, catching up with Heather.

"Where?"

"The blond girl . . . over there." He pointed to a young skater halfway across the rink. "What do you think of her skating?"

Heather spotted the girl. She was short and squatty—all

hips. But her purple practice pants were eye-catching. "I'll let you know in a minute," she told him.

"Promise?"

"Of course I promise," she said. Her brother was acting so weird today. Demanding and pushy. In fact, all he'd wanted to talk about on the trip down was a skating replacement.

While she stroked around the rink, Heather kept her eye on Miss Purple. The girl was a so-so skater, in Heather's opinion. She knew she'd have to be careful what she said to her brother. Kevin would think she was being picky. Actually, she was trying to be as objective as she could about Kevin's choice.

Meanwhile, Mom was busy chatting with several coaches. Heather glanced her way every so often, wondering if her very particular mother might be lining up interviews for next week. Of course, Heather knew she'd have to convince Mom that she could actually pull off the jumps and spins required to be a free skater.

"So . . . what's the verdict?" Kevin was back. He'd snuck up behind her while she was watching Mom in the stands.

"To be honest with you, I think you can probably find someone better than Miss Purple."

"Okay, then, what about the pink number over there?" Kevin said, a twinkle in his eye.

The skater in pink was perky and cute—about Heather's build and height. She had long, graceful lines and the shiniest, bounciest brown hair Heather had ever seen. And she could do flying spins like nobody's business!

Kevin stayed close to Heather as they moved around the rink. Occasionally, he touched her elbow or waist the way he often did during their dance routines. Heather found it both annoying and amusing, thinking it was most likely second nature to him.

"Wow, she's really good," she heard him say.

"Better introduce yourself quick," Heather suggested, "before she gets away."

"Come with me, okay?" Kevin asked, looking unusually shy.

"No . . . you go by yourself," she insisted. "This isn't my thing anymore." With that, she sped up, gliding across the rink.

"Heather, come back!"

Deep in her heart, she felt a stabbing pain. Never before in all her life had she turned her back on Kevin this way. She had done it twice, really. Once when she'd quit dancing with him and now today, when he'd asked for her input.

What's wrong with me? she thought. *What's happening to us?*

Then she remembered what Livvy had said about skating couples who split up. *"They mess up their relationship,"* Livvy had said. *"And sometimes set their careers off course."*

But Heather didn't think she had to worry about spoiling their relationship. After all, she and Kevin were brother and sister. Nothing too terrible was going to happen. They lived in the same house, shared the same parents and the same younger brother and sister. She was sure things would be just fine.

Watching from afar, Heather found herself holding her breath. Kevin skated up to the girl in pink, and the skater burst into a big smile. Kevin was smiling, too.

Before long, he began skating with the girl. They talked and laughed, stroking leisurely around the rink. At one point they stopped, and he showed her a step sequence. The skater watched carefully, then imitated Kevin's footwork almost perfectly.

Girls will be lining up to skate with Kevin. . . .

The twosome skated around the rink two more times. But when they stopped to talk to her mother, Heather knew Kevin must be thinking seriously about auditioning the girl. Had he found his new partner?

———

"Cynthia's strong and very athletic, don't you think, Mom?" Kevin babbled all the way home.

"We'll see how the two of you work together" came Mom's answer.

"But she's so expressive," Kevin continued.

Mom nodded. "Yes, I noticed that. But she's never had a partner before. That will take some getting used to."

"So when can we start?" he asked, obviously eager.

"Let's discuss it with Dad," Mom replied. "He'll want to meet Cynthia. So will Coach McDonald."

Kevin grinned. "Fair enough."

Heather was sure her brother had his heart set on the brunette skater. "She might be a good choice" was all she said.

"Might be?" Kevin replied, looking wounded. "Cynthia's my age, for pete's sake!"

Leaning against the window, Heather thought about her brother's reaction to the prospective partner. She wondered if he was really all that excited about ice dancing with her. Maybe he was, but she suspected there was more to it. Kevin had all the signs of a major crush on Cynthia Whoever.

Best of all, though, Heather was soon to be off the hook. Ice dancing with Kevin was completely over. Now, if she could just make it till Monday morning and impress the socks off Livvy's coach. And Mom!

A Perfect Match
Chapter Fourteen

Sunday after church Heather phoned Miranda Garcia. "How's it going?" she asked, making small talk.

"Busy. You know how it is with ballet and school and stuff."

"Do you have any extra time to, like, join a club?" she asked right off.

"What sort of club?"

"It's called *Girls Only*. So far there are three of us," she explained. "Jenna Song, Livvy Hudson, and me."

"Really?" Miranda seemed interested. "What do you do?"

"Last month we presented a Christmas show for our families. Right now we're working on a dance festival for spring. We like to practice ballet moves and, you know, hang out at Jenna's house—that's where we meet."

"I heard she has a barre and a huge wall mirror in her bedroom," Miranda remarked.

"That's true. Jenna's bedroom is in the attic. There's lots of room for all of us to practice at the barre."

"Good, then, count me in."

"We're mostly about athletic goals and Olympic dreams," she went on to say. "I think you'll get a better feel for it when you come."

"When's the next meeting?" asked Miranda.

"We get together on Fridays, right after school. And we always eat healthy snacks, so don't worry about junk food or sweets."

"Great. Thanks for inviting me," Miranda said.

"Uh, you might wanna keep it a secret because so far it's just the three of us—with you, four. But we'd rather not get too big, you know what I mean."

"Sure do. Thanks, Heather. See you at ballet."

"Okay. Bye."

Heather hung up the phone. *That was easy,* she thought and hurried downstairs.

She found Kevin whispering in the kitchen with Tommy and Joanne. He turned around quickly, like he'd been caught red-handed. "Oh, it's you. That's okay," he said.

"What's up?" she asked, opening the fridge.

"Keep your voice down," Tommy bossed.

Joanne was gesturing for her to come over. "We're

talking about the tooth fairy's birthday," she said. "He's turning the big four-oh."

Kevin smiled. "We're pooling our allowance," he explained for Heather's sake.

"To get something really special for Daddy," Joanne whispered.

"Does Mom know?" asked Heather, glancing over her shoulder.

"It's just our secret," Tommy said. "And you have to promise not to tell."

Heather laughed. "Oh, I'm good at keeping secrets. Trust me."

The phone rang, and Kevin ran to get it. Heather stayed with Tommy and Joanne because she was certain the call was for Kevin. Probably from Cynthia, the skater they'd met yesterday.

"That's Kevin's girlfriend, right?" Tommy asked.

"Beats me," she said.

"Kevin acts real silly all the time," Joanne piped up.

Heather agreed but kept her thoughts to herself.

When Kevin came back, he looked mighty happy. "That was Cynthia. She's coming to Alpine Lake tomorrow afternoon to meet with Coach McDonald."

"Really, that soon?" Heather tried not to show her surprise.

"Yep. Everything seems to be working out." Kevin opened the cupboard and pulled out some beef jerky. He pulled it apart, dividing it into four pieces. "Who wants to share this?"

Tommy and Joanne did, of course. Heather refused.

The kids decided how much money the four of them had between them. All totaled: twenty dollars. Enough to buy a brand-name tie for their dad.

"A really *special* tie," Joanne insisted.

Before church that evening, Heather went upstairs to her room and rested. She fell asleep, dreaming that she was skating alone under a starlit sky. One of the stars seemed so bright, she just assumed it was a spotlight. But when she looked again, she saw that it was the moon.

———

Livvy Hudson was at church that evening. She seemed delighted when Heather invited her to sit with them. "We're one big, happy family," Livvy said, sliding in next to Kevin.

"Better watch it," Heather warned. "My brother's got a girlfriend."

"Who?" whispered Livvy.

"Tell you later." And she did. Right after the benediction, Kevin got up and filed out of the church. But Heather and Livvy stayed in the sanctuary for a few minutes longer.

Quickly, Heather filled Livvy in on the latest. "Her

name is Cynthia Something, and she's coming to meet Coach McDonald. Tomorrow!"

"Aw, phooey," Livvy said, eyes downcast. "I was hoping he'd pick *me* for his skating partner."

"You?"

"Sure! I'd love to skate with someone like Kevin."

Heather could hardly believe her ears. "You're the best free skater around here. What're you talking about?"

"Gotcha," Livvy said, wearing an ear-to-ear grin. "I think you'd better relax about this."

"I'm trying. I really am."

"Could've fooled me," Livvy said as they walked toward the church foyer. "See ya tomorrow, bright and early?"

"You're coming?"

Livvy gave her a hug. "I wouldn't miss it for anything."

"Thanks." Heather went home and counted the hours, minutes, and seconds till her appointment with Livvy's coach. But when she prayed, she told God she was definitely nervous. "But you'll be there to help me, right, Lord?"

The moon was nowhere to be seen as she slipped into bed. The light from the back porch spilled out far past their snowy yard. The night was bright enough.

So was her future.

A Perfect Match
Chapter Fifteen

Heather and her mom arrived at the mall rink ten minutes early. She laced up the boots of her skates, keeping the skate guards on. Leaning on the rail, she watched a skater at the far end of the ice.

The girl skated across the ice toward Heather. With a solid, upward motion she brought her right leg up and forward, then shot into the air. Her legs flew apart into a wide, clean split high above the ice. Then she landed on one skate, dipping down to a sit spin position. Spinning around in a blur, she came to a stop with her hands raised overhead.

"Wow," whispered Heather. "That's exactly what I want to do someday."

"You'll have to work very hard," Mom said, offering an encouraging hug.

"I know, and I'm ready for it." She looked at her watch. "Coach Sterling's late."

"Here he comes now," Mom said, looking over her shoulder. "And Livvy's right behind him."

Heather felt herself relax a bit. She knew she was psyched for this moment—had even worried that something might happen to prevent or delay the jump lesson. But seeing Livvy and her famous coach, Heather breathed a deep, confident breath.

———

She circled the rink several times to get the feel of the ice beneath her skates. *A single loop jump—an edge jump,* she thought. Livvy's coach had picked the easiest jump of all.

Concentrating on her feet, Heather took a deep breath. She enjoyed the feeling of freedom. No one holding her hands or waist. She could move at will. On her own!

She was ready to try the jump. Off from the back, outside edge of her skating foot, she lifted herself up. One rotation—to form the look of a loop in midair— and down. She landed on the back, outside edge of her takeoff foot.

"Excellent!" Coach Sterling called to her.

The loop jump was too easy. She should try something

harder this time. And Livvy's coach didn't disappoint her. "Let's have you attempt the flip jump next," he said, motioning to her.

Listening carefully as Mr. Sterling described the jump, Heather remembered how the jump looked when Kristi Yamaguchi or even Livvy Hudson performed it. Same as the Lutz, but it took off from the back, inside edge of the skating foot—not the outside edge. And it was a toe pick-assisted jump.

When it was time, she stroked hard to build up speed. Then, turning backward, she glided across the ice. She used her toe pick to help her spring into the jump. But she fell on the landing. "I'll try it again," she said, getting up.

This time she landed on the wrong foot. But she wasn't one to give up easily. She tried again—four times more. By the fifth try, she landed on the back, outside edge of her free foot.

"Yes!" Livvy shouted, clapping on the sidelines. "You did it!"

The flip jump hadn't been perfect, but Heather was excited. And by the end of the hour, she'd landed two more single flips and was trying for the next hardest— the Lutz.

"You're super incredible!" Livvy said, hugging her after the session.

"Thanks. I wanna get much better at jumping. And

soon." Heather had to look down at the ice to make sure she wasn't walking on air!

Coach Sterling was nodding and rummaging around in his coat pocket. "Here, Miss Heather," he said, handing her a business card. "Give me a call when you want to get together again."

Heather could hardly stand still. "Mom?" she pleaded. "Can we make another appointment? *Please?*"

"Absolutely," Mom said, taking the card from Heather. "How about this Wednesday and Friday mornings?"

Mr. Sterling wrote in his pocket notebook. "I'll see you soon, Heather."

She walked to the mall entrance with Livvy. "Thanks for everything, Liv."

Livvy frowned, shaking her head. "You did all the work. I'm super proud of you!"

"You shared your coach with me, and I'm so excited," Heather replied, waiting for her mother to catch up.

"The sky's the limit now," Livvy told her. "Someday we'll be in the same competitions."

Heather hadn't thought of that. "Wow—that's hard to believe."

Livvy's eyes danced. "You've got what it takes. Coach Sterling wouldn't be offering you lessons if he didn't think so."

"You're probably right."

"Well, I better get going," Livvy said. "Coach'll be waiting. I'll see you at ballet."

"Okay. Thanks again!" Heather held the door for her mom, and the two of them walked to the car. "Thanks for believing in me. You don't know how happy I am."

"I think I do. Happiness is written all over your face."

Heather remembered what Kevin had said about her emotions showing on her face. He'd said, *"It's easy to read you."*

Well, for a change, she didn't mind. Not one bit! She was on her way to becoming a free skater. What had Livvy said about competing in the same events? Seemed next to impossible, but Heather thrived on a challenge.

"Are you coming to meet Cynthia Ganesford this afternoon?" Mom asked just as they pulled up to the house.

"I don't know. Kevin might not want me there."

Mom parked the car next to the sidewalk and pulled the key out of the ignition. "Well, I think you might be surprised."

"What're you saying?"

"Kevin asked if you'd come," Mom replied. "He wants you to meet Cynthia."

Heather wasn't sure how she felt about meeting her replacement. "I'll let you know after lunch."

"Okay with me."

They got out of the car and picked their way up the

snowy front steps. All the while, Heather's thoughts were on her jumps. She had more important things to think about than Kevin's new ice-dancing partner. The way she felt now, she'd probably stay home. Let Mom and Coach McDonald do the audition. Wasn't her decision anyway.

A Perfect Match
Chapter Sixteen

Mom and Kevin left at three o'clock to meet with Coach McDonald. They wanted to talk with him before Cynthia Ganesford showed up. Heather decided to skip the audition and stay home.

"Why didn't you go?" Joanne asked, plopping down next to Heather on the sofa.

"It's all up to Kevin now," she said, hugging a round pillow.

"But you *know* ice skating," her little sister insisted. "Maybe you could help Kevin decide if Cynthia's the right partner."

She turned to look at Joanne. Here was a first-grade munchkin far older than her years. And Joanne was probably right. She should've gone along.

But, no, it was much better this way. With all the

talk of Cynthia, she didn't need to add her two cents. Besides, Kevin had already made up his mind. She was almost sure of it.

When the phone rang, Heather ignored it. She wasn't going to bother. She and Joanne were in a close game of tic-tac-toe.

"Aren't you gonna answer it?" Joanne asked.

"Don't feel like it," she said.

"Why not?"

"Just don't."

"Are you upset about Cynthia?" asked Joanne.

Heather frowned. "Why would you say a dumb thing like that?"

Joanne's eyes blinked rapidly, like she was in trouble. "Because I think it's true," she said softly.

The phone kept ringing.

Heather shook her head. "How could I be upset?" She wished Joanne hadn't brought this up. Not now.

"Because ice dancing is your life, and you know it." Joanne smashed her lips together, eyes wide. "I . . . I didn't mean to say that."

Standing up, Heather tossed the tic-tac-toe tablet onto her sister's lap. "I think you did mean it, and I'm outta here."

"Where are you going?" Joanne demanded.

"To my room."

The phone had stopped. And she could hear Joanne

complaining about the unfinished game on the stairs. Closing her door, she wished she and Joanne hadn't fought. None of this stuff with Kevin and Cynthia was worth hard feelings in the family.

When she felt calmer, she went to her parents' bedroom and phoned Livvy. "How was school?" she asked.

"I've got way too much homework," Livvy said. "I tried to call you earlier."

"Oh, was that you?"

"So you were busy or something?" Livvy asked.

"Yeah, with my little sister." She didn't want to say that she was bummed out in general. "What'd you call about?"

"I just happened to run into Kevin and your mom."

"You're kidding. How'd it go? With Cynthia, I mean."

Livvy paused for a second. "If I tell you, promise not to be upset?"

"How can I be upset? If my brother's found the perfect replacement, I'm thrilled. Case closed."

"She's an amazing skater, Heather. I watched them try out some dance steps and patterns. You should've been there to see it. I could hardly believe it was their first time on the ice together."

"That's definitely good news. Thanks for letting me know, Livvy."

Livvy talked about school and the outrageous amount of homework she already had for the week. But when

Heather hung up, she hardly remembered much of anything Liv had said. Except for the report of Cynthia's *amazing* audition with Kevin.

———

During every minute of supper and dessert, her parents talked of nothing but Cynthia's performance. But it was Kevin who beamed whenever the skater's name was mentioned.

He's nuts about her—on and off the ice, Heather decided. And the way she saw it, that alone was a problem. If Kevin really liked this girl, he'd be shy about putting his arm around her waist or holding her hand. There'd be no way he'd dance close to her on the ice, the way the judges required for good marks. Choosing a girl Kevin was attracted to was a big mistake.

But she wasn't going to intrude. If Kevin made a bad choice, he'd find out sooner or later. The first real practice session would tell him.

"It's for sure . . . about Cynthia, I mean?" she asked her mom in the kitchen during cleanup.

Mom poured detergent into the tiny cubicles in the door of the dishwasher. "Coach McDonald will be working with them in Colorado Springs next Saturday. We're going to take turns driving back and forth between there and here."

"Sounds like a good trade-off," she said. "Have you met her parents?"

"Very nice people," Mom replied. "Might even be Christians. But I guess we'll find out."

"That's great." She finished wiping the counters and dried a few pans that didn't fit into the dishwasher.

They had family devotions, and then Heather went to her room to work on unfinished schoolwork. Mom was a stickler about following through on things.

Ice dancing is your life. . . .

Joanne's childish words kept intruding into her thoughts off and on all evening. Not until she got wrapped up in a library book on free skating was Heather able to nudge the ridiculous assumption out of her mind.

A Perfect Match
Chapter Seventeen

Making birthday party plans for her dad and practicing jumps consumed most of Heather's free time. There were occasional spats with Kevin, but they seemed to occur during homeschooling sessions. The disagreements had nothing to do with skating, either free skating or ice dancing. For the most part, their relationship was still intact.

By Wednesday, she found herself enthusiastic to work with Livvy's coach once again. Mr. Sterling was the most helpful, kind coach she'd ever known. Not any more than her former coach, of course, but he had a wonderfully encouraging way about him. Made you want to work till you dropped.

Livvy didn't show up for Heather's second jump lesson with Coach Sterling. Just as well. Heather wanted to make her own connection with the kindly gentleman.

"You are improving so rapidly, Miss Heather, you make my head spin," Coach Sterling told her after the lesson.

"Thank you very much." She could hardly wait to tell her parents. And Livvy, too.

The walk home seemed shorter than usual. Maybe it was because she was so jazzed up about her progress. Yet in spite of her development as a free skater, something seemed not quite right. Try as she might, she couldn't put her finger on it.

After the supper dishes were cleared from the table, she asked permission to use her father's computer. Checking her library book, she found a listing of the top-ten ice-skating Web sites.

In an instant, she located the Kristi Yamaguchi Web page and info about the Stars on Ice tour and other skating news. There were many Internet links to figure-skating tidbits and bios of the most famous free skaters in the world. For an hour, she was lost in a world of extraordinary people—brilliant skaters and lavish costumes.

Lying in bed, her head buzzed with high hopes of becoming a Junior Olympics gold medalist. Her focus, hard work, and determination would get her where she wanted to be.

Had to!

On Thursday morning, she went to the mall rink to practice. Kevin did the same. In fact, they shared the ice, but not their practice. It seemed terribly odd to Heather, and she did her best not to keep watching her brother. But it was hard to focus on her own work.

Kevin worked through his solo stroking as usual, then went right into his half of the cha-cha dance pattern. She tried to ignore his marvelous, intricate footwork and turns. Of course, the only thing missing was his partner.

Heather busied herself with preparations for the flip and Lutz jumps. The setup for the Lutz had her stumped nearly every time. Skating backward in a curve—and the long glide into the jump—was definitely difficult.

Once, when she fell, she felt stunned for a moment. Both Mom and Kevin came running. But it was Kevin who picked her up gently and held on to her while she got her bearings again.

"Maybe you oughta take a break for a while," he said, guiding her off the ice.

"I'm fine," she said. "Thanks."

He stood there, looking down at her. "You sure you're all right?"

She nodded, waiting till he'd turned and stepped back onto the ice to rub her leg.

"Are you hurt, honey?" Mom asked, hovering over her.

"Just a little bruised, that's all."

"Maybe Kevin's right about taking it easy. You've been pushing yourself really hard these days." Mom sat beside her, looking on with sympathetic eyes.

"I can't slow down, Mom. You know I can't." She sighed. "I'm so far behind."

Mom patted her hand. They stared out at the ice—at Kevin executing one beautiful dance pattern after another. Alone.

———

Heather sat on a soft chair in Jenna's bedroom later that afternoon. Her leg still hurt from her reckless fall, so Jenna and Livvy babied her by giving her the chair. Actually, she was hurting in two places. Her leg hurt because she'd pushed herself too hard at practice. The second hurt was deep in the core of her stomach. The pain wasn't a typical stomachache—like from something she'd eaten or the flu. Nothing like that. The ache was more like the squeamish, worrisome feeling she often experienced before an ice-dancing competition. But she knew that was ridiculous. There were no events coming up very soon. This was mid-January. The next big event was the Summer Ice Spectacular.

Oops . . . she'd forgotten. She almost laughed out loud. Once again she was thinking about her former interest. Ice dancing was none of her concern. She was something else now. A free skater with the brightest future ever.

Why do I feel so miserable? she wondered.

The pain in her stomach didn't go away. Not even when the *Girls Only* Club was called to order. There was no following the bylaws this meeting. And Miranda Garcia was the reason. She had asked if it was possible to have the meeting a day earlier this week because she was already busy during their normal Friday meeting. Jenna, the prez, wanted to make sure their ballet friend was comfortable. So they threw out the rule book and just had a good time chattering about school and boys . . . and of course, sports.

When they went to the barre and warmed up, she partnered with Livvy. Jenna put on a CD of Chopin waltzes, and Heather began to relax.

Halfway through the stretches, she started to laugh. She couldn't stop, either. Livvy, not knowing what was so funny, began to laugh, too.

At that moment—sharing the barre with Livvy—Heather realized what was causing the pain in her stomach. She missed her partner. In spite of her longings, she honestly wanted things to return to the way they had been. Before she'd decided to go it alone. Before she'd given up the best partner ever. "I have to talk to my brother," she said through her laughter.

Livvy was nodding. "It's about ice dancing, isn't it?"

Heather pulled herself up to a standing position. "How'd you know?"

Livvy grinned and tossed her hair. "Just guessed."

They fell into each other's arms. Giggles spilled over into the attic bedroom-turned-clubhouse. Jenna turned up the volume on the Chopin, while Miranda kept at her warm-ups.

"Are the meetings always this wacky and wonderful?" asked Miranda over raspberry lemonade.

"Pretty much," Jenna said, smiling. "Wanna see a teeny, weenie gymnast?"

"Sure do," Miranda said.

Jenna said, "Follow me," and the three of them headed for the nursery to see the amazing left foot of baby Jonathan.

The club meeting ended with a swing dance runthrough. "The choreography was created by none other than Heather Bock!" Jenna announced.

"Go, girl!" Miranda said, thumbs up.

Once again, Heather teamed up with Livvy for the practice. While she danced with her partner, the pain in the pit of her stomach began to disappear. And soon, it was completely gone.

Now, how to break her news to Kevin. Was it too late?

A Perfect Match
Chapter Eighteen

Heather had a tough time finding Kevin alone without either Joanne or Tommy hanging around. What she had to tell him might change their travel plans tomorrow. Might change both their athletic futures, too.

Finally, after family devotions, she nabbed him. "I need to talk to you," she said, cornering him in the upstairs hallway.

"Sure, what's up?" His eyes seemed to look through to her heart.

"You won't yell at me, will you?"

He looked thoroughly confused. "About what?"

"About me not wanting to skate solo." There, she'd said it. Now what would he do?

His face lit into a smile. "What did you just say?"

"I said I miss skating with you. I . . . I made a big

mistake." Tears were stinging her eyes. "I was crazy to give up everything we'd ever worked for."

Kevin put his arms around her and patted her head. "You're crazy, little sister."

"Will you let me skate with you again?" she sobbed into his old flannel shirt.

"On one condition," he said, holding her at arm's length. "Are you through with free skating?"

"Do I look like Kristi Yamaguchi to you?" She spun around in front of him, bursting into laughter.

"Man, will Mom be shocked," Kevin said, pulling her arm and racing down the stairs. "But it'll work out. You'll see."

Leave it to Kevin to be optimistic at a time like this. No matter what, though, Heather knew she could count on her partner.

"What about Cynthia?" she said as they hurried to the kitchen.

"What *about* her?" He was laughing, too. "I've got the perfect partner right here."

No matter what she might've thought about other days in her life, this day—this moment—was the very best of all.

Definitely.

Reach for the Stars

AUTHOR'S NOTE

Special thanks to the International Ski Federation, the U.S. Olympic Committee, and various ski instructors at Ski Cooper, Silvercreek, and Winter Park in Colorado—where else!

My heartfelt appreciation to Allison Jones, who has won numerous awards in Alpine skiing, placing First *four* times at the '98 National Winter Paralympics (Juniors Category) and who graciously answered my questions. Allison was featured in the January/February '98 issue of *American Girl Magazine*.

Hugs to my daughter Janie, who helped with research on bone fractures for this book.

Information about Picabo Street (Alpine skier and Olympic gold medalist) can be found on the ESPN SportsZone Web site.

To

Allison Jones,

an extraordinary Alpine skier
who reaches for the stars . . .
and beyond!

Reach for the Stars
Chapter One

Twelve-year-old Miranda Garcia gazed down the black diamond slope. "Ski your heart out," she whispered to herself.

Falcon Ridge lay below her, rigorous and still. The first practice run of the day always left her a bit breathless. But she liked it that way.

Long and steep, the course required extraordinary courage. But Manda, who liked to refer to herself as "Downhill Dynamite," was ready to seize the challenge.

Pairs of closely spaced flags, called gates, waved gently in the frosty morning air. The slope was as familiar to her as the downhill skis on her feet. After all, the finish line was only a few blocks from her back door. She'd grown up here. Alpine Lake, Colorado, was the ideal hometown for a downhill skier with her heart set on Olympic gold.

Miranda rocked back and forth on her skis at the starting gate. She focused on the course ahead. *Ski, baby, ski,* she thought.

She'd memorized every inch of the dangerous slope. The steep drop-offs, the midsection "Corkscrew" with its series of sharp turns, and the sizzling-fast beeline to the finish.

The practice run would require concentration and energy, but she remained cool and confident. She took several deep breaths—her customary approach to waiting for the starting signal.

If she skied well today, Coach Hanson would be glad he'd entered her in the Dressel Hills Downhill Classic. The annual race was only six weeks away—on St. Patrick's Day—one ski resort to the north of Alpine Lake. *This* year, the competition was open to intermediate through advanced skiers, with categories for both girls and guys. She was eligible in more ways than one!

"I can't wait to see you compete at Dressel Hills," her mom had said that morning at breakfast. "I'll watch you float through the air like an eagle. And those jumps of yours, especially before the final stretch . . . well, you're amazing!"

"Thanks, Mom. You're my biggest fan," she'd replied.

Then came a big hug. "I'm so proud of you, Manda!"

Miranda liked her nickname far better than her given

name. Manda was short and to the point. Not as flowery as Miranda. More like who she *really* was.

After the kitchen was made spotless once again, they'd gone their separate ways. It was typical for most winter Saturdays at the Garcia home. Manda headed off to ski with her coach; her mom to the Alpine Ski Academy at the base of Cascade Peak.

Manda had decided years ago that snow skiing must be in their genes—hers and her mother's. Adelina Garcia, Manda's mom, was a certified ski instructor. She specialized in preschool-age beginners. For as long as Manda could remember, her mother had been passing on her love for Alpine skiing to little tykes. Including her own daughter!

Manda could hardly remember *not* being on skis. From her earliest little-girl memories, she was either skiing with her mom (or alone) or mountain biking on long trails during the summer, working out and waiting for the first snowfall.

Winter was by far the best season of all.

At last, the starting signal came from Coach Hanson.

Manda shot out of the gate. She pushed off with her poles and charged onto the course. Quickly, she dropped into her speed tuck, folding her body into a crouched position. Her hands were close to her chin, and she moved her elbows next to her body.

Tight as a Tootsie Roll, she thought, curling herself down. It was the best way to slice the air at top speeds. Sometimes sixty miles an hour . . . or more!

Swish!

She flew over the icy snow, carving her turns by digging her ski edges into the slope. She zipped past the sharp drop-off to her right and headed for the first jump.

Whoosh!

For several seconds, she was airborne. But Manda was careful to remain in her racing tuck. She landed gracefully, like a feather caressing the snow.

At moments like these, Manda felt she could conquer most any mountain. Even Eagle's Point in Dressel Hills seemed within reach. She'd had a few practice runs on it—enough to know how dangerous and exciting it was. She loved a good challenge, and Eagle's Point was definitely that.

Downhill Dynamite!

Manda took the sharp turns as solidly as she could. Her legs felt each bump and jolt beneath her skis. But this was an excellent run. One of her best all week.

The Corkscrew was next. A succession of zigzagging turns, it marked the completion of the middle section. Manda slowed just a bit, enough to make the turns without losing control completely.

The dizzying-steep part of the course was now in sight.

It was a straight path to the finish line—at breakneck speed—with two enormous jumps coming up fast.

Her poles flapped in the air, but Manda fought to keep her cool. The first jump and landing. High and up she soared. Down she came with a perfect landing. Easy enough.

Next, the second big jump. Towering high above the course, she saw Alpine Lake, the ski resort valley below her. Though she didn't have time to fully enjoy the view, she could hardly wait to tell her mom about this amazing run. She could feel the confidence in her bones.

Her second landing was slightly harder than usual, but the finish was less than two seconds away. She'd beaten her all-time fastest record. She was sure of it!

Wrapping herself into the tight tuck again, she high-tailed it toward the finish line. On the way, the wind caught her right ski pole, and it flew out of her gloved hand. But Manda let it go. She could retrieve it later—after she was clocked.

Swoosh!

She flew past the finish and slowed, making a hockey stop by tipping her skis on edge.

"Wow, Manda—way to go!" Benny the timer called.

She skied over to the young man in the blue-and-white ski outfit. "How'd I do?" she asked, breathing hard.

Wide-eyed, Benny read his stopwatch. "One minute, thirty-nine and a half seconds. On the button." He looked at her, grinning. "You shooting for Junior Olympics this year?"

"Sooner or later—you bet I am!" Manda pumped her fists into the air. Her time was far better than she'd thought possible, at least for a practice run. Usually, it took a cheering crowd to get her adrenaline going.

Just then she heard the familiar *swish* of skis behind her. She turned to see Coach Hanson, tall and lean, taking wide, careful zigzags as he headed toward her and Benny.

What's Coach doing? she wondered, surprised to see him.

He waved her wayward ski pole as he came to a quick stop. "I just received a message for you," Coach Hanson said, his eyebrows knitting into a deep frown. "Manda, your mom had an accident. She's on her way to the hospital."

Manda's heart sank. "The hospital? What happened?"

"She had a bad spill on the slope," he replied, handing her the ski pole. Then he removed his cell phone from his pocket. "Here, use this to call the hospital," he offered.

A vision of her mom strapped to a stretcher made Manda shudder. "No . . . thanks anyway. I want to be there with her," she whispered. "As soon as possible."

Reach for the Stars
Chapter Two

The smell of rubbing alcohol made Manda cringe as she scurried down the hospital corridor. She darted ahead of her coach, arriving at the information desk nearly out of breath.

"My mother's here . . . in the emergency room," she told the receptionist. "An ambulance just brought her in."

The blond woman offered a kind smile. "Does your mother have a name?"

"Oh yes . . . yes, she does. Sorry." Manda gave her mother's full name. "And she hates hospitals," she blurted.

"Well, who doesn't?" the information lady said cheerfully. "Yes, your mother's in the ER at the moment. Let me show you the way." She led Manda and her coach down the hall to the double doors that opened into the bustling emergency room.

"Thank you," Manda remembered to say. Then she followed Coach Hanson past the swinging doors. Several doctors and nurses were busying themselves behind a long counter.

One of the nurses looked up. "May I help you?"

"Yes, I'm Adelina Garcia's daughter," Manda said. "Please, may I see her?"

"Ah yes. The ski instructor's daughter." The nurse motioned for Manda to follow her. "Your mother's been asking for you, dear."

Coach shrugged and jerked his head in the direction of the double doors. "I'll wait for you, okay?" he said softly.

Manda waved her thanks and hurried to catch up with the petite nurse. "Is my mom going to be all right?" she asked when they arrived at the curtained-off area.

"Your mother may seem a bit groggy. Pain medication has a way of doing that," explained the nurse. "But I think she'll be very glad to see you."

"Thanks," Manda said and pulled back the white curtain.

There, lying in the hospital bed, was Mom—bruised and injured. Her left leg was hoisted up slightly off the bed, and her face was bruised on the left side. She'd taken a pounding.

Manda flew to the head of the bed. "Oh, Mama," she whispered, touching a limp hand. "I'm here. It's me, Manda."

Her mother stirred, eyelids fluttering briefly, then closing. "I was so stupid," she whispered. "It's my own fault."

Manda shook her head. "If there's anything you are *not*, Mom, it's stupid. I won't let you lie here and say crazy things like that just because you're hurt." She fought back tears.

Her mother's lips formed a weak smile. "That's my girl. Always tough and tumble." She opened her eyes for a moment. "How was your run this morning?"

"That can wait," Manda insisted. "If we're gonna talk about anything, we're talking about *you*." She squeezed her mother's hand gently, staring at the fractured limb. "Will they have to operate?"

Before her mother could answer, a doctor and two nurses came in. No warning, just breezed past the cotton curtain. Like skiers past a flagged gate.

Manda's question was left hanging in the air.

———

The rest of the week, Manda spent every spare minute with her mom after school. Each day, she rode the bus with her girl friends Livvy Hudson and Jenna Song.

Sometimes Heather Bock, a homeschool friend who practiced skating at the mall ice rink, rode along, too. Heather and her older brother, Kevin, were hotshot ice dancers headed straight for star status. Manda thought it the first time she saw them skate.

Manda, Heather, Livvy, and Jenna belonged to a club they called *Girls Only*. The exclusive club was for girls who had one thing on their minds: excellence in athletics. Most of the time, anyway. Every now and then, the foursome admitted to having lingering thoughts of boys. But for the most part, they talked about Olympic this or gold medal that. Just the way Manda liked it.

When the bus came to a stop at Sundown Avenue, Manda slid out of her seat. "Here's where I get off," she told her friends.

"Tell your mom I'm praying for her," Livvy Hudson said with a big smile. Her bright eyes sparkled beneath a full head of auburn hair.

"So am I," said Jenna Song, offering an eye-squinting smile. Her black hair was bouncy and cute as always.

"My mom's making a secret basket of goodies," blond Heather Bock called. "But don't tell *your* mom!"

"Okay, see ya!" Manda said, waiting for the bus doors to open.

When she was safely on the snow-packed sidewalk, she picked her way over the next half block to Memorial Hospital. She was grateful for true friends like Heather,

Livvy, and Jenna. They and their parents had pitched in and helped, even invited Manda over to spend the night several times.

Manda had enjoyed the home-cooked meals, but she always refused the overnight invitations. Politely, of course. She didn't mind staying home alone. She needed time to think . . . and to make some very special plans. Besides, she could take care of herself.

There was one thing that worried her, though. It was about missing nearly a week of practice. Skipping her usual habit of training could set her back—too far back to compete at Dressel Hills next month. Yet she knew her first concern was and always would be her mother.

Coach Hanson had been very understanding when she told him the serious nature of the fracture. He'd nodded and patted Manda on the shoulder. "You only get one mom, you know," he'd said.

Wasn't that the truth! And Manda had only one parent. She wasn't going to let anything happen to *this* one—no sir! She and her mom had hung in there, through thick and thin. Mostly thin. Her dad had literally vanished one day when she was only two years old. He simply never came home from work.

Weeks passed. No divorce papers. No note . . . no nothing. When Manda tried to explain the "single-parent thing" to friends other than her *Girls Only* friends, they'd look at her, heads half cocked and mouths wide. "You've gotta be kidding. Your dad just left and never called your mom or wrote or anything?" one girl had asked back in fourth grade.

"Zip, zilch," was Manda's casual comeback.

Her father's leaving was no big secret. She didn't try to hide the fact that her dad had abandoned them. Anybody who left his beautiful wife and baby girl for absolutely no reason at all had to be a loser.

Because of her family history, Manda had decided at a young age to "wear the pants" in the family, so to speak. She was going to look out for her mom—make sure she was happy.

Most of all, Manda tried not to think about the other thing that gnawed at her. What if there *was* a good explanation for her dad's leaving? What if he knew he was dying and didn't want them to know? Wanted to spare them the pain . . .

But no, Manda honestly didn't believe that. Not for a single second.

———

Manda opened the door to her mother's semiprivate room and tiptoed inside. "Hey, good, you're conscious for a change," she teased.

A nurse helped prop some extra pillows under the

broken leg, now hooked up to a pulley system overhead. "Right on time," the nurse said with a smile.

"That's my girl—pert, persistent, and pretty," Mom said, waving.

Manda clicked her fingers. "Three *p*'s—hey, you're really with it today," she said, laughing. "Did they cut off your morphine supply or what?" She knew better. The medication was necessary to take the edge off the worst pain. Otherwise, her mom would've continued to suffer unbearably.

"Come here, you," Mom said.

Like a puppet doll, Manda jerked back and forth, inching her way to the hospital bed. "I love you, Mama."

Her mother reached up for a hug. "I missed my girl," Mom said, whispering.

"I came the instant school was out." Manda watched the nurse stroll to the door. "I know how you hate this place."

"Oh, it's not so bad, I guess."

"Just not quite home?" Manda remarked.

"Right." Mom's big brown eyes held a hint of worry.

Manda pulled up a chair and sat down. She took out a harmonica from her schoolbag and began to play. Self-taught, she liked to play when things seemed out of whack, which happened to be a lot during her younger growing-up years.

After a while, she paused to catch her breath. "Any idea when they'll let you out of here?"

411

Her mother sighed. "First things first. The operation is scheduled for next Monday. After that, I'll be in a leg cast for a month or so."

Sighing, Manda looked around at the plants and flowers lining the windowsill. There was a TV hanging in midair, it seemed, against the opposite wall. And a cream-colored, not-so-opaque draw curtain hung between Mom's bed and that of the other patient, Ethel Norton.

Ethel, gray-haired and wrinkly, had asked to be called either Auntie Ethel or Nana Ethel. "You pick," she'd said on the first day when Manda met her.

Hesitant about it, Manda had chosen Auntie. It seemed to work better with Ethel than Nana. Besides, Nana reminded her of a goat or something.

She fidgeted. This place was too confining—too smelly—for her outdoorsy, robust mother. She scooted the chair closer to the bed.

Mom wore a forced grin. "I'm doing just fine. Don't worry."

"C'mon, Mom. You've got a full-blown fracture to the fibula. You're *not* fine." She scratched her head. "Besides, I've been doing a lot of thinking. . . ."

"Uh-oh. Should I be worried?" Mom smiled.

"Listen to me." She glanced at the curtain between the beds. Yep, Auntie Ethel was listening, too. Manda lowered her voice. "Since you're gonna be laid up for a while, I've made some plans. I have a fantastic idea."

Mom pretended to faint, her hand on her forehead. "Please, don't tell me."

"Seriously, I have this great idea," she repeated. "I'm taking over your job till your leg heals." She stole a quick look at the gauzy curtains. Auntie Ethel turned on her bed light, making it easy for Manda to see her "thumbs-up" approval. "Thanks, Auntie Ethel," she said.

"Good for you, honey," the old woman replied.

"Whoa . . . wait a minute. You're *what*?" Mom seemed upset.

"I've already worked through the angles—talked to your boss and everything," Manda told her. "He thinks it's a terrific idea."

Mom leaned her head back against the pillow. A tear escaped the corner of her eye and rolled down the side of her cheek. "Oh, sweetie, you don't have to do this," she whispered.

"Please don't cry, Mom."

But it was too late. The tears were already coming fast. Manda found a box of tissues and handed it to her mother. "Oh nuts . . . go ahead," she mumbled. "Sometimes tears are just what the doctor ordered."

Taking a deep breath, Manda played two church songs, one right after the other. The harmonica blocked out the sound of sniffling.

Reach for the Stars
Chapter Three

The next day, Manda was in charge of the preschool instruction program at Alpine Ski Academy. The job was the ideal solution, even though the pay wasn't the same as the school was required to pay a certified adult instructor. But she didn't mind. She could hold the job while her mom's leg was healing. Besides, the ski classes would keep Manda busy. And she enjoyed working with kids.

Between her own ski practice and filling in at the ski school, Manda figured she'd be able to squeeze in an occasional baby-sitting job, too, along with her homework—in spite of the computer being on the blink. Yep, she could even fit in her once-a-week *Girls Only* Club meeting on Fridays.

She liked to keep busy. She could pull it off easily enough. And with the help of Uncle Frank—her mother's only brother—they would do just fine financially. Money had never really been much of a problem after her dad left. Uncle Frank had always come to the rescue.

Manda hoped to pay him back someday for his kindness. Someday, when she won certain big competitive ski events, she would. That desire, coupled with the fact that she loved the daring aspects of skiing—just like Olympic gold medalist Picabo Street—was the reason for her passion and drive.

———

Manda surveyed the enthusiastic lineup of four- and five-year-olds. "Good morning, students. My name is Manda."

"Good morning, Manda," the kids chorused back.

"Is everybody here who's supposed to be?" she asked.

The six children were adorable ski bunnies, dressed in everything from designer ski outfits to makeshift ski attire. All tiny . . . and cute!

"Somebody's missing," a little brown-eyed beauty spoke up.

Manda counted heads. "You're right, but who *is* it?" she asked.

"Tarin's in the bathroom," another child volunteered.

Quickly, she searched through the student roster. "Tarin . . . Tarin who?" she muttered.

The children giggled.

"What?" she said, looking up. "What's so funny?"

The same girl raised her hand. "Teacher?" she said.

Manda couldn't see her name tag. "What's *your* name?" She motioned the girl to come closer.

The girl looked down at her skis, then back at Manda. A fearful expression crossed her tiny face. Then she began to shake her head. "I'm Shelley Rolland, but I can't move," she said, staring back down at her feet. "I'm stuck on my skis."

Of course you are, thought Manda. She skied over to the girl. "I'll teach you to ski like a pro. But first, can you tell me Tarin's last name?"

She blinked her eyes. "Sure you wanna know?" Shelley replied in her husky, childish voice. She pulled on Manda's sleeve. "Bend down. I'll whisper it in your ear."

Playing along, Manda leaned over.

"He's Tarin the Terrible," Shelley said, her nose tickling Manda's ear.

Manda straightened to her full size. "Well, what an interesting name!" She observed the youngster. "Are you sure about that?"

Shelley began nodding her head up and down. "You'll find out why," she volunteered.

Tarin the Terrible . . .

417

Flipping through her schedule for the day, Manda located the boy's name. Sure enough, Tarin was listed. But his last name wasn't Terrible. It was Greenberg.

She was smart enough to know, from the numerous baby-sitting jobs she'd had over the years, that you never got anywhere by debating with a preschooler. Nope. She wasn't going to set herself up on her first day as ski instructor.

"Okay," she said, offering a smile. "So Tarin the Terrible is missing. I think we'd better find him."

As if on cue, a youngster emerged from the shadows. He was dressed in an orange, waterproof, one-piece suit. If she hadn't known better, she might've blurted out that a miniature pumpkin had just shown up. But she smiled at the boy who, just a few seconds before, had been absent from the lively group.

She took a deep breath. "Welcome to the beginner's ski class," she began again.

"*I'm* not a beginner," the pumpkin kid piped up.

Manda paused. "Then maybe you're in the wrong class."

He shook his head. "I'm in the precisely correct class."

Precisely correct?

Who did this kid think he was?

She was about to ask when Shelley Rolland pointed at the pumpkin-suited boy. "It's him," she exclaimed. "Tarin the Terrible's right here!"

Oh terrific, thought Manda.

"And he's not called terrible because he's a *bad* boy," not-so-shy Shelley continued. "He's terrible because he's real smart."

Manda wasn't sure whether to ignore the statement or respond to it. Fortunately, she didn't have to decide at that moment. Another class was forming off to the left of her group. "Let's move closer together," she said.

"Motion to unify is good," Tarin said unexpectedly.

"No kidding" was all Manda could say.

A light snow had begun to fall. The sun continued to shine down on her wee bunch, in spite of the feathery flakes.

"Look!" Shelley exclaimed. She stuck out her tongue— way out—to catch snowflakes.

Soon the others were imitating her. All except Tarin the Terrible. He was holding his ski goggles up to the sky, letting snow land on them. Then he began to clean his child-size goggles with a handkerchief he pulled from his pocket.

Tarin caught her watching him and hurried to pull the goggles down onto his face. He picked up his ski poles, bent his knees, and leaned forward on his skis. "Schussing, anyone?" he said with a mischievous grin.

Schussing? she thought. *He's right . . . he's no beginner!*

Manda called to the rest of her class. "Okay, enough

snow-feasting." She began her talk on carrying skis and putting them on. Next, she demonstrated the ski stance. "Always keep your head up, eyes looking straight ahead, and make sure your neck is relaxed."

They practiced limbering up their arms. She showed them how to place the weight of their bodies over the front portion of their feet. "Whatever you do, don't stick your rump out like this," she said, illustrating her point.

Giggles flurried like snowflakes from everyone but Tarin. He stuck out his chin and stared her down. No laughter, no smiles.

I need to talk to Mom about this boy, she thought.

Reach for the Stars

Chapter Four

"He's such a cute little thing," Manda told her mom about Tarin Greenberg.

"They're all cute at that age," Mom said, smiling, her brunette hair pulled back on both sides.

Manda described each of her groups of skiers. "Tarin's the only one who doesn't seem to fit in," she said. "Did you meet him?"

"I guess I would remember if I had," Mom said.

"Maybe you blocked out the memory of him when you fell," Manda suggested.

"No . . . I do remember a precocious young boy, now that you mention it." Her mother's smile wavered a bit. "He liked to use big words."

"That's the kid. He throws words around and watches

how you react to them." She glanced up at the rings and pulleys that held her mother's broken leg in place.

Trying not to let the worry show, she talked about other things. Like how pretty the snow was, falling so gently before lunch. How outspoken little Miss Shelley Rolland was. And somehow or other, the conversation swung back to Tarin Greenberg.

"He seems determined to outsmart me," she admitted. "I can't let a five-year-old take over that way. It's not fair to the others in the group."

Now Auntie Ethel joined the conversation. "Don't let that young Einstein get the best of you, honey," she croaked and pulled the curtain open between the two beds.

"Well, good afternoon," Mom said, being polite.

Manda, on the other hand, wasn't too pleased with the old lady's eavesdropping. How much had she heard, anyway?

"Youngsters like that usually have something amiss at home. That's generally the case," Auntie Ethel continued.

Mom chuckled. "And sometimes it's just that they've grown up around serious, academic types."

Manda listened, curious about Ethel's comment. "You sound like you know children," she ventured.

"Oh, I don't claim to know very much. But I did teach school for many years before I retired." The exactness of the woman's words hinted at such professional things.

"But I daresay your young fella has some problems, one way or the other."

Manda glanced at her watch. It was almost time for her own skiing session. "Coach Hanson will be waiting," she said, giving her mom a kiss and a hug. "I better scoot."

"Come again soon," Ethel called with a wave of her wilted hand.

"I'll be back tomorrow after Sunday school and church," she said.

"Have a splendid run," Mom said.

"Downhill Dynamite will do her best," Manda replied.

I always do, she thought as she left the hospital room and headed for the elevator.

———

The practice run was as smooth as any. Even for having missed several days in a row, Manda was still on top of things. She was a hard hitter when it came to pushing herself. The mountain existed for the beauty of it . . . and to be conquered. That's the way she lived life. Conquering one challenge after another.

She thought of young Tarin Greenberg. Nobody deserved a nickname like Tarin the Terrible, even though he did seem to flaunt his IQ. Still, she'd have to be cautious in her approach to the boy.

Yet she found herself thinking about Tarin throughout the evening, curiously drawn to the brainy kid. While she did her homework, she caught herself doodling—writing his nickname. And while she talked on the phone with Heather Bock, she doodled some more.

The phone rang much later in the evening, after she'd had her bath and was dressed for bed. "Hello?" she answered.

"Hi, Manda." It was her mother. "How's everything going?"

"I'm doing okay. How're *you*?"

Mom sighed. "Missing you. I'm antsy to come home."

"I miss you, too, Mom."

There was a long silence. But she heard her mother's unsteady breathing on the line.

"Are you all right?"

"Oh, I was just thinking back to the day you were born," her mother replied. "It was the best day of my life."

Manda couldn't help but smile. "For me, too."

They went on to chat about schoolwork and their defunct computer. But it was obvious to Manda that her mom was avoiding the subject of her upcoming leg surgery. She simply didn't want to talk about it.

The topic of Tarin came up again. "I'm gonna find out what makes that kid tick," Manda declared. "One way or the other, I'm going to be a friend to him."

"Sounds like a good idea," Mom said. "Just don't let it get in the way of your skiing goals."

"You don't have to worry. I'm totally focused on Dressel Hills next month. Coach Hanson thinks I have a good chance at placing—high."

"*I'm* convinced," Mom said with a chuckle. "Well, I'd better let you go. Get a good night's sleep, kiddo."

"I will," she promised. "See you tomorrow."

"It's a deal." Mom's voice sounded strong and courageous, but it had an empty ring to it.

Manda hung up the phone after they said good-bye. But she was worried. Besides her mother's physical condition, what was bothering her? Was she suffering the effects of being isolated in the hospital?

"That's it!" she said out loud, startling herself. "Mom's been cooped up too long."

She wondered what she could do about it and felt as helpless as a skier off course, barreling down a treacherous slope. Out of control.

Poor Mom, she thought. *What can I do?*

Then an idea struck hard. Since her mom couldn't go to the mountain and experience the great outdoors, Manda would have to do something about that. She'd just have to bring the mountain to her mom!

That's what she'd do.

Easy!

Reach for the Stars
Chapter Five

She had everything planned.

Everything!

Right down to the video camera she was going to borrow. But church attendance came first. Even so, Manda found herself excited about her idea, thinking how pleased her mom would be when she presented the mountain—Cascade Peak—tomorrow afternoon.

Mom would be needing something to boost her spirits after surgery. She'd feel totally lethargic and bummed out. It was the perfect timing.

At the church, after Sunday school class, Manda shared the plan with her friend Heather. "The guy who times my runs is going to videotape me skiing tomorrow. Isn't that cool?"

Heather's blue eyes brightened. "Hey, and while you're

at it, get him to tape you doing your thing with those tiny preschool skiers. Your mom'll definitely love it."

"Maybe you're right," she replied, wondering how some of the children might respond to being filmed at ski school. But she didn't voice her concern.

"Think it over," Heather said.

"I will, and thanks for the suggestion." She was actually delighted with the idea. Heather and the other *Girls Only* Club members often came up with fantastic ideas for using their athletic talents to encourage others.

"So . . . wanna come over for dinner after church?" Heather asked as they headed toward the church lobby. "You could use our computer to check up on the history facts for class."

"Okay with your mom?" asked Manda, grateful for the offer.

"I wouldn't be inviting you if it wasn't, silly." Heather motioned for Manda to sit with her and Kevin, her older brother and ice-dancing partner. Heather's parents and younger brother and sister were already seated in a long pew near the front of the church.

"Thanks," Manda said, feeling much better now. Hanging out with God's people always made her feel good. At times like this, she wondered if her wayward father had ever settled things in his heart with the Lord.

The hymns the congregation sang were old songs, yet Manda gladly joined in. Even though she could jam up a storm on her harmonica, she couldn't carry a tune all that well. She kept wondering when Heather might glance at her cross-eyed. Or tell her to pipe down. But Heather was kind and shared the hymnal without covering her ears.

The minister's sermon text was easy to understand today. " 'Be kind and compassionate to one another, forgiving each other, just as in Christ God forgave you.' "

Manda listened carefully. This was the sort of verse she could put into practice with her ski students. Especially Tarin the Terrible!

There was someone else she probably ought to apply this verse to, along with her brilliant ski pupil. Even though her dad wasn't anywhere around, she had to forgive him. It was the right thing to do. Just not the easy thing.

She'd never thought of forgiveness quite this way. So she sat motionless on the cushioned seat next to Heather and the rest of the Bock family.

Your young fella has some problems. . . .

Auntie Ethel, the retired schoolteacher who shared the hospital room with Manda's mom, had commented on little Tarin. Probably with some professional insight, too.

Manda decided it might be a good idea to pay attention to the woman. Maybe by showing kindness to Tarin, she could help him fit in with the group.

Maybe.

———

The dinner table at the Bocks' house was set with red heart-shaped place mats. Manda suspected they were homemade, probably created during a homeschool art session, as all four Bock kids were taught by their mother.

"We made them for Valentine's Day," Joanne Bock, Heather's six-year-old sister, told her as they were seated.

"Pretty," she said, smiling across the table at the toothless grin.

Again, her mind wandered to Tarin Greenberg. Maybe it was Joanne's missing front tooth that triggered the thought. Or was it the youngster's wiggly excitement at having a Sunday dinner guest?

Dessert was being served when Joanne spoke up again. This time she was giggling. "There's a new boy in my Sunday school class."

"Joanne, please," her father said. "It isn't polite to talk and giggle at the same time."

"I'm sorry, Daddy," she said, continuing on. Her eyes blinked several times while she pressed her small hand against her mouth. Probably trying to hold in the giggle.

When Mrs. Bock returned with additional servings of cherry pie, Joanne took her hand away from her mouth. "I think I'm ready to talk now and not laugh," she said softly.

"Go ahead, then," said her mother.

"We have this boy . . ." She paused, her mouth turning up hard on both sides. "He's got a strange nickname."

Before she could finish, Heather jumped in. "You're not talking about Tarin Greenberg, are you?" She looked at her little sister. "Because if you are, I've heard his nickname, and I don't think it's very nice."

Joanne's eyes fluttered. "But he calls *himself* that!"

Manda could hardly believe this conversation. "Are you talking about Tarin the Terrible?"

Joanne nodded her head up and down. "He's the smartest boy on earth," she said.

"Well, I wouldn't know about that," Mr. Bock said, chuckling.

Heather spoke in her sister's defense. "He *is* smart, Daddy. So smart he keeps scaring off his baby-sitters."

Manda's ears perked up. "Why would a bright kid like that frighten anybody?"

"I guess, from what I've heard, Tarin's quite sophisticated," Heather explained.

"You mean his vocabulary is very advanced for his age?" asked Manda.

Heather cocked her head. "Yeah, how'd you know?"

"Because he's in one of my classes at the ski academy," Manda said, folding her hands in her lap. "Is he new to Alpine Lake?"

"I don't think so," Heather replied.

Joanne was grinning now. "Tarin's just new to our church," she said. "He and his dad changed churches recently."

Manda observed Joanne's childish mannerisms. Light-years difference between the girl across the table and Tarin Greenberg. Joanne was a normal first-grader. Tarin, even though he was a year younger, was out in the nebula somewhere intellectually. Just how far, Manda didn't know.

"It's very sad. Tarin's got no mother," Joanne said.

The little girl's comment was revealing, especially because of Ethel Norton's remark. So there *was* a problem at the Greenberg home. Aunt Ethel was right, after all.

Eager to see her own mother at the hospital, Manda spent only an hour with Heather after the meal. She stayed till the dishes were stacked in the dishwasher and the leftovers were cleared away. Then, because Heather pleaded with her, she played through her entire repertoire on the harmonica.

"You should come over more often," Heather teased, putting away the dishrag. "Nobody I know plays the harmonica like you. It sounds cheerful and soothing at the same time."

"I try to avoid playing in public," she said, laughing. "But thanks."

"You ought to share your musical talent with the world,

the way you perform for the public on skis, you know," Heather said.

She ignored the comment and changed the subject. "Thanks for inviting me. I had a great time."

"It was my mother's idea." Heather went to the walk-in pantry and brought out a basket of homemade treats. "Take this along when you visit your mom."

Peering into the basket, Manda saw several kinds of cookies, candies, and even a miniature nut bread. "This is incredible." She gave Heather a hug. "Mom'll love it, believe me."

"All of us helped with it. Even Kevin and Dad."

Swallowing hard, Manda said, "You have no idea what this means to my mom and me."

Heather reached out and hugged her again. "We're glad to do it. Blessing others is what life's all about, right?"

Just then Mrs. Bock came into the kitchen. She smiled when she spied Manda with the basket. "Enjoy the goodies. We used stone-ground whole wheat flour, sweetened with honey."

"So they're safe?" said Manda, laughing.

"Oh, we have to watch our junk food intake here, too, you know," Heather volunteered.

Kevin peeked his head around the corner. "Don't let the goodies distract you from your skiing," he said. "We'll be cheering for you in Dressel Hills next month."

Manda was surprised. "You know about that . . . the competition, I mean?"

"Your coach knows our ice-dancing coach, Mr. McDonald," Kevin said. "Everyone's excited about the Downhill Classic."

Manda smiled. "Thanks," she said, hoping the warmth in her cheeks wasn't showing. Kevin Bock was *so* cute!

She thanked Mrs. Bock for inviting her to dinner. "And for the basket," she said.

On the drive home, Mr. Bock said he and his family would be praying for her mother "during her surgery tomorrow."

She nodded her head in gratitude, because she knew if she tried to speak she might cry. Hard-driving Alpine skiers didn't give in to their fears.

At least, *she* didn't!

Reach for the Stars
Chapter Six

Her mom was the one with glistening eyes when Manda showed up that afternoon. Manda carried the care basket from the Bock family like it was something precious.

"What thoughtful people," Mom said, pulling out each section of goodies, individually wrapped in various colors.

"I wish you could've been at the Bocks' today." She explained young Joanne's playful banter with her father. "They're really very close as a family. They work together and play together, too."

Her mother cast a look of concern. "I hope you're not thinking about . . ."

"Not really," she was quick to say. And it was true, she really hadn't been thinking about her own loss of a father. It had more to do with the way the Bock family interacted. She believed they truly loved and respected one another.

She and her mom easily fell into a long talk about the Bocks, including Heather's adorably cute brother. But Manda was careful not to reveal too much about her attraction to Kevin. She preferred to like a boy in her own way. Secretly, and from a distance.

Later, she talked about the announcement Joanne had made at the table. "I couldn't believe my ears, but she started chattering about Tarin the Terrible. The new boy in her Sunday school class."

Mom gasped. "She actually called him *that?*"

"I guess everyone does, but *I* don't. Not to his face, anyway." She shrugged. "I think a name like that might feed his attitude, you know." She wasn't sure why she felt that way. "I know! I'll make up a new nickname for him," she said. "Something more positive."

"Something that would bring out the best in him?" Mom said.

"Exactly!"

Before Manda left the hospital, she pulled back the curtain between the beds. Auntie Ethel was awake and trying to sit up in bed. Quickly, Manda rang for the nurse.

As they waited, she told the woman about young Tarin. "Remember, you said he might have some problems at home? Well, I heard today that he doesn't have a mother."

Ethel's brow wrinkled into a deep frown. "Everybody has a mother, honey. What you're saying is his mother doesn't live with him, or she's passed on. One of the two."

"That's true." Once again, Manda was intrigued by the elderly woman's quick thinking.

"He's going to need your emotional assistance when you see him next," Ethel pointed out.

Manda agreed. "I'll give it my best shot."

Mom was all smiles. "That's my girl."

Turning, Manda went to stand at the foot of her mother's bed. "If you're excited about that, just wait'll tomorrow. But you have to be wide awake from surgery before you'll have any idea what I'm talking about."

Mom leaned forward a bit, wincing when she did. She glanced toward the ceiling where the traction pulleys did their thing, then back to zero in on Manda. "Promise me . . . no big surprises, please," she said. "I'm not kidding."

Manda went to her mother and kissed her cheek. "I won't agree to anything, but I can promise you one thing—you'll be absolutely jazzed."

She could hardly wait to start filming.

Tomorrow!

———

The afternoon was extra cold, and the windswept slope was slicker than usual. With the sun on her face, Manda prayed that all would go well.

"This is important stuff," she told Benny, who held his video camera. "It's for my mom. She needs a piece of the mountain." She gave him a few instructions about the sort of angles she hoped he might capture on video.

"I can handle that," he said, hoisting the camera onto his right shoulder.

"Don't worry about this being too professional." She patted him on the arm. "It's the thought that counts."

She prepared to ski the short distance, waiting for Benny to give her the high sign. The plan was to ski out the gate and down the first one-third of the course. No need to capture the entire run.

"When you're ready, just whistle," she called to him.

Benny skied down the first section of the run, using wide, banked parallel turns, taking things slow and easy due to the camera perched on his shoulder.

Manda had to smile to herself, the excitement building. "Mom's gonna love this," she said to Coach Hanson at the starting gate. "You have no idea how much!"

"Ski cautiously," Coach advised her. "There's a lot of ice out there today."

Another challenge. But she was ready. "Hear anything?" she asked Coach.

His ruddy face broke into a smile. "Sounds like a whistle to me."

"Benny's ready." She was off, down the slope, thinking only of her mom's soon-to-be look of surprise. Manda felt the ice when she hit several patches of extremely hard snow made by the harsh daytime wind.

Adjusting to the conditions at hand, she used the absolute minimum of edge on her skis. And she avoided hanging on to the traverse too long. *Just like the best skiers,* she thought as she spotted Benny and the camera.

The first section of taping went too quickly, so Manda asked Benny to ski down another long section, toward the Corkscrew. The perfect place for some additional footage. The real exciting stuff!

Although Manda had been filmed frequently, never had it been under a circumstance like this. The tape was for pure entertainment. Possibly therapy.

She could just imagine her mother's face light up when Manda took the tape to the hospital. She'd already arranged with the nurses to borrow a VCR for the showing. "The video might help her get better quicker," she'd told them.

Now, preparing to ski the wild turns of the Corkscrew, she glanced at the sky. It was bleak and gray, yet pieces of blue tried to peek through the cloud layer.

She peered down the course through her goggles.

"Go, girl," she said into the icy air. "You're Downhill Dynamite!"

Benny gave the whistle sign again, and she was off. She zigzagged and swooped past the sharp turns of the familiar run, enjoying the thrill of it—the stimulating tingle of a job well done.

At the designated spot, she turned her skis quickly and came to a swooshing stop as snow billowed about her like a misty fan. Satisfied that Benny had captured enough footage, she thanked him. Then, winded but pleased, she headed down to catch the ski lift, feeling as happy as if she'd actually won a race.

But the serious hard work of the day was still ahead. In five short weeks she'd be competing in the Downhill Classic. If she was to place anywhere near first, she needed more practice time on the slope. Shouting "Go, girl!" to the sky wasn't going to cut it in Dressel Hills.

She knew that. The next hour would be a test of her raw nerve. *Do I have what it takes to win?* she wondered on the ride back up to the summit of Falcon Ridge.

Do I?

Reach for the Stars
Chapter Seven

She didn't have to wonder long. Manda's last practice run of the day, followed by a stiff set of pointers from Coach Hanson, had been a blazing success.

"Move over, Picabo Street," she said.

Coach agreed. "You really pushed your limits today, Manda. Keep skiing like that, and I'll be following *you* to the Olympics someday."

"Thanks, Coach."

"Don't thank me. You're the one with the bite."

They laughed together, but she knew he was right. There was something burning inside her, driving her . . . pushing her to the very edge of human endurance and courage.

Manda never questioned what that something was. But she knew it was there. Sure as the stars in the sky.

And she would use it to kindle her strength to compete.

To win!

———

On the way to the ski lodge at the base of Cascade Peak, Manda bumped into Mr. Greenberg. She had secretly observed him before, after ski class when he came to pick up his son—super intelligent and smart-mouthed Tarin the Terrible.

"Aren't you Tarin's father?" she said, propping her skis up against the log-frame exterior.

"Why, yes, I am." His clean-cut face was friendly and warm. When he smiled, his slate gray eyes twinkled. "And you're Tarin's new ski instructor, I believe."

"Just till my mother's leg heals," she explained. "She has a badly broken leg, and I'm filling in for her."

His eyebrows rose slightly. "I see, so you must be a very good skier yourself."

"I'm pretty good for my age." Laughing about her mildly boastful comment, she was about to excuse herself.

"Uh, Miss Garcia—"

"Manda," she interrupted. "Call me *Manda*."

His smile was contagious. "All right, then, Manda." He looked at her the way she assumed a father might look at his own daughter. "I was wondering, would you happen to know of a responsible sitter? Someone who might be interested in spending time with Tarin a couple afternoons a week?"

Instantly, young Joanne Bock's comments came to mind. But Manda dared not let on that she knew Tarin had scared off several baby-sitters.

"I would be glad to pay more than the usual hourly rate," he added quickly, almost before she could reply.

She smiled politely. "Let me think about it. I might know someone who could help you out." She didn't say that *she* was the one. She didn't want to let on that she was intrigued by both Tarin . . . *and* his father.

"Very good," he said, offering his business card. "Would it be too presumptuous to ask if you'd mind giving me a call? That is, if and when you might come up with someone?"

She accepted the card, noting that he was a computer analyst. "Sure, I could do that."

He turned to go, then stopped and looked back at her with a kindly nod of his head. "Thank you, Manda. I'd like very much to interview someone soon."

Interview? What on earth for?

Hardly anyone interviewed baby-sitters in Alpine Lake. Not unless there were certain health concerns involved. Things the prospective sitter might need to be aware of. Stuff like that.

But for the life of her, she couldn't think what Mr. Greenberg might need to discuss with her or any sitter. Was Tarin so terrible that his father had to interview someone for the job?

She left for home, head reeling. Thankful that her ski videotape was ready to present to her mother, she picked her way across the well-lighted streets.

Up and down Main Street, lights began to come on in the front windows of the old Victorian houses. Livvy Hudson, vice-president of the *Girls Only* Club, lived in a gray-and-white three-story house just a block from where Manda turned to head home.

Maybe Livvy would know what sort of sitter interviews Mr. Greenberg was conducting these days. After all, one of Livvy's school friends had baby-sat some of the worst-behaved kids in town. Livvy had told her so.

Manda came close to going the extra block, just to stop in and ask her ice-skater friend her opinion. But at the last minute, she decided not to. It really wasn't her duty to dig up dirt on Tarin Greenberg. She would find out the whole story for herself when *she* attended the interview for the job.

Long after her ski-lodge encounter with Mr. Greenberg, Manda continued to think about him. He was so thoughtful, it seemed. And his words were kind, almost gentle. Yet his son was fiery and determined. How could that be? Surely, there was something of his father lying silent in the rambunctious and outspoken boy.

I'm going to find out, she decided as she waited for the pedestrian light to turn. *I won't waste a single second.*

It was a promise she'd made to herself yesterday, after the Sunday dinner with her friends the Bocks. She wouldn't forget. No matter what, she was going to get to the bottom of this Tarin thing!

Reach for the Stars
Chapter Eight

"You're doing *what?*" Livvy Hudson practically howled into the phone. Raising her voice was highly unusual for Livvy. She was soft-spoken most of the time.

Manda continued. "You heard me . . . I'm interviewing for a baby-sitting job . . . with Mr. Greenberg."

"I don't believe this," Livvy muttered.

"Well, it's not the end of the world."

"Don't be so sure," Livvy retorted, then fell silent.

"C'mon! You can't mean that. What could be so horrible about sitting for Tarin Greenberg?"

Livvy spoke up. "They don't call him Tarin the Terrible for nothing, do they?"

"Maybe not. But I've seen the way he operates in my ski class, and to be honest with you, there's nothing scary about that kid." She was being straight with

Livvy and, at the same time, trying to check out some things.

"You better think this through super carefully," Livvy said. "Before you do something you might regret."

"What's to regret? I need the money for lift tickets and other ski stuff, and it sounds like Tarin needs a good sitter." She sighed. "Where's the problem?"

Livvy huffed into the phone. "Go ahead . . . learn the hard way."

"Just give me something solid to go on," Manda insisted. "Tell me something I don't already know about this kid. Then maybe I'll think about dropping it."

"Okay, I'll get the lowdown for you. Soon as I talk to someone . . . a friend of mine."

Manda assumed the friend was Suzy Buchanan, Livvy's school friend. Suzy was one of the town's busiest sitters. "We're talking straight from the horse's mouth?" asked Manda.

Livvy chuckled. "You got it."

They chatted about the upcoming *Girls Only* meeting and, later, how Manda's mother was doing. "Mom should start improving soon," she told Livvy. "She had her leg surgery today. I'm heading off to the hospital now."

"Need a ride?" Livvy asked.

"Thanks anyway. I'll catch the city bus."

"Are you sure?"

"Positive," she said. "See ya tomorrow at school. And don't forget the buzz on Tarin."

"Don't worry. Bye."

Manda said good-bye and hung up the phone.

She tossed a frozen dinner in the microwave. The chicken and rice dish had a flat, cardboard taste. She couldn't wait for her mother to come home from the hospital. Even if Mom couldn't stand up and cook, she could tell Manda what ingredients to throw together. Anything would taste better than nuked fast food!

After eating, she washed up and changed clothes. Then, before leaving the house, she called the hospital. "How'd the surgery go?" she said when her mother answered.

"I survived, and now I'm ready and waiting for some entertainment. Namely, you."

"Remember, you promised to be wide awake when I get there," Manda reminded.

"My eyes are propped open, and I can't wait to see you. Hurry!"

Manda smiled into the phone. "Okay, I'm leaving now. I'll see you in less than ten minutes."

Actually, the walk to the bus stop was less than two minutes from the house. The bus would take her the rest of the way. Five minutes—max!

———

When Manda arrived, both her mom *and* Auntie Ethel were sitting up in bed. A row of cut flowers—yellows, blues, and reds—and plants lined the wide windowsill nearest Mom's bed. Ethel's side of the room was decorated with a pink-and-white balloon bouquet and at least a dozen get-well cards.

"I've got a big surprise!" Manda announced, motioning to the nurse in the hallway.

"You're surprise enough for me." Mom reached out for a hug.

Manda hurried to her bedside and squeezed her gently. "What did your doctor say about the operation?"

"That I slept through it," Mom joked.

"Well, now, that's a *good* thing, I'd say," Ethel commented with a chortle.

Manda joined in the laughter. "No, really, how'd everything go?"

Mom was still smiling. "The surgery was a snap. No complications. My leg should be back to normal in six weeks or so." She was wearing a pink bow in her shoulder-length hair.

Manda touched the bow. "Where'd you get this?"

"Oh, one of Ethel's grandchildren gave it to me." Mom looked especially bright, nearly childlike, with the pink touch in her dark brown hair.

Auntie Ethel grinned, showing her gums. "Yes, indeed, we had a whole roomful of company today."

"Sorry I missed it," Manda said. "But I think you'll understand when you see the surprise."

Almost on cue, two nurses came in and set up the VCR. "It's show time," one of them said, waving as they left the room.

"Show time?" Mom asked.

Manda stood in front of the two beds, her arms out like a choir director's. "Both of you need a bit of fresh air, a blue sky, and . . . a very tall mountain!"

Mom started clapping as if she knew the surprise. Ethel burst in with short applause, too. "This is such fun," said Mom.

"Wait till you see the show, then you can decide." Manda pressed the "play" button on the remote and went to sit on the edge of her mother's bed. "Ta-dah!"

She played her harmonica as background music, though the video was quite short. But it was accompanied by numerous "oohs" and "aahs"—from Mom especially.

Ethel mostly panted and gasped when the Corkscrew section came on the screen. "Oh, dear me, how in the world does she ski like that?" the woman said.

Mom was obviously proud for the chance to crow about Manda. "You should've seen her when she was a little thing . . . skiing down the easy green slopes in no time at all. I taught her almost as soon as she could walk and, well, you know the rest." Mom beamed as she related Manda's past athletic history.

When the "stop" button was pressed, both women pleaded for Manda to rewind and show it again. So she did. Her mom kept going on about how she'd used her ski edges in dealing with the icy surface. "You're looking good, Miranda!"

"Thanks." She smiled at her mother. "Since you couldn't go to the mountain, I had to bring it to you."

"And it was wonderful," Mom said, her eyes shining. "I loved every one hundredth of a second of it."

Manda thought about the precision of speed. One hundredth of a second could mean the difference between first and second place. She fully intended to cut off another full second from her present time. She must do it before competition!

She began to rewind the short video and was getting ready to eject when the nurses came back. They wanted to see it, too. So she showed the video once more, insisting on the "full treatment"—the harmonica tunes played live and in person.

Ethel was the first to mention it. "All of us should go and cheer Manda on at the Downhill Classic. What do you say?"

The nurses glanced at the woman, nodding their heads kindly. Ethel Norton was in no shape to travel even the short distance to Dressel Hills. She'd had her share of physical ailments, the most recent being her knee-replacement surgery.

"If nothing else, you'll get the play-by-play from me," Mom spoke up. "I'll come visit you whenever I can."

"You'll tell me all about Manda's win?" Ethel asked, her watery eyes pleading.

"I promise," Mom said.

When all the talk of skiing and competition died down, Manda brought up the subject of the sitter interview. The one with Tarin's father. "Ever hear of a formal interview for a baby-sitting job?" she asked her mom.

Mom glanced at the ceiling. "Let me think," she said. "Yes, as a matter of fact, I did conduct an interview . . . several different times." She glanced at Manda. "You were just a toddler when I had to go back to work. I never would've considered leaving you with a sitter I didn't know inside and out."

Auntie Ethel was getting a kick out of the story. She'd folded her arms low at her waist, like an awkward Girl Scout, hanging on to every word.

"Well, if *you* interviewed formally, I guess it's okay," Manda remarked. She couldn't help but notice the similarities between her mom's gentle, almost soft-spoken approach and Mr. Greenberg's. Of course, she didn't *really* know the man. But what she'd seen so far, she admired. A lot.

She decided on the spot that the interview should be

as much about herself—and her mom—as it was about Tarin the Terrible. And his wonderful father.

How to pull off such an interview, she had no clue.

I'll play it by ear, she thought. *Like my harmonica.*

First thing tomorrow afternoon, she would call for her appointment. Secretly, she was counting the hours.

No, the seconds . . .

Reach for the Stars
Chapter Nine

Manda met Suzy Buchanan at Livvy's locker. Suzy was a short, perky girl with stick-straight brunette hair. Shiny clean, her hair framed her face, falling past her shoulders.

"You remember Miranda Garcia, don't you?" Livvy said to Suzy, glancing at Manda.

Suzy nodded, wearing a smile. "Hi," she said. "We were in second grade together. Remember?"

Now that Suzy said it, Manda did remember. Fuzzy memories were clearing up fast. "We sat together in reading group sometimes, right?"

Suzy's big brown eyes widened. "Weren't we the Blue Jays, or something feathery?"

"Hey, you're right!" Manda was aware again of Suzy's winning smile. Here was the girl who'd graced the art room walls with smiley faces cut from construction paper. A birthday surprise for their second-grade teacher.

Livvy closed her locker door. "Manda's thinking of interviewing for a baby-sitting job. It seems Tarin Greenberg has run out of sitters. Again," she said out of the corner of her mouth. "Any advice?" Livvy spoke directly to Suzy but ended by looking at Manda with big eyes.

Suzy frowned. "Better think twice about sitting for him."

"I'm not thinking," Manda replied. "I've already decided."

Suzy's smile flickered and died. "Well, I think you might be sorry."

"Really?" Manda was all ears. "Tell me more."

"Let's put it this way," Suzy continued, "the kid's a sitter's worst nightmare."

"He seems harmless." She thought of her interaction with the boy at ski classes. Sure, he was a clown . . . even a show-off. But a nightmare?

Suzy scanned the row of lockers—up one side and down the other. Like she was about to tell an enormous secret. "Tarin's smarter than all of us put together. No lie!"

Manda laughed. "You're not telling me anything new!"

Suzy was shaking her head. "His IQ is over 140."

Manda gulped, looking at Livvy for some moral

support. "Is *this* what you were talking about on the phone? You actually knew all this heavy IQ stuff about Tarin?" she asked.

"Nothing too specific." Livvy twitched her nose. "But now you know something *solid*."

The bell rang.

"Consider yourself warned," Suzy said, shifting her books. "You'd have to tie me up and drag me over there. I'd *never* willingly sit for that boy again. He reads dictionaries for entertainment and talks in riddles. And that's not all!"

"What else?" she asked.

"He knows three languages . . . at least!" Suzy said.

Three?

Manda was impressed. "Wow, maybe he'll teach me one."

"Don't be sarcastic," Livvy said, eyes flashing.

"It's true. Tarin can read three languages . . . that I know of," added Suzy.

Manda tossed her hair and shrugged. "Are we talking counting in a foreign language and easy stuff like that? Because I was saying the Greek alphabet when I was four years old."

"Way *more* than that," Suzy said. "I'm telling you, the kid's an undersized egghead."

Students around them slammed their lockers and hurried down the hall in response to the bell. Manda, Livvy, and Suzy parted ways, shuffling in different directions. No formal good-byes were said.

But Manda wasn't discouraged. She was looking forward to the interview. In fact, she could hardly wait.

―――――

After school, Jenna Song made herself a human blockade at Manda's locker. The Korean-American gymnast, petite but strong, held out her sturdy arms and stared Manda down with her dark eyes.

"What're you doing?" Manda asked. She reached around her friend to get to her locker combination.

"I'm here to talk some sense into you, girl."

"Let me guess. You don't think I should waste my time sitting for Tarin Greenberg—"

"Since you have an important skiing competition coming up," interrupted Jenna, finishing the sentence.

Jenna had no business interfering like this. "I'll handle my skiing, you do your thing in gymnastics," Manda protested.

Lowering her arms, Jenna gave in. "Fine. Do what you want, but don't come crying to me when you don't place at Dressel Hills."

Manda shut her friend out. "I know what I can and can't do." It was a statement—cold and probably a little abrupt. But nobody was going to call the shots for her. Not even the president of the *Girls Only* Club!

Jenna flounced off without saying more. But Suzy Buchanan had overheard. "That's two," she said, offering a sweet smile. "My dad always says there's safety in numbers—which means you might wanna skip out on that interview. Whenever it is." Suzy waved to her and turned to dash down the jammed hallway.

Manda reached for the combination lock on her locker door. *Everyone's trying to run my life,* she thought. *What's the big deal?*

But she knew.

Deep down, she understood the reason for Jenna's warning. It *would* be tough trying to cram everything into her already tight schedule.

In spite of herself—and her skiing goals—she honestly wanted to pass the interview and baby-sit for Tarin the Terrible. If for only one reason. . . .

Reach for the Stars
Chapter Ten

Mr. Greenberg's house was a short five-minute walk from the hospital, on Wood Avenue. At first Manda thought the door was slightly ajar. Taking a second look, she spied a note—evidently from the paper carrier—shoved into the crack between the storm door and the doorjamb.

She stood on the front porch, curiously spying out the place. There were Swiss-style window boxes adorning each of the four windows at the porch level. A few dried-up flowers and leaves remained. An iron-footed plant stand posed in the corner of the porch, empty. Probably, it had been home to geraniums or other colorful flowering plants during the summer. She wondered, too, if Mr. Greenberg had a green thumb. The notion made her snicker.

Of course, a man with a name like Greenberg surely

could grow most anything. Easy! Plenty of flowers . . . vegetables, too. Probably in the backyard, which she hadn't seen just yet.

About the time she felt the urge to tiptoe around the side of the house to see if there might be a cozy little garden plot, the front door opened. All by itself!

She stood there, staring at it. "Anybody there?" she said softly.

The main door continued to open, leaving the storm door undisturbed. "Enter at your own risk," a voice boomed overhead.

Quickly, Manda looked up, trying to locate the origin of the deep voice. Was this some kind of trick?

Confidence rose in her. "I'm coming in!" she announced to the unseen voice and reached for the storm door.

"Beware! The inhabitants of this dwelling tolerate nothing less than total compliance" came the strange voice.

Manda listened, her gloved hand resting on the storm door handle. She'd heard this sort of voice before. It sounded like a computerized telephone message.

Ignoring it, she pressed the doorbell and heard it ring.

Then, without warning, the front door slammed shut. In her face. Not willing to give up, she remained standing. Waiting for exactly what, she didn't know.

Still, she waited.

After a time, she rang the doorbell again. Once more,

she waited. This time the voice did not continue, and finally—about the time she'd thought of leaving—Mr. Greenberg appeared at the door. "Ah, wonderful." He sported a grin. "You're right on time."

She decided not to inquire about the peculiar, warbled voice. Or the fact that the front door had mysteriously opened and closed at will. Instead, she paid close attention to Mr. Greenberg's directions, assuming that he might be testing her—taking mental notes on how well she followed his instruction.

"Please have a seat, Miss Garcia." He motioned to a chair near the fireplace.

She almost corrected him, wanting to remind him that she preferred Manda. But she was cautious, a bit worried about sounding rude. She really wanted this job!

Across the room, leaning against one long wall of the parlorlike living room, were four tall bookcases. Two exceptionally wide ones reached high to the ceiling.

Everywhere she looked—at the swept hearth, dusted curio cabinets, and polished upright piano—everything seemed to be neat and orderly.

Interesting, she thought, recalling that Tarin and his father lived alone in the house. No maid that she knew of. And no wife or mother.

Her eyes roamed the bookshelves, coming to rest on the middle shelf—precisely eye level to a five-year-old.

Standing on end was a portly dictionary, tattered on its top edge. Probably where small hands had pulled it away from the shelf. Over and over again.

She remembered both Suzy's and Jenna's words of caution. *"The boy reads dictionaries for entertainment."*

"Let's start by talking about you," Mr. Greenberg began, taking her by surprise.

"Well, let's see. I like kids . . . a lot." She didn't hesitate to remind him of her instructional skills—at the ski lodge. "And I've been baby-sitting since I was about nine." She thought about that, wanting to be accurate. "Yes, that's right. Nine probably seems young to be taking care of children, but I really do like kids. I think I'm good with them. People have told me that."

"I see." He leaned back in his chair and nodded. "And who might those people be?"

Ready for anything, she pulled out her list of references—parents of the babies, toddlers, and preschool-age children she'd baby-sat for over the past three years. "You may keep the list," she said, hoping she seemed businesslike.

Silently, his eyes ran down the list. "Very well," he said, smiling his wonderful smile. "Tell me more."

Yes! A chance to pour it on. She took a deep breath. "I'm very responsible, Mr. Greenberg," she bragged, going on to detail an incident that happened while baby-sitting a four-month-old baby boy. "He had a high fever, and I handled things perfectly. The mother said so—even called my own mother to tell her."

"That's very good to know. Now . . . what about your vocabulary skills?" Mr. Greenberg said unexpectedly.

She chuckled, almost without thinking. "I, uh, have a good understanding of the English language, if that's what you mean."

"Precisely. Now, if I might ask you about your ability to carry on several tasks at once," he said. "In other words, are you able to receive input and respond to it simultaneously?"

She was beginning to wonder if Suzy and Jenna were right. Was this going to turn into a nightmare, after all? Was she going to be asked to demonstrate her ability to speak French and Chinese, and who knows what else?

"I'm fast on my feet," she spoke up, thinking about skiing.

Mr. Greenberg grinned at that. "Yes, I expect you are."

"Is Tarin home?" she asked, eager to get on with it.

"Of course." He got up and went to the long staircase. He called for his son to join them. "Miss Garcia, your ski instructor, is here."

"I hope you don't expect Tarin to call me that," she said softly as he returned.

His eyebrows became butterflies. "Excuse me?"

"Manda . . . or Miss Manda will be fine. But nothing formal, please," she insisted.

He nodded. "I understand."

Tarin dashed down the steps, scurrying into the room where she and his father were chatting quietly. The chubby boy stood there without speaking.

"Tarin? Please greet Miss Manda," said Mr. Greenberg.

"Hello," said Tarin with a blank expression.

"How's it going?" she replied.

"How is *what* going?" Tarin asked. A frown planted itself between his blond eyebrows.

She smiled at him, hoping to defuse the tone of the conversation. "It's just a saying," she remarked, shrugging. "Nothing to dissect or analyze."

Mr. Greenberg was grinning at her response. Yes! She was getting somewhere. At least with Tarin's father.

The boy seemed somewhat defenseless against the two of them. "No need to elucidate, Miss Manda," came the tiny voice. "I fully assimilate the significance of the phrase."

If the blond-haired boy with the babyish voice hadn't seemed so serious, it would've been something to laugh about. But, bless his heart, this kid knew what he was talking about. Manda figured she had better just keep the expressions rolling. Turn the interview into a game.

"I'm going to be your new sitter," she announced, turning to look at Mr. Greenberg just to be sure.

Tarin's father was nodding his head, an enormous grin spreading from ear to ear. "Yes, I do believe this arrangement is going to work out quite nicely," he said, getting up. "Three afternoons a week."

"I haven't offered *my* assessment yet," Tarin whined, on the verge of a tantrum.

"Very well, the interview continues," Mr. Greenberg said, glancing at Manda. Quickly, he sat down again.

Tarin gladly took center stage, which happened to be the carpeted living room floor. He stood with his knees locked and his round head tilted to one side, probably thinking.

Manda could almost hear the wheels of his mind turning. Turning . . . What would he ask her?

"I'm intrigued by your qualifications," Tarin began, eyes blinking. "Please specify."

She drew a deep breath. "In what aspect of my achievements are you most interested?" she asked.

Nice comeback, she thought, congratulating herself.

The boy's eyes were bright blue, the color of the ocean in summer. His plump face was flawless and clear, but it held a permanent look of mischief. "What genre of cuisine would you say is your specialty?" he asked.

Easy!

"Well, I've been known to make a mean spaghetti and meatballs dinner," she said.

Simply and without another word, Tarin turned to his father. "Employ her."

Manda was shocked at the kid's power. Tarin the Terrible clearly ruled the roost. The occasional after-school job was going to be a battle of wills. Hers against his.

Who would win?

She was eager to find out!

Reach for the Stars
Chapter Eleven

"I'm coming home tomorrow," Mom told her later that afternoon. "Doc says I'm ready."

Manda was thrilled. "This is great news." She hugged her mother, enjoying the smell of her perfume. The familiar scent made her wish her mom could skip out of the hospital this minute!

The semiprivate room seemed smaller today. Manda wondered if it was because the Greenberg home had been so spacious.

"How'd the interview go?" Mom asked.

"It was crazy. Very different."

"What do you mean?" Mom looked worried.

"It's just that Mr. Greenberg and his son have an unusual relationship, to say the least." She was careful not to reveal what she thought of Mr. Greenberg himself.

"So tell me all about these people," Mom said, appearing to be well rested as she sat perched on the hospital bed.

"Let's see, uh, Mr. Greenberg is . . ." She paused. "Oh, I don't know. There's just something very individual . . . intriguing about him." She wished she had the nerve to say that her mom ought to meet him sometime. Maybe invite him over for coffee or something. But that would mean Tarin might have to tag along. Big mistake!

She was probably way out in left field. Such wild and wacky thoughts. There was no hope that her mother would ever be interested in getting to know the man anyway.

"How's your work with Coach Hanson coming?" Mom asked.

"I'm right on schedule for Dressel Hills, but I'm really glad you're coming home. It'll make things much easier." She figured she'd still have to do some of the cooking and cleaning up. Her mom's leg was going to be in a cast. It would be tough going on crutches for many weeks. At least Manda wouldn't have to be running back and forth to the hospital every day.

"I really hope I'll get to see you compete," Mom said, smiling. "It might be kinda hard." She glanced at her broken leg. "With this cast, you know."

"You'll make it, Mom. I'll make sure you're there." Once again, she thought of Mr. Greenberg. She pictured him, his strong arms carrying Mom up the slope partway—getting her situated at the finish line. Easy!

Shaking off that surprising thought, she went over and parted the curtains. "W-where's Auntie Ethel?"

The hospital bed was empty!

"She was released at noon," Mom explained. "My roomie's gone home. But don't worry, I have her address."

"That's good." She paused, remembering how happy the dear lady had seemed two days ago when Manda played her ski video. "Maybe my piece of the mountain got her inspired enough to check out of here."

Mom laughed. "There might be some truth to that."

Manda was pleased all around. Ethel Norton was back home, Mom soon would be, and she'd landed herself another job . . . right under Mr. Greenberg's nose!

Things were absolutely ideal.

———

Tarin the Terrible acted out the next day during ski class. He followed Manda around on the bunny slope, asking for special favors. Constantly. What bugged her even more was his endless intellectual talk. It was put-on . . . so unnatural. And by the end of the session, she wondered if she should mention something to his father.

Unfortunately, the opportunity never presented itself.

So she decided to wait and discuss it tomorrow afternoon, the next time she was scheduled to baby-sit. She hoped there might be time to talk to Mr. Greenberg before he slipped out the door.

Meanwhile, she endured the endless barrage of Tarin's articulate prattle. She couldn't help but count the minutes till her first ski class was finished. She worried that she might feel frustrated like this while baby-sitting the boy. Was it worth putting up with such nonsense just to get better acquainted with Mr. Greenberg?

As it turned out, she completely missed Tarin's father after class. Little Shelley Rolland needed some assistance with her skis, so Manda helped her unsnap the bindings. "How's that? Now you'll know how next time, right?"

Shelley nodded her head. "Thanks." She reached for Manda's gloved hand. "You're the best ski teacher in the whole world!" she said as they walked toward the ski lodge together.

Manda chuckled. Shelley was so young it was hard to imagine her ever having had another ski instructor. She led Shelley up the wooden ramp, to the west door of the lodge.

"I've got a secret," Shelley said, button nose upturned in the frosty air.

"You do?"

"Yes, and it's a big-girl secret." Shelley's eyes were

wide, waiting for Manda to take the bait. "I'll tell you if you make me a promise."

Manda reached for the lodge door and held it open. "What promise is that?"

Shelley did her usual motioning so Manda would bend down to her level. "I'm in love with someone," she lisped.

"Should I guess?" Manda asked, playing along.

"No," Shelley insisted. "Let me *tell* you!"

Manda wondered if all five-year-olds were this outspoken. "I'm ready for the secret," she said, leaning down.

"I'm in love with Tarin," whispered Shelley. "I think he's *terribly* terrific!"

Manda nodded. She couldn't say that she agreed. The boy was a spoiled, brainy brat, and she was going to do her very best to tame him. And . . . to find out what made him tick!

She had a scheme, and it wouldn't be easy. But she wasn't a quitter. She wasn't giving up!

Tomorrow she'd lay down the ground rules. *Rules!* Wouldn't Tarin the Terrible be surprised?

Well, it wouldn't matter what the boy thought. He'd have to comply, one way or the other. Starting with letting *her* call the shots!

Shelley pulled on her sleeve again. "Don't you think we'd make a cute couple?" she said.

Manda snapped back to attention. "Oh . . . yes, I think you'd be very cute together."

The little girl's eyes were dreamy now. "I think Greenberg is such a nice name." Then she started muttering, "My name is Mrs. Shelley Greenberg. . . ."

Manda couldn't help hearing the childish mutterings. She remembered her own kindergarten daydreams about boy classmates. Except she'd never have been interested in a kid like Tarin. She liked the overly confident types best. The kind of boys who popped off huge mounds of snow, soaring on snowboards at twenty-five feet into the air. Or . . . daring aerial skiers and bungee jumpers. Her kind of guy.

But she did agree with her young student on one thing, at least. Greenberg was a *very* nice name. She thought it would be a fantastic change from Garcia—the name her father had given her mother when they married, and passed on to her. Maybe *that* was the reason she caught herself thinking so much about Mr. Greenberg. Maybe she wanted Mr. Greenberg for her father. It was time for a real father, one that would stay with her and her mother forever.

After all, Tarin's father was a single man; probably a lonely one, too. He needed a wife and daughter to round out his life. . . .

Reach for the Stars
Chapter Twelve

Promptly after school on Friday, the *Girls Only* Club members gathered for their once-a-week meeting. It promised to be a short meeting because two of the members had other appointments. Manda didn't say that she had an appointment, too. With Tarin's destiny.

"Let the meeting come to order," Jenna Song said, sitting cross-legged on the rug near her bed.

Jenna's attic bedroom was more like a hideaway clubhouse than a bedroom. Everything a girl gymnast could possibly want was available. Things like a four-poster bed and dresser, a computer desk, an Olympic rings wall hanging, and a shelf for displaying competition medals.

Unlike most girls, Jenna had floor-to-ceiling mirrors and a barre to practice ballet in her bedroom. The size of the room, the barre, and the fact that it was high in the attic were the main reasons why they'd chosen to have club meetings here. After all, the four club members were each enrolled in the same ballet classes!

"Old business first," Jenna said.

The girls shook their heads. Nothing.

"New business?" the president asked.

Heather Bock had something to say. "I think we should offer to help Manda's mom. She's home from the hospital with a badly broken leg."

Jenna and Livvy agreed. They liked the idea. So did Manda, of course, but she felt awkward about commenting. After all, it was *her* mother!

Then Jenna spoke up. "Since Manda seems to be spreading herself thin these days, we oughta make sure her mom's doing all right. You know, help out."

Manda resented the comment. Jenna made it sound like Manda was too busy to help her own mother. "My mom's just fine, thank you. And what I do with my free time is my business." She hadn't planned for the words to slip out quite so spitefully.

"Thing is," Jenna continued, "in order to be an *active* member of this club, you need to be focused on your competitive skiing." She glanced at the wall calendar. "There isn't much time left before the Downhill Classic . . . is there?"

Sounded like a threat—like Jenna thought she didn't deserve to be in the club anymore.

Jenna pushed on. "Dressel Hills is going to be packed with competitive skiers," she stated.

Manda knew all about that. No one had to remind her what she was up against. "I'm on top of things," she said. "Coach Hanson thinks I have a good chance at first place this year."

Jenna looked puzzled. "How can you possibly pull it off?"

"I just will," she replied, feeling more and more resentful. Then, not thinking, she let it slip that she was headed for her first baby-sitting afternoon with Tarin Greenberg. Starting today. "I know I can handle everything."

Jenna slouched down and clammed up. Livvy Hudson tried to carry the rest of the meeting, handling duties as vice-prez, while Jenna had her silent tantrum. Heather Bock also seemed unhappy and embarrassed about it.

As a result, the meeting was adjourned twenty minutes early. And not a single thing was accomplished, except for the annoying, bossy words dished out by the president.

Manda was thoroughly upset with Jenna. She didn't hang around for refreshments—healthy snacks, of course. Since the four of them were aspiring athletes, it was important to serve up finger foods like celery sticks and carrots, raw cauliflower and broccoli. Today, they could enjoy their snacks, just the three of them. Without her!

She headed for the door, hoping to sneak out unnoticed.

"Psst, I'll call you," Heather whispered.

"Okay, see ya!" Manda wiggled her fingers at her friend. She wanted to tell her to say hi to her cute brother Kevin but didn't.

Thank the Lord for Heather, she thought. Without Heather Bock in her life, she might've felt truly alone. But she knew the blond-headed ice dancer was a loyal friend, if there ever was one!

Manda was gone and glad to be out of there. She was off to her baby-sitting job on Wood Avenue. Tarin the Terrible was waiting.

So was his father!

———

There was no time to chat with Mr. Greenberg before he left. Manda wanted to complain about Tarin's extremely advanced vocabulary and the fact that she thought it was something he was putting on just for show. But all too quickly she was left solely in charge of the bland-faced kid, without a clue as to his true mental abilities.

Tarin began spewing out long sentences in something that sounded like Swahili. He kept it up until she thought she'd have to leave the room.

What a way to start the first day, she thought.

Then, attempting to investigate his book, she went to sit next to him. Tarin's legs were too short to hang down off the sofa. They stuck straight out, extending from his little lap, where he held the book.

"What're you reading?" she asked.

He sat still, staring at the book and mumbling the foreign language. He was ignoring her.

Again, she tried to make polite conversation. But the boy was simply not interested. He was probably bored with her, she decided. Bored with a sitter of average intelligence . . .

She decided *she* was going to be the one to pick their battles. Not the other way around.

Silently, Manda rose and went to the desk in the corner of the room. There she took out her homework and spread the papers out neatly. She sat down and began to work her math problems. She wished she'd asked about using Mr. Greenberg's computer for some history research. Her mother's PC still wasn't working properly.

Five minutes passed till she felt Tarin standing behind her. She sensed it from his breathing and the smell of him—the clean, fresh scent of little boyhood.

Slowly, she turned. "Do you need something?"

"Nourishment," he said, pouting.

"You're hungry already?" She'd forgotten to speak his level of speech, quickly changing her comment to "You're experiencing insatiability?"

His eyes fluttered almost uncontrollably. "Did you allude to spaghetti during the interview?" he asked.

If he hadn't been standing there, within inches of her, she wouldn't have believed Tarin was so young. He was tiny—just a whiff past toddlerhood—yet here he was conversing like a college professor.

She checked her watch. "Your father will be home in time to cook your supper. But if you're hungry for a snack—"

"My appetite is voracious!" he hollered.

He might as well have yelled that he wanted his supper right this minute and not an instant later. But it was so weird to hear this kid carrying on in adult lingo.

"Okay," she said, getting up. "Let's find something to snack on."

That didn't seem to account for much. Sure, Tarin wanted a snack, but he wanted her to play along with his cerebral game. Or *was* it a game? She wasn't sure. Maybe the poor little kid talked this way because he didn't know any other way to express himself. But how could that be?

While she spread peanut butter and jelly on several crackers, she wondered if it was because Tarin hadn't had a mother cooing over him as a baby. Maybe his father had never talked baby talk to him. Maybe that was the reason!

She was about to ask him, inquire into his private five-year past, when the phone rang. "Why don't you sit here and eat your snack," she said, pulling out a kitchen chair.

"My father permits me to consume food elsewhere," he piped up, eyes daring her to stop him.

The phone continued to ring.

"All right, but be very neat," she said, handing him a napkin.

He frowned at her again and headed back toward the living room, muttering something in French. Or was it Italian?

Quickly, she reached for the phone. It was her mother.

"Hi, Mom. What's up?" asked Manda.

"Coach Hanson called just now. He says you might have an opportunity to practice skiing on the run at Dressel Hills tomorrow morning. Interested?"

"Sure am! When?" She stretched the phone cord, trying to see where Tarin had wandered.

"Early . . . before seven," Mom said. "That okay?"

"Actually, it's perfect. I can get back to the lodge in time for my first ski class."

"Bright and early won't hurt, right?" Mom said.

"Tell Coach I need a ride," Manda reminded.

"I already mentioned that to him." Mom sighed into the phone. "Oh, I wish I could drive you, honey."

"Don't worry about it, Mom. You'll be back on your feet in no time. I know you will!"

"How's everything going there?" Mom asked.

"It's a conversation contest at the moment," she said, laughing. "But it's far from boring."

Mom chortled about it, then they said good-bye and hung up.

Manda scurried through the dining room and into the living room. She found Tarin sitting at the desk, doing her math homework. Peanut butter and jelly smudges were all over her important pages.

"Excuse me. I don't think my teacher's going to be too thrilled about this." She picked him up out of the chair.

"Put me down!" he began to holler. "Put me right down! Right now."

She burst out laughing. "So you *can* speak normal English! This is quite a discovery. You had me worried." She set him down in front of her and knelt down to face him. "I think it's time we had a talk, you and I."

Tarin folded his pudgy arms over his chest, his lower lip protruding. "I won't allow you to address me in that manner."

"I'm your sitter, and I certainly will if I want to!"

He squinted his eyes at her. "I thought you were intelligent. That's why my father hired you."

She burst out laughing. "And I thought you were hopelessly cerebral. But guess what? You ain't!"

He must've thought that was funny. Tarin's arms dropped to his sides, and he began to laugh. "I like that . . . my baby-sitter is insane!" He kept shouting it over and over.

Finally, to get him to stop, Manda pulled out her harmonica. She began to play her favorite hymns. After the second phrase, Tarin became completely silent. And wide-eyed.

I'm going to tame him, she thought. *I've got to!*

Reach for the Stars
Chapter Thirteen

The sun was just beginning to peek over the icy horizon as Manda prepared to ski down Eagle's Point. No wind today. The ideal way to practice her technique on the steep and menacing slope.

Get your mind in gear, she told herself as she awaited the starting signal. But it was difficult. More than ever, her thoughts were caught up with Tarin and Mr. Greenberg. She'd made the mistake of calling her friend Heather last night. They'd talked about everything under the sun and then some. She'd actually confided in Heather about Mr. Greenberg!

Stupid, she told herself. *What were you thinking?*

She had no idea how ridiculous her comments might sound. Not until she had spoken them. Not until she'd sat through Heather's long, blank silence on the end of the phone.

"Reach for the stars," her mom had always said. And whether it was skiing or mountain biking—no matter what it was—Manda always approached life like an astronaut. She figured if she reached for the distant nova, she might lariat the moon. Or something else equally terrific.

Somehow or other, she'd got it stuck in her mind that Mr. Greenberg was the perfect man for her mother. And the perfect dad for her.

Of course, there was always the problem of Tarin the Terrible. No girl in her right mind would want *him* for a brother—stepbrother or otherwise! But then, what had Tarin accused her of being? *Insane?*

Well, maybe she was out of her mind for wanting something so far out of reach. She burst out laughing at the starting gate. She couldn't help it; the pressure had built up in her.

Coach Hanson looked at her with concern. "Are you all right?" he asked, coming over quickly.

The laughter subsided. "Have you ever aimed to reach for an impossible goal?"

Coach's eyes were sincere. "Manda, listen to me. Nothing . . . I repeat, *nothing,* is impossible!"

He must've thought she meant the Dressel Hills Downhill Classic. She recognized the look in his face. He was determined for her to win. At least place high.

"What if I told you this isn't about skiing?" she ventured.

He leaned his head back and looked at the pink hues in the morning sky. Exhaling, his breath cast a wispy cloud over his head. "I'd still say reach hard and high. You'll always accomplish your dreams that way."

She was pretty sure his answer dealt with athletic goals. He had no way of knowing what her deepest heart longings were. Not now. Now that she was almost a teenager. The private thoughts she had these days—this far past twelve—well, he just couldn't possibly know. Or understand.

Truth was, she wanted a father. Someone just like Mr. Greenberg. Someone with a sharp mind and a warm smile. Maybe it wasn't such a stretch after all.

When she was ready to conquer the mountain—respect the work of God's creative hand—about that time, the go-ahead came. With a surge of renewed dash and determination, she shot out of the gate and skied hard and strong. Her way! The difficulty of Alpine skiing was always inside a person—never outside. At least, that's what she'd been taught. And she believed it.

With that in mind, Manda pushed off and skied down Eagle's Point—her best time yet.

———

The second she got in the front door, the phone rang. "I'll get it, Mom!" she called, dashing to the phone. "Hello?"

"We're having an emergency meeting for *Girls Only*," Heather said. "Are you coming?"

"What emergency?" she asked breathlessly.

"Don't worry about that," replied Heather. "Just come this afternoon, right after lunch, okay? I really have to go. See ya at Jenna's. Bye!" Heather hung up.

What's going on? she wondered. Was the president calling a meeting to vote her out? Jenna's snide comment about the club's *active* member requirements still bugged the daylights out of her.

Sure, she'd go. She would go and defend her right to belong to *Girls Only* . . . no matter what kind of weird stuff Jenna Song was pulling!

Manda strolled into the living room and sat in the chair across from her mother.

"Who was on the phone?" asked Mom.

"Heather Bock . . . we're having another club meeting."

"Oh? Sounds important," Mom remarked. "When?"

"Around one-thirty." She leaned back and stared at the oil painting above the sofa. Aspen Highlands had always inspired her. The mountain had the most double black diamond trails in America. A Christmas gift years ago from Uncle Frank, the picture was easily one of the coolest things in the whole house.

Because of her young, "rich" uncle, so to speak, Manda had been able to follow her dream of someday going to the Olympics. He wasn't exactly loaded, but her mother's brother had insisted on paying for her ski training from second grade on.

"Do you think Uncle Frank will ever get married?" Manda asked, feeling more relaxed now that she was sitting.

"He's talking about proposing to his girlfriend," Mom replied. She was propped up on the sofa like a rag doll. Her feet stretched out in front of her, taking up the length of the couch. "I do think he'll marry someday."

"What about *you*?" The question burst out before she'd thought over whether or not it was the right thing to ask.

Mom, however, didn't seem too frazzled by it. "Well, I doubt at my age anyone would be interested," she said softly. "Though I have thought it would be nice to get married to someone who stayed around. You know, a permanent fixture."

Manda knew, all right, and she was dying to bring up Mr. Greenberg again. But she knew she'd talked her poor mother's ear off about the man. No sense opening up that topic just now.

"What do you want for lunch?" Mom asked, stirring around like she was going to zip right off the sofa and cook up something.

"You name it . . . I'll cook it," Manda said, leaping up. "You stay right there. I'll bring the food in to you, okay?"

Mom decided on tuna salad sandwiches and tomato soup. A good combination for a winter day. And as she went to the kitchen, Manda thought of Tarin the Terrible— the way he'd insisted on taking his peanut butter and jelly crackers into the living room. How he'd managed to smear them on her math homework.

Yet as she recalled her fury that day, she was surprised that she didn't feel anger anymore. The kid was clearly *not* a brat. He was a dear, lost boy . . . needing the tender touch of a mother's hand. Or someone who could possibly take his mother's place.

She understood where he was in life. Fully understood! At that moment, as she chopped the hard-boiled eggs for the tuna salad, she knew why she was drawn to the boy. And she knew just how to help him—starting with giving him a new nickname.

But first she had an emergency to attend to. Jenna Song's emergency club meeting.

What could possibly be so important?

Reach for the Stars
Chapter Fourteen

Jenna Song kept a journal. She was dedicated to writing in it. Every day. Her favorite place to write private thoughts was curled up next to Sasha, her golden-haired cat. At times, Manda wondered if Jenna's obsessive journal keeping was a clue to her personality. She wasn't sure, though, because she was still getting to know Jenna Song.

The Song family had arrived in Alpine Lake just as school was starting last fall. Jenna's father had come to fill the pastorate of the local Korean church.

Jenna clutched her small leather journal as she called the *Girls Only* Club meeting to order. Not a single sign of slouching today. Nope, the prez was back to her normal self. "We're here for an important reason," she announced.

"What's going on?" Manda finally spoke up. "What's the emergency?"

Jenna smiled, opening her diary. "It seems to me that it's time for the four of us to unify. You know, merge our feminine skills."

The strange grin on her face worried Manda. "What's that supposed to mean?" she asked.

Heather Bock was fidgeting like crazy. Like she was uneasy. "Wait . . . I have to tell Manda something first, uh, before you keep going." Heather said this to Jenna, but she looked Manda square in the face. "I have a confession to make," she said, her face pinched a bit.

Manda was thoroughly confused. "What's to confess?"

Heather's fair-skinned complexion began to redden. "I'm embarrassed to say this, but I told the girls about our phone conversation. The one about . . . Mr. Greenberg."

"You *didn't*!" Manda was shocked. "That was a complete secret! How could you?"

Heather grimaced for a moment, then continued. "The three of us—three-fourths of the *Girls Only* Club—have a great idea."

"What're you talking about?" she asked, almost afraid to hear the answer.

Livvy Hudson piped up in her soft voice. "We've dreamed up a way for Mr. Greenberg to meet your mother."

This was insane—to use Tarin's word!

"You've got to be kidding," she heard herself say.

"No, actually, we think you'll be pretty wild about it," Jenna said, her finger stuck in her diary. "After Heather told Liv and me how you thought Mr. Greenberg and your mom should go out, well, you know . . . I started jotting some ideas down. About how to get them to meet."

"All of us did," Livvy said, holding up a piece of paper. "We each interviewed someone, asking how they met their spouse. I talked to my grandma. Jenna asked her parents."

Heather's turn. "My mom let me read the journal my dad kept right before he met my mom. It was definitely interesting."

"And then after we discussed this stuff," Jenna jumped in, "we decided how we can get your mom and Mr. Greenberg together."

Manda felt limp. "You *discussed* this . . . without me?"

Heather touched her arm. "It's okay, really, Manda. I think you'll like our idea."

She wasn't so sure. "Well, what is it? What's the great idea?"

Heather's blue eyes shone. "Here's what you do. Get permission to sit for Tarin at *your* house one day next week. When Mr. Greenberg comes to pick him up, leave

493

the door unlocked with a note for Tarin's dad to come in."

"But, of course, you and Tarin will make yourselves scarce—maybe outside or something—so your mom and Mr. Greenberg will meet each other," Livvy added.

"Right in your own living room," said Jenna.

"Yeah, that's right, Mom *would* be sitting there—a captive audience—because of her leg cast," Manda said, visualizing the whole scene. "Yes! I like it. You guys are nuts, but this is pretty great." She was looking at Heather now. "Honestly, I don't think you ever promised not to tell on the phone, did you?"

She ran her fingers through her short hair. "If I had, I wouldn't have breathed a word to the club. And we wouldn't be having this very important emergency meeting, either."

Jenna, Livvy, and Heather seemed excited with their matchmaking idea. Manda was, too. And she decided to forget about Jenna's hot-under-the-collar approach to the baby-sitting job. This plan of Jenna Song's would be easy enough.

Now, to actually pull it off!

Reach for the Stars
Chapter Fifteen

Mr. Greenberg was in a rush when Manda arrived on Monday afternoon. He said something about having to meet with a new client. Ruffling Tarin's hair, he waved and hurried out the door.

No time, once again, to talk to the man. She'd wanted to set up the location for retrieving Tarin. Yes, *the* setup— setting up Mr. Greenberg with her mother. Possibly for the rest of their lives.

So Tarin wouldn't be coming to her house today. Just as well, because the boy became sick soon after she arrived.

"My head hurts . . . bad!" he told her minus the brainy gibberish.

"I know just the thing for headaches." She led him upstairs and had the boy lie down. Then she found a clean washcloth in the bathroom closet and dampened it with cool water.

He eyed the wet washcloth. "What're you gonna do?"

"Don't ask so many questions," she said, deciding not to say a word about his lack of eloquent speech. "It makes your brain busy. When you have a headache, it's best not to think too hard."

"Whoever told you a dumb thing like that?" he asked.

"My mother."

He didn't say anything for a moment. Then he took a long breath. "Maybe it's okay, then. I mean, if your *mother* said it."

Folding the washcloth in thirds, she placed it over his forehead. "There, isn't that nice and cool?"

She almost expected one of his smart-aleck comebacks. But he was quiet. She sat on the edge of the bed, watching Tarin's flushed face.

"Is it nice having a mother?" he asked softly.

She hardly knew how to respond. Instead of speaking, she touched his warm cheek with her hand.

"I never, ever saw mine," he whispered. "She died when I was born."

Taking a breath, Manda replied, "My father left when I was real little, so I sorta know how you feel." She offered the comment out of empathy for the boy.

"My head's getting better," he said.

"That's because you're resting." When she was

convinced that he would lie still and not chatter off a million questions, she pulled out her harmonica and began to play. The tune was actually a song, but Tarin had no reason to know the words. It was one of Manda's favorite nursery songs. "Gentle, Sweet Child." Her mother had sung it to her many times when she was sick or just frightened by the dark.

When she finished, Tarin's eyes opened. He blinked several times before speaking. "I like your music, Miss Manda."

"And I like *you,*" she replied, though she was hesitant. And quite surprised at herself.

"Do you like me because I'm Tarin the Terrible?" he asked, staring back at her.

She smiled down at him. "To tell you the truth, I like you just because you're you. But I'm not crazy about your nickname."

He snapped out of the blues. "Why not?" he demanded, trying to sit up.

"Just relax," she said, getting him to lie back again. "You don't want that headache returning, do you?"

He shook his head slowly. "What's wrong with my name?"

"I think there might be a better one for you. One that fits you just right."

His mouth turned crooked, like he was interested but trying to hide it. "Like what?"

"Tarin the Terrific. It's much better."

"Play another tune on your harmonica," he said, battling a smile.

She sighed. "Make a deal with me first."

He bit his lip. "Not now. I don't feel good."

"I know, but just promise me one thing," she pushed. "No more of that grown-up talk, okay?"

"How about some French?" He was smiling now.

"Only if you teach me." She picked up her harmonica. "Is it a deal?"

He nodded, watching her closely. "Okay. No more advanced communication."

"*What* did you say?"

A little laugh burst through his lips. "Just kid talk from now on."

"You got it." She played the same song again on her harmonica. Three times.

When she finished, little Tarin the Terrific was sound asleep.

———

"I think I might've tamed him," she told her mother on the downstairs phone. "At least for today."

"You're the genius."

"All I did was play music. It seemed to soothe him." *Like it does me,* she thought.

"Your father used to play, you know," Mom said.

"He did?" Unexpected news.

"At night, when you had trouble falling asleep." Mom's voice was sure, unwavering.

"I never knew that," she said.

Mom changed the subject, asking what Manda wanted to eat for supper. "I think I might be able to stand and fix something special," she said. "I'll lean on my crutches."

"Give it a few more days," Manda insisted. "I'll be home in a couple hours. I'll make something for us then."

She heard her mother sigh into the phone. "Well, I *am* just a bit tired. Someone from the church dropped by to look at my computer. I'm ready to get off my feet."

"That's good news," she said, eager to use the online encyclopedia for her latest homework. "Take it easy, Mom. I'll be home soon."

The fact that her mom was still pretty much house-bound was ideal. Especially because she planned to ask Mr. Greenberg to pick up Tarin at her house this Wednesday. She hoped her mother would be her cheery self when Mr. Greenberg walked into the house un-announced.

She stifled a giggle and headed back upstairs to look in on Tarin. To say that she could hardly wait for Wednesday was the absolute truth!

Reach for the Stars
Chapter Sixteen

Tuesday night, the evening before the big day, Manda stood outside in the backyard, looking up at the stars. She had decided long ago that just before all the light disappeared from the sky—that second before dusk—something wonderful happened. There was the slightest pause, soft and still. In the evergreens just beyond the city, near the foothills, a whisper of twilight lingered. Then it happened. One by one, thousands of stars made their appearance until the whole sky was filled with flickering light.

Tonight, not feeling the least bit self-conscious, Manda reached up and swept her fingers and hand across the sky. *"Scoop up some stars,"* her grandmother used to say when Manda was little. *"Scoop up and make a wish."*

Making a fist, Manda captured her stars and held her

breath. But she didn't make a wish. She was too grown-up for such silly things. She would pray instead. Praying to God, the Creator of the stars, was far better.

"Please, dear Lord, could you let Mr. Greenberg like my mother? Somehow, if it is your will, may they like each other."

She didn't go on to say anything about marriage or having Mr. Greenberg for a stepfather. None of that. God already knew how she felt.

———

Manda talked to Mr. Greenberg first thing when she arrived the next afternoon. "Would it be all right if Tarin and I walk to my house?" she asked politely.

He agreed. "That's fine. I'll pick him up there around five-thirty."

"Okay, thanks!"

As soon as he was gone, Manda sat with Tarin. "Before we go to my house, I'm dying to know something," she said.

"My headache's over," he volunteered. "Is that what you want to know?"

She stroked his soft hair. "I'm glad you're feeling better, but that's not my question."

"Do you want to learn French?"

"This isn't a guessing game, Tarin," she said. "I

wondered why you talked that way before . . . you know, all grown-up? And why did you want to scare off your baby-sitters?"

He was grinning. "That's *two* questions. Which one first?" He turned to face her on the sofa.

"You choose." She felt completely comfortable with this little guy, and yet it had happened so quickly. She was grateful about that.

He sucked in a deep breath, then forced it out. His tiny chest rose and fell as he did. "I talked grown-up because I sometimes feel that way inside. I never have any kids around me, except at ski school. Just grown-ups. And my dad's friends are always very smart . . . just like me."

She chuckled at the admission. "Was there another reason?" she asked, guessing what it might be.

"Sure," he said, his eyes shining. "I get lots more attention when I act like a thirty-year-old."

She laughed out loud. "No kidding. Okay, so what about all those sitters—Suzy Buchanan and the others?"

He folded his arms and sighed. "None of them were right for me," he said. "I was waiting for someone like you, Miss Manda."

She couldn't help herself; she hugged him. And she felt his fingers squeeze around her arm in response. "Want to go to my house?" she said, letting go. "We can walk through the snow. It'll be fun."

"Can we pretend we're skiing?" he asked, face aglow.

"We'll practice our gliding strokes," she said.

"Can we make a snowman at your house?"

"Sure . . . in my big backyard," she said, remembering the plan to keep Tarin occupied for his father's grand entrance.

Then she gasped. "Oh no!"

"What's wrong?" Tarin said.

"Your father doesn't know my address, does he?"

Tarin nodded. "I think Daddy wrote it down that day we interviewed you," he told her and ran to find his father's notes.

How could I have been so stupid? she thought.

Tarin came running back. "Here it is," he said, pointing to a small notebook.

"I can only hope he knows where to come," she whispered.

"There's always the phone book," Tarin suggested.

She groaned. "Our number's unlisted."

Without revealing her concerns, Manda hurried to the hall closet. There she bundled up Mr. Greenberg's son with his own favorite wool scarf, mittens, and snow boots.

Outside, Tarin held her hand as they walked the short distance. "Let's race on our pretend skis," he hollered, running ahead.

"Look out for Downhill Dynamite!" she called back.

He turned around. "Is that *your* nickname?"

She was surprised at his perception. "How'd you guess?"

"It's perfect for you," he replied. "That's how."

They bent their knees and leaned forward, pretending for more than a block. At the intersection, they stopped and waited for the traffic. "Have you ever wanted a new father?" the boy asked. "Since your first one went away."

She thought about it. "Sure . . . someday I'd like . . . to have another father."

If he only knew, she thought, watching for cars as they crossed Wood Avenue.

"Me too . . . only I want a mommy." Tarin the Terrific looked up at her and grinned shyly. "Maybe *you* could adopt me, Miss Manda," he said. "Maybe when you're all grown-up."

She didn't have a good comeback for that. Not even a ho-hum one. But she'd seen something of his father in Tarin just now. That kind and thoughtful look in his childish eyes. Something very special, indeed!

Reach for the Stars
Chapter Seventeen

Manda's mom was comfortably situated on the couch when Manda and Tarin arrived. "This is Tarin Greenberg," she introduced her young charge.

"It's very nice to meet you, Tarin," Mom said, offering her hand.

The little boy shook her hand and stood near the sofa. "Miss Manda says you told her not to think too much if you have a headache." Politely, he waited for a convincing reply.

Mom smiled her broad grin. "That's right, honey. I did tell her that."

The remark seemed to satisfy him. "Thank you," he said. "Nice to meet you, too." He looked at the leg cast. "Take care of your leg."

"I sure will," said Mom with a wink.

Manda helped Tarin out of his jacket and things. "Want to see my room?" she asked, leading him toward the stairs.

"You have lots of ski posters?"

"At least four," she said. "Ever hear of Picabo Street? I have one of her."

"That's a funny name."

"Her parents named her after a trout stream called Picabo, which means 'silver creek,' " she explained.

"Couldn't they think of something else, like Annie or Shelley?" he asked.

"They wanted something unique, just like you wanted to be called—"

"But I'm *not* that name now, am I?" he interrupted. "I'm Tarin the Terrific, aren't I?"

"Yep," she said as they headed upstairs. "So . . . you must like the name Shelley?" She couldn't resist. She had to know what he'd say about the little girl at ski class.

"Shelley's a nice name. I think she likes me," Tarin said with a big grin. "I can't wait to go to ski school again."

Manda didn't press for more, although she could see the twinkle in the boy's eyes.

———

Before they made the promised snowman, Manda sneaked around the house. She stuck the note—*Just walk in*—on the front door, still hoping Mr. Greenberg might find his way to them. She hoped increasingly harder while she helped Tarin pack and roll the white stuff for their snow creation.

Then, at close to five-thirty, she made an excuse to go inside. "I'll be right back," she told Tarin.

Praying and hoping that things might work out perfectly, she tiptoed into the house. She crept past the dining room and toward the living room.

Yes! She could see past the front window. Mr. Greenberg had just pulled up. Good, he'd found them.

Her heart was thumping hard as she waited—not for the doorbell, but for the sound of the front door opening. What would her mother say to the tall, handsome man? How awkward would it be for a stranger to come in the door?

Manda decided she wouldn't observe the two of them for very long. She'd make herself scarce once the first hellos were exchanged.

Then the front door opened. Mr. Greenberg stepped inside cautiously. He spied Manda's mother propped up on the sofa. "Well, hello again, Adelina," she heard Tarin's father say.

"How are you, Matthew?" came the curious reply.
Adelina? Matthew?

They knew each other! But how?

Mr. Greenberg smiled at her mother. "How's your computer running now?" he asked.

"Perfectly fine, thank you," Mom replied.

So that's who had repaired their computer! She couldn't wait to report back about this at *Girls Only* on Friday. Her friends would love every minute of it.

Manda turned and tiptoed to the back door and went outside. Tarin was delighted to show off his half-made snowman.

"Guess who's here?" she said.

"Daddy?"

"Yep."

He frowned briefly. "Can we finish Mr. Snowman on Friday?"

"If the weather stays cold, sure."

By the time she got Tarin inside, his father was seated on a chair near the sofa. Still chatting with Mom, he seemed in no hurry to leave.

A good sign, thought Manda, thoroughly surprised at the amazing turn of events.

"I want to come back to Miss Manda's house. Please, Daddy?" he asked, describing their partially completed snowman.

"Well, let's have a look at your handiwork, young man," Matthew Greenberg said. "Miss Manda can lead the way."

She was glad to. Anything to keep this man and his son on the premises a bit longer!

———

Later, when Mr. Greenberg and Tarin were gone, Manda sat on the floor beside the sofa. "Somebody's been holding out on me," she began, watching her mother's face closely.

"Yes, I suppose you're right," Mom replied.

"You must've gotten acquainted with the computer man the other day."

Mom's face lit up. "Honestly, I don't know what it was about him, but we just clicked. Right away."

Manda could hardly believe her ears. "So . . . are you, I mean, is he going to ask you out to dinner or anything?"

"Well, let's not rush this," Mom said. " 'Good things come to those who wait'—you should know that by now."

She wasn't too keen on waiting. "My motto is: Take the bull by the horns, or in other words, take control of the mountain!"

"Speaking of which, you've got an important competition coming up in less than a month," Mom said, adjusting her leg.

"I'll reach for the stars," Manda said.

"And maybe catch the moon, right?" Mom glanced at the mountain painting above her.

"No maybes for me. I'll make you proud of me, Mom."

"You already have, honey."

Manda stood up, ready to make supper. "Downhill Dynamite needs a great, big bite. I'm starved."

"Count me in," Mom said, putting her thumb up.

"So . . . are you gonna invite *Matthew* Greenberg to the Downhill Classic?" Manda probed.

"I think that's your department," Mom turned the question back to her.

"Sure, I'll invite him . . . and Tarin, too. Easy!" And she knew it would be. As Coach had said, "Nothing's impossible."

After all these years, she was beginning to believe it. With God's help, of course.